EDS

EDS

Medical Kidnap Files #2

P.D. WORKMAN

ISBN: 9781988390383 (IS Hardcover)

ISBN: 9781988390376 (IS Paperback)

ISBN: 9781988390338 (KDP Paperback)

ISBN: 9781988390345 (Kindle)

ISBN: 9781988390352 (ePub)

ALSO BY P.D. WORKMAN

YOUNG ADULT FICTION:

Medical Kidnap Files:

Mito

EDS

Proxy

Toxo

Pain (Coming soon)

Between the Cracks:

Ruby

June and Justin

Michelle

Chloe

Ronnie

June, Into the Light

Tamara's Teardrops:

Tattooed Teardrops

Two Teardrops

Tortured Teardrops

Vanishing Teardrops

Breaking the Pattern:

Deviation

Diversion

By-Pass

Stand Alone YA novels

Stand Alone

Don't Forget Steven

Those Who Believe

Cynthia has a Secret

Questing for a Dream

Once Brothers

Intersexion

Making Her Mark

Endless Change

Gem, Himself, Alone

MYSTERY/SUSPENSE:

Reg Rawlins, Psychic Detective

What the Cat Knew

A Psychic with Catitude

A Catastrophic Theft

Night of Nine Tails

Telepathy of Gardens

Delusions of the Past

Fairy Blade Unmade

Web of Nightmares

A Whisker's Breadth

AND MORE AT PDWORKMAN.COM

That the truth may be known.

CHAPTER ONE

Katt let herself into the house and immediately turned on the TV. After finding the remote and turning to the right channel, she headed into the kitchen to pull together a snack. She had timed everything perfectly so that she had five minutes before her show came on. She danced around the kitchen, tossing her blond hair and sweeping her long arms out like a ballerina before deciding that was a bad idea if she didn't want to risk smashing into something.

An apple, peanut butter, some milk because milk was important to build strong bones. If anyone needed to build strong bones, it was Katt. She pulled open the fridge and grabbed the big milk jug. It was full and it was heavy. Katt's mind was already on her next movement, two steps over to the fruit bowl. She wasn't thinking about bracing herself properly or pulling the milk jug out straight or about sliding one hand under it for extra stability. She just put her hand through the handle and jerked it off the shelf.

There was a loud pop in her shoulder and Katt yelped and let go of the milk jug. There wasn't even time to swear as the jug fell and she realized that it was going to hit her foot. She was still reaching for her right shoulder with her left hand when the jug hit her foot. Katt gasped with pain.

"Ow, ow, ow!"

She hopped on her left foot, grabbing her injured right foot with her left hand while her right arm hung loosely at her side. Then she swore. Not again. How could she be so clumsy? The pain in her foot was worse than when she stubbed her toe on the iron frame of her bed. But she decided she'd better stop jumping up and down, or she was going to fall and break her tailbone too. Standing on one foot, she leaned against the central island of the kitchen, probing the bones of her right foot delicately. She was slender and her skin was so fair that the veins showed through the skin, and in the right light she could just about trace the bones beneath the skin without an x-ray. Almost without thinking of it, Katt transferred her grip to her right shoulder and eased the joint back into place with another loud pop. She rolled both shoulders and returned her attention to her foot.

The small bones in the top of her foot didn't feel right. Unbelievable. It was like the boys at school said, all they had to do was look at Katt and she'd break a bone. Katt put her foot down, and balanced on the heel, not laying it flat on the floor. She bent down and used both hands to pick up the milk jug, which miraculously had not popped its top and hadn't leaked a drop onto the floor. One less thing to worry about. She put it back into the fridge and opened the freezer to take out an ice pack. They were all arranged in the door of the freezer waiting for her.

Walking on her right heel, Katt minced through the kitchen, grabbing an apple from the fruit bowl, but abandoning her plans for peanut butter and milk. She settled herself carefully into the easy chair just as the opening notes of her show started to play on the TV.

Katt raised the footrest and carefully arranged the ice pack over her foot, settling back to watch her programs.

———

"I'm home," Karina called out to Katt as she walked into the kitchen through the garage entrance and put her purse down on the counter. "How was your day?"

Karina rubbed her back with long, slender fingers as she went into the living room to greet her daughter. She instantly took in the ice pack on Katt's foot.

"Uh-oh. What happened?"

Katt looked at her with luminous blue eyes. Her face was even paler and more angelic-looking than usual. Her wispy hair was tousled by the wind outside. Karina automatically gathered her own dark hair, pushing it behind her ears and back over her shoulders.

"I dropped the milk jug," Katt said, apologetic.

"Anything broken?" Karina bent over Katt's foot and pulled the now-warm ice pack away for a look. The foot was obviously swollen; the skin pulled tight. "Oh, damn."

"I'm sorry, Mom. I didn't mean to. I just wasn't paying any attention when I picked it up…"

Karina returned the ice pack to the freezer and retrieved a cold one. She handed it to Katt to replace, knowing that Katt would tolerate the pain better if she were the one laying the ice pack over the injury. She went back to the garage and grabbed a pair of crutches, hardly even having to look to lay her hands on them. She took them over to where Katt was sitting.

Katt eyed the crutches and sighed. "Can we have dinner first?"

She was probably more concerned about watching the rest of her show than she was about eating, but it was a valid request. They both knew the menu in the hospital cafeteria sucked and that they would be waiting for at least a couple of hours before getting the foot set. They had to eat something at some point. It might as well be in the comfort of home.

"Fine, all right," Karina agreed. "I'm just going to make mac and cheese. We'll want to get over there before the evening rush."

Katt looked at her watch and didn't say anything. They were probably going to get there right in the middle of the evening rush, but Karina wanted to remain optimistic. Maybe there would be a lull, and they could get in and out in good time.

"How was school?" she asked, as she moved back into the kitchen to get started on cooking supper. "And how much homework do you have?"

CHAPTER TWO

George Buckskin had already put in ten hours when he entered the curtained area where patient Katt Lindholm was sitting on a bed waiting. Like pretty much every other kid who went through the ER, she had a phone in front of her face while she texted, chatted, or played games to pass the time.

She was a lovely-looking girl, fifteen or so with blond hair, bright blue eyes, and pale, almost translucent skin. His skin was almost ebony compared to hers. When George walked in and picked up her chart, she set the phone down in her lap and gave him a tolerant smile. She'd already been there a couple of hours and was probably in considerable pain. But she and her mother, a brunette sitting beside the bed, didn't jump all over him about the wait.

"So, it sounds like we've got a broken foot," George offered, scanning the details on the chart. He lifted the ice pack off of her foot to take a quick glance at it, confirming that it was very swollen. Not much else he could do without x-rays. He could manipulate it, but with the amount of swelling, that would be excruciating and probably wouldn't give him any answers. "What exactly did you do?"

Katt sighed and rolled her eyes. "I'm such a klutz," she said, "I sort of… dropped a full jug of milk on it."

George frowned, squinting at the notes that the nurses had made, which confirmed that she had told them the same story.

"And how did you do that?"

He proceeded to give her a quick exam, checking vital signs. The staff hadn't bothered to hook her up to a monitor, so he took her pulse and blood pressure manually and listened for a moment to her chest. With the speed of her pulse and how high her blood pressure was, she was obviously in more pain than she was letting on with her calm, good-humored manner.

"Well, I just grabbed it out of the fridge," Katt explained, making a brief motion, miming the movement. "But I wasn't really paying attention to how heavy it was. My shoulder popped out, and I dropped it."

"This shoulder?" He tapped her right shoulder lightly.

"Yes."

George examined it, but could find no swelling or tender spots as he manipulated it.

"Is that something that has happened before?"

"Yeah. I kind of get hurt a lot. Some of my joints pop out more than they should."

"So when you say it pops out, you mean it clicks? You get a little twinge of pain?"

"No," Katt shook her head. "The joint pops right out."

"And that doesn't hurt?"

"Yes, it hurts. But when I pop it back in again—"

"How do you do that?"

Katt put her left hand over her shoulder and made an explanatory motion. "Just like that…"

"Hmm. Well, we need to get you down to x-ray to have a look at that foot. And I'd like to put you on a monitor so we can keep tabs on your blood pressure. You haven't been given anything for the pain?" George picked up the clipboard again, scribbling his instructions and looking for any meds administered.

"No."

"Do you have any drug allergies?"

"Uh-uh."

"Have you had Demerol before?"

Katt nodded. "Yes. I don't react to it."

"Okay. Let's get you some of that and down to x-ray."

"Thank you," Katt's mother said. George had been ignoring her during the interview. Katt was old enough to answer his questions herself, and it was better not to have a third person filtering information and obscuring any signals.

"Mom, why don't we have you go on back to the waiting room for now? Someone will come and get you when Katt is done in x-ray," George suggested.

"Oh, I'll stay with her."

"You can't go with her to x-ray. She's a big girl; she'll be okay. We'll take good care of her. Why don't you get yourself a magazine and a bite of supper from the cafeteria? It will be an hour before she's done."

"We already ate. I don't need anything…"

George just looked at her, waiting. Eventually, she got the message that he wasn't going to let her go down to x-ray with the teen. Her mouth a thin line, she stood up.

"I'll see you in an hour, baby," she told Katt, touching her on the arm, and then she headed back toward the waiting room.

George put the sides up on Katt's bed to transport her. No point in her hobbling around on a broken foot or wasting time on a transfer from bed to wheelchair. It was easy enough to just transport her on the gurney.

"You have bruises on your legs," he murmured to her, quiet even though her mom should have been well out of earshot.

"I have very fair skin and I'm a klutz," Katt explained, as he put the clipboard down and started to push her. "I always have bruises."

"Tell me again how you broke your foot."

"I dropped the milk carton on it," she said in an exasperated voice.

"Have you broken any bones before?"

"Yes. Arms, legs…"

"How?"

"I don't know… I broke my ankle getting off of a trampoline. Tripped and fell and broke my wrist. Got knocked down playing hockey at school and broke my arm. I told you, I'm just clumsy."

"Okay," he agreed, not wanting to get her worked up, especially not with her blood pressure so high already.

Katt's anxious expression smoothed. She nodded and relaxed, her eyes closing part way as he pushed her down the corridor and she watched the ceiling whip by overhead. George settled her in the x-ray intake waiting area and went to find a nurse to get Katt's IV and monitor set up.

———

Marshall, the x-ray tech, stared down at the yellow requisition sheet that George had filled out. His brows drew down as he compared it to Katt's chart.

"This is the girl with the broken foot, isn't it?"

"Yes."

"Then what is this?" Marshall flapped the yellow paper at him. "Why would we be doing full body x-rays on a kid who dropped something on her foot?"

"Follow me. I'll show you."

George led Marshall out of the x-ray room to where Katt was waiting.

"How's that feeling now, Katt?" he asked, checking the drip on the IV.

"Lots better," Katt said, her voice sleepy.

"Good. Your blood pressure is coming down. I just want to listen to your lungs, can you sit up for a minute?"

She swayed a little when she sat up, obviously woozy from the Demerol. George steadied her shoulder and placed his stethoscope on her chest over the hospital gown. Marshall was still looking at him like he was crazy. George switched the stethoscope to Katt's back, pushing the gown to the side. As he rested the stethoscope on her back, not even bothering to listen to it, he looked at Marshall and then down at Katt's bare back. Marshall got the hint and looked down. Katt's white skin was discolored with several dark bruises. George avoided touching them as he moved the stethoscope around, instructing Katt to breathe. He withdrew the stethoscope and closed Katt's gown.

"Great. Go ahead and lie back down. They're just about ready for you."

He walked with Marshall back into the x-ray room.

"Who's been hitting her?" Marshall demanded.

"Mom or Dad, probably. You'll do the whole thing?" George nodded to the requisition sheet still in Marshall's hand.

"You bet. You putting in a call to Social Services?"

"Right now. I'll have someone on it once you've got results for me."

"Have you checked her history?" Marshall nodded to his own computer terminal.

George sighed. "Tell me you'd be surprised that she has multiple hospitalizations every year since she was born."

"Yeah. They've never done anything?"

"No. Been investigated, but never any action. Which is why I want everything done and Social Services talking to the girl before the mother knows anything is going on. She can obviously sweet talk Social Services, and that's not happening this time."

"Bravo. I'll be a while on this imaging. You should get her admitted in case the social worker doesn't get here right away. Block her from going home immediately."

"Good thinking. I'd like to keep her here for a bit anyway. Evaluate for soft tissue injuries."

George left Katt in Marshall's capable hands.

———

George managed to persuade Sarah Wolfe to join him to see Katt once she was finished in x-ray.

"Don't you think you should wait for the results of the x-rays before calling Social Services?" Sarah suggested, irritable after having her growing pile of paperwork interrupted yet again.

"I don't know what x-ray will show, but I know she has some pretty nasty looking bruises and a broken foot, and that she's broken limbs several times before in accidents that sound a little suspicious."

"A broken foot, that's not usually abuse. You don't see a lot of parents breaking their kid's feet."

"Maybe not. And maybe it wasn't abuse this time, but looking at her… I have to believe she *is* being abused. That foot could have been broken by dropping something on it, or she could have been pushed and landed on it wrong. Or a piece of furniture could have been shoved over in a fight. Just because it's not a twisted arm, that doesn't mean it isn't abuse."

"No." Sarah sniffed and didn't argue it any further.

They didn't go straight to Katt, but stopped at a computer terminal to take a look at the x-rays first. Marshall had been thorough. There were dozens of films, and a number of them already had markings and annotations on them. George started to go through them, translating the various points for Sarah who sat beside him looking at the screen.

"There's her foot. Three bones broken. That's pretty extensive for a 'dropped something on my foot' injury. You drop something on your foot, and you usually try to avoid it. Get a glancing blow. Maybe one small bone broken. Not several. Ankle on the same foot has been broken before. This is an old, healed injury. She said she broke it getting off a trampoline."

"That could be true."

"Yes. Could be. Moving up to the pelvis…" He traced a line on the x-ray. "There's an old break here. Pelvic bones are big. It takes a lot of force to do this."

"How would she break her pelvis?"

"Most likely a car accident. But I didn't see anything on her record about a pelvic fracture. I don't think it was ever treated."

Sarah nodded, her expression stony. She was on his side now. She believed that Katt was being abused or at least neglected.

George swore, looking at films of Katt's torso, especially the posterior views.

"What?"

"You see these rib fractures? One, two, three, four, five… and the vertebrae themselves. Old fractures here, here, here, and here."

Sarah's eyes widened. "Five ribs and four vertebrae? And she was never in a car accident?"

"You can look at her record. She's had a lot of ER visits, but not anything like that."

Sarah shook her head, scribbling quickly in her notebook now. "What else?"

"Wrist, she says she fell down. Radius and ulna, she said she was knocked down at school. Like I said, nothing that you would expect to cause these types of injuries. Oh, collarbone too. She didn't mention that one. But it's not like she would have forgotten."

"Maybe it happened when she was very young? A baby?"

"No…" George studied it. "I don't think it's been that long since it healed. I wouldn't put it over a year old."

Sarah continued to write. "I'm glad you called me on this one. Sorry I gave you a hard time. Sometimes we get called and it's just a simple case of bruised shins from playing sports…"

"I told you you would want to see her."

"Yes. Let's go have a little visit."

———

It was late, and Katt was doped up on painkillers, so she was asleep when George and Sarah got to her bedside.

"Katt…" George nudged her. "Katt, I need you to wake up and talk to me for a few minutes."

At first, she didn't stir, then she jumped at his touch and her eyes went wide. She clutched at the sides of the gurney like she was afraid that she was going to fall out of it. George made a soothing humming sound.

"There, you're okay," he told her softly. "Calm down. You remember me? Doctor George."

Katt nodded slowly. She looked around and rubbed her sleepy eyes. "Can I go home now?" she ventured.

"No, dear. I think we're going to keep you here overnight. We'll get your foot set and then we'll find you a room for the night. Okay?"

"I don't want to stay." She yawned. "I want to sleep in my own bed. It's just a broken bone; I don't need to stay overnight."

"We're concerned about complications. It won't hurt you to sleep here one night."

Katt's eyes fixed on Sarah. She shifted, propping herself up on her elbows. "Who are you?"

She probably had more than enough experience with hospitals and Social Services investigations to recognize a social worker when she saw one.

"Hi, Katt. I'm Sarah Wolfe." Sarah extended her hand and Katt politely took it but didn't shake. She just inserted her hand for a moment and then pulled back again.

"You're not a doctor," Katt said.

"No. I'm not. I'm just here to ask you a few questions about your injury and how things are going at home."

"Things are fine at home." Katt's eyes went back and forth. "Where's my mom? You said she could come back after I was done my x-rays."

"She'll be joining you again soon," George assured her.

"Why don't you tell me how you managed to break your foot?" Sarah encouraged, giving Katt a friendly smile. "I bet there's a story there."

"I dropped a milk jug on it," Katt snapped. "I don't know who you are, and I don't want to talk to you."

"I'm with Social Services, Katt. Was your mom at home when this accident happened?"

"No. I get off school before she gets off of work. But it was just my own clumsiness, and I was fine and safe there. I just waited until she got home. I knew it wasn't an emergency."

"So there wasn't anyone at home with you?"

"No. But I'm fifteen. I don't need a babysitter. I can take care of myself for an hour or two."

"What about your dad? Was he at work too?"

"There is no dad. He abandoned my mom when I was born."

Sarah nodded. "So it's just you and your mom, huh? How do the two of you get along? Mothers and teenage daughters... things can get pretty intense sometimes, all those hormones."

"We're good friends. We get along."

"Uh-huh." Sarah nodded as if she believed it. "That's nice. No boyfriend...?"

Katt's skin flushed a little pink. "No, no," she laughed. "No one is interested in me."

"You're a pretty girl; I find that hard to believe."

"No. Guys aren't interested. I'm not popular. I'm a klutz and everyone knows it. And... I'm just not one of the cheerleader types. I'm not... very good with people."

"Do you play sports?"

Katt frowned, looking sideways at Sarah. "Why does that matter? I got hurt dropping something on my foot, not playing sports."

"I just wondered. Sometimes you can get hurt playing sports and not realize how badly you hurt yourself. Or you can get bruises."

"Oh, bruises." Katt straightened the blanket over herself as if making sure that there were no bruises visible to Sarah. "I'm always covered with bruises. But that's just because I bruise easily. Not because anyone's hurting me. I don't do sports because I'm clumsy, and I get hurt, even in gym class." She shook her head. "I always have bruises, but they don't mean anything."

Sarah moved a chair closer to the bed and sat down, studying Katt. She moved up close like they were girlfriends gossiping together. She gave George a look that was clearly one of dismissal. He shrugged and moved away.

"Someone will be in to set that foot shortly."

———

Sarah looked into Katt's eyes. The girl was scared. Of course she was. She didn't know who she could trust. She'd probably been told that if she said anything about her mother's abuse, she'd get taken out of the home and terrible things would happen to her. There were always threats to keep children compliant. She wanted her mom there to answer the questions so that she wouldn't have to expose herself.

"Katt… it's more than just bruises, isn't it?" Sarah said softly. "I know, some kids do bruise really easily. I remember when I was seven, my shins were always covered with bruises from kicking the boys at school! Sometimes I get bruises and I have no idea where they came from. But that's not all that we're talking about. You know that we took x-rays of your whole body, not just your foot."

"Yes," Katt agreed, her voice petulant. "I kept telling them that it was my foot and they kept saying they needed to x-ray other stuff as well. My mom is going to be really mad about exposing me to that much radiation. Radiation can make you sick. It can cause cancer later in life. We only get x-rays when we absolutely need to."

"It wasn't up to your mom. It was up to us to make sure that you are okay."

"And now you know that I am."

"Do you want to know what we found on the x-rays?"

Katt's shoulders lifted and fell again. She didn't answer aloud. Of course, she already knew what they had found on the x-rays.

"We found that you have had a lot of broken bones in your life."

"I know. I told that to Doctor George. Stupid accidents. Not abuse."

"You told him some of your injuries. Some of the times that you broke bones…"

"Yeah."

"But not all of them."

Katt's mouth pursed, considering. She shifted around in the bed, looking for a comfortable position. Considering her injuries, there probably wasn't a position that would be comfortable for her.

"I have a high pain tolerance," she explained. "And with some kinds of breaks… there isn't anything that the doctors can do. They can't set them, all they can do is wait for them to heal."

"You've had a number of broken ribs and vertebrae. Even pelvis, and that's a big bone that's hard to break."

Katt didn't say anything right away, smoothing the blanket over her body. "I don't remember," she said. "Some of them probably happened when I was too little to remember. That's why I didn't say. My mom could tell you and Doctor George about it."

"When did you break your collarbone? George said that was in the last year."

Katt frowned and ran her fingers along her clavicle. "I'm… not sure. I got hurt at school in September, some guy crashed into me in the hallway and smashed me against the lockers. It really hurt… Mom put my arm in a sling until it healed. I never thought it was broken."

"That seems unlikely. You know what a broken bone feels like. And your mom just putting it in a sling and not taking you to the doctor is medical neglect."

"My mom takes me to the doctor all the time!" Katt's voice rose until she was almost yelling, her voice echoing off the hard tiles. "She'd never neglect me! That's garbage! If I went to the hospital every time something hurt, I'd be here all the time. I don't unless we know something is really wrong. If it's just random pain from getting banged around, I stay home and ice it."

Sarah wrote down a few more notes. She started a checklist at the side of her paper. Talk to the school. Talk to the family doctor. Review previous hospitalization records. Try to get the mom to identify how each broken bone occurred. Start making phone calls to find a long-term foster care home for Katt. She was fifteen now. If they were lucky, they might find someone who would take her until she aged out. Get a written opinion from George for the court file. Get affidavits from any other experts they could recruit.

Sarah looked over at Katt, who was watching her scribble her notes with wide eyes.

"I want my mom now," Katt insisted.

"She'll be here before long."

Sarah would need to get an emergency hearing to confirm Social Services apprehending Katt as soon as possible. Before Mom had a chance to start getting doctors and experts on her side. The last thing they wanted was for Katt to end up back home in a day or two.

CHAPTER THREE

When Karina was finally shown to Katt's bedside, she was almost beside herself with anger and worry. Anger because they had kept her and Katt apart for hours, constantly telling her it would be just a few more minutes. And worry that maybe Katt's injury was worse than it looked. Did she need surgery to pin the bone back together? Were they calling in experts to figure out how to best treat it? Had Katt reacted to the Demerol and they didn't want to tell her?

It was such a relief to finally be escorted to Katt. She was okay. She had gone to sleep, so she wouldn't know Karina was there until morning. But they both knew that Karina would never be away from her side any longer than necessary.

Karina noticed the woman beside the bed with a clipboard and no stethoscope. She obviously wasn't a doctor or a nurse. And as Karina entered the room, a hospital guard followed her in. It was a private room. Karina had never seen them put Katt into a private room without a special request and credit card.

"What's going on here?"

"Sarah Wolfe, Mrs. Lindholm. I have a few questions for you regarding Katt's medical history."

"Who are you?"

The woman didn't answer right away, but Karina knew the answer before she opened her mouth.

"I am a social worker. For now, Katt's social worker. We're pretty concerned about your little girl here."

"Is that why no one would let me near her? How long were you interrogating her? I have rights, you know. You can't question my daughter without me present."

"I think you know that I can, and in fact, I needed to. Your daughter has quite a laundry list of injuries. The broken foot is just one of many current injuries, and she also has a number of healed breaks, which we could see on her x-rays. Katt needs someone advocating for her."

"That's *my* job. That's why I'm here. I brought her here and had her treated. I'm the one who is always harassing the doctors to take care of her injuries when they think that there isn't really anything wrong. Do you know how many times I've been told that you can't break a bone from tripping over a crack in the sidewalk? Well, guess what? Katt can. And does. I'm out there advocating for her every single day. You don't know anything about her."

"I was hoping that you and I could go somewhere private to discuss it."

"No." Karina was adamant. "I've already been kept from her for hours. I'm not leaving her side again."

Sarah Wolfe's smile at this assertion was not comforting.

"You can sit with her for a while, but I would still like to ask you some questions."

Karina sat down beside Katt's bed with an exasperated sigh. As much as she hated answering social workers' questions, she knew that she'd better cooperate. She needed to reassure Sarah Wolfe that Katt was safe and well before the woman decided to do something stupid. So far, Karina had always been able to talk with social workers and to prevent Katt from ending up in the system. After they had spent some time with her, they could see how much Karina loved Katt and could understand about her difficult history. They could see that it was just a medical challenge and that Karina wasn't doing anything to hurt her daughter.

"Katt has always had medical problems," she told Sarah. "Right from the day she was born. Even before she was born. I can see how you might look at her medical history and think that someone is doing something to hurt her. But if you talk to those doctors and listen to what Katt and I have to say, you'll see that you don't need to worry about it. I'm doing everything I can to get Katt the help that she needs."

"I assume she's been tested for brittle bones and osteoporosis and that type of thing," Sarah said flatly.

"Yes. All of that. But they still can't explain why she breaks bones so easily. And as far as why she keeps getting into these accidents… that's just the girl she is. She does things impulsively and ends up landing the wrong way and getting hurt. The doctors say that she just needs to look before she leaps, there's nothing wrong with her."

"I'm sure some children are just accident prone… but it is a red flag for us."

"Of course. I understand that. But if you'll look at each case separately, you'll see that it's not a pattern of abuse… just of clumsiness and bizarre injuries."

Sarah made a point of writing something down on her notepad. She looked at Karina, eyes narrow.

"Maybe you would like to explain the broken bones which Katt has had which have not been treated."

"Not treated…? What hasn't been treated?" Karina demanded.

"Her collarbone injury earlier this year. A large number of broken ribs and vertebrae. One of the bones of her pelvis."

"Well… no. She did hurt her collarbone, but we didn't know that it was broken. It didn't swell very badly, and it felt fine as long as she had her arm in a sling. I figured it was a muscle or ligament pull. It healed on its own…"

"And the others?"

"I… don't know. She hasn't had any untreated breaks that I know of. Ribs? She's never had broken ribs."

"She's had quite a number."

"And spine… I would definitely have brought her in if I knew that she had fractured vertebrae. That could be dangerous."

"Yes, it could. And they were not treated."

Karina shook her head, at a loss to explain it. "She has so many accidents… if something doesn't seem very bad, I don't bring her in. She'd be in hospital all the time if we brought her in for every little trip and bump."

Sarah wrote more notes on her clipboard. They both looked up at the door when footsteps approached and then stopped in the doorway. A black-uniformed police officer stood there, looking at the two of them.

"Sarah Wolfe and Karina Lindholm?" he asked.

Karina's heart sank. A policeman. Who had called the police? They already knew her name and where to find her, and that meant it was too late. She had been trying to head off any charges by Social Services, but they had already been made.

"I'm Karina Lindholm," she said, standing slowly.

The policeman looked her up and down and nodded. "Karina Lindholm, you are under arrest for child abuse and neglect," he told her. He read her her rights, just like they did on TV, and pulled her hands behind her back to handcuff her. Karina winced in pain.

"My wrist," she protested. "It's injured. You can see I have a brace on."

The policeman grunted.

Sarah shook her head. "Like mother, like daughter," she suggested. "How did you hurt your wrist?"

"I just got a mild sprain, taking out the garbage…" Karina trailed off. She hated explaining her own injuries even more than Katt's. Especially because her problems were so mild when compared to Katt's and she always felt like people would think she was trying to upstage her daughter.

"Katt is being placed in state care," Sarah told Karina, in case she hadn't understood that part. "You are not to contact her directly. You may speak to me if you want to set up a meeting, and any meetings will be supervised. We'll have a court hearing as soon as possible to prove that her safety is in jeopardy with you."

Karina's eyes burned. Tears brimmed over and traced down her cheeks. "Take care of my baby. Please be careful, she's so fragile. People don't understand just how careful you need to be with her…"

"She'll be fine, Mrs. Lindholm. She'll be just fine under our care."

The policeman escorted Karina from the hospital room, leaving Katt sleeping peacefully, completely oblivious to what had just happened.

———

Katt still felt tired and dopey when she woke up, but she rubbed her eyes and looked around for her mother. Karina was not there. Katt sat up, careful not to pull the IV in her arm, which was hurting. Her foot didn't feel too bad, but it was encased in a cast to keep it rigid until the bones had mended. The cast was a bright orange. They hadn't had any pink, which was what Katt usually liked to get.

She pressed the call button beside the bed. It was unusual for her to have a room to herself. She was almost always in with someone else when she had to stay over at the hospital. Sometimes even parked in a hallway because there were no rooms available. Now and then she got lucky and was given a room with another empty bed in it and no roommate yet, but that was pretty rare. A private room by herself was… never.

It was a while before a nurse bustled into the room. Pretty, slim, her skin almost as dark as Doctor George's.

"You're awake, are you, miss?" Her voice rose and fell in a Jamaican-sounding lilt. "What can I do for you?"

"Where's my mom? Is she around? Did she go to the cafeteria or something?"

"Your mother had to go. Now, don't you worry, we'll take good care of you until you're ready to go home."

Katt's heart sped, alarmed. "What? What do you mean she had to go? You make it sound like she's not coming back! What do you mean?"

"Now, don't be getting worked up about it. We need you to stay nice and calm so that you can heal faster." The woman patted her on the hand. She seemed hesitant to tell Katt anything more. Katt tried to remember all of the details of the previous evening, but it was clouded by painkillers.

"Where is she? Where did she go? Tell me what's going on!"

"If you get too worked up, we will have to be giving you something to keep you quiet, so please don't be getting upset."

The nurse turned away from her to check the IV, but Katt was sure the IV was just fine, and the nurse just didn't want to look at her.

"Your mother had to leave with the police," the nurse said finally. "We will just have to wait while they get it all straightened out."

"The police? Why would she go with the police?"

"What's going on in here?" another female voice asked. "What are you getting our patient all upset about?"

The woman who had come in looked tired, as if she had stayed up all night. Her dark blond hair was in disarray and there were lines around her eyes. "I'm just clocking out," she advised, walking up to Katt's bed. "I thought I would check in on you before I go."

"Who are you?" But even as Katt asked, she remembered. Sarah something or other. A social worker who thought that Katt was being abused. Katt suddenly understood the nurse's oblique statement about Karina leaving with the police. She had been arrested! "What did you do? I told you my mom isn't hurting me! No one is hurting me. I'm just a klutz. You can't have my mom arrested; she didn't do anything!"

"We have enough evidence to charge her, and we'll be collecting more to prove our case. I hope that you'll be cooperative and come to see that we are trying to help and protect you, not hurt you more. It's normal to be sad and angry when you're taken away from your parents, even though they hurt you."

"They don't—she doesn't hurt me. You're wrong. I'm just clumsy. Please don't do this!"

"We've already done this. Don't worry, Katt. It will all work out. You'll be safe."

Katt slapped the mattress beside her angrily. She knew better than to hit the rail of the bed, even though that was what she wanted to do. She wanted to make a noise. To show Sarah that she meant business. That she was really serious and upset about it. But she also didn't want to break her hand on the railing. She'd never be able to manage crutches with her hand in a cast too.

"Why don't we leave Miss Katt alone, now?" the nurse suggested. "It isn't good for her to be so upset. She'll settle down faster if you're gone."

Sarah nodded her agreement. She put a business card down on the table next to Katt's bed. "That's my contact information if you need it. You'll be assigned a full-time social worker soon, but for now, I'm your contact point."

"I don't want your stupid card."

The nurse and the social worker left and Katt was alone in the room. Tears prickled her eyes. She couldn't believe that Karina had been arrested. But Karina was good at explaining about Katt's injuries. She would be out soon. And then she'd be back at Katt's side, laughing about the whole thing and taking care of her.

Katt closed her eyes and tried to go back to sleep. Maybe when she woke up the next time, Karina would be there.

———

But when Katt awoke next, Karina was not there. Instead, there was a policeman shaking her gently by the arm. He was young, handsome, the kind of boyish charm that would normally have resulted in a crush. But Katt wasn't falling for him. He was there to gather evidence against her mother and she wasn't going to give it to him.

"Hello, Katt." The man gave her a friendly smile. "I'm Officer Borden. How are you feeling today?"

"Pretty ticked off," Katt growled. "I can't believe that you arrested my mom! She hasn't done anything!"

"We want to help you, Katt." He sat down on the chair beside her. Katt had her suspicions that it wasn't because he was tired or felt like resting, but because he wanted to be closer to her level and look nonthreatening. Because then she would spill her guts out to him about how her mother abused her. Except that Karina didn't abuse Katt. Or neglect her. She was the most devoted mother a girl could hope for. "Why don't you tell me all about your mom? In your own words."

Katt breathed out, trying to calm herself and give the impression that she was being open and honest with him. He needed to see that she was telling the truth.

"My mom and I are best friends," she said. "I do get hurt a lot, so I've spent a lot of time home or in the hospital recovering. And she's always there for me. She's always here," she gestured to the chair that Borden was sitting in, "making sure I've got everything that I need, and that the doctors and nurses are giving me the proper care."

"But sometimes you don't get the proper care. Sometimes you have injuries, broken bones even, that are not dealt with. That's pretty serious."

"But they can't do anything with breaks like that," Katt protested. "They can put a cast on an arm or a leg, but they don't do anything about a toe or a rib or any of those other bones that they can't splint. I mean, unless you need surgery to pin something back together, all they can do about those other bones is to give you painkillers and tell you to ice it and take it easy. And we don't need to come to the emergency room for five hours—or overnight—just to be told that. I've had enough injuries to know how it works."

"You told the social worker that you don't even know how you broke your ribs or vertebrae."

"Well, yeah…" Katt shrugged. "Sometimes I get hurt and it takes a while to heal… I guess it's possible that I've broken bones without realizing it. Like my collarbone. I knew it hurt, but I didn't know it was broken. We just iced it and put my arm in a sling, because that made it feel better. After a few weeks… it was okay and I didn't need the sling anymore."

"I find it hard to believe that you wouldn't know something was broken."

"I can usually tell… with an arm or leg, anyway. But sometimes something really hurts, and it's only sprained or bruised. There's no point in coming in here when it just needs to be wrapped or iced."

"Tell me about school."

His change in direction confused Katt. She had to stop and think for a minute. What did he want to know? If she was doing well in school? If she had friends? If someone at school was abusing her? That was closer to the truth than he knew.

"I like school," Katt said tentatively. "I don't always do very well at it. Sometimes I need tutors. I do a lot of homebound study." She gestured to her foot. "There are so many stairs at the school and no elevator. It's impossible to get from one class to another when there are so many stairs if I have a broken foot or something. Or sometimes I get a sick stomach, too. I have some food sensitivities, and I pick up viruses whenever they are going around. Mumps went through the school earlier in the year and the principal told me to do home study until they were done with it. Because he knew I'd pick it up if I was around the other kids."

"So you've missed a lot of school."

"Well, I haven't missed it, I've still kept up my studies. Just not *at* the school."

"I see." He paused to write something down in his little notebook. "What's your favorite subject?"

"Ummm… art and English language arts, I guess. I really like both of them. I'm not the best at math. And you can imagine how I suck at phys ed."

She actually got a little laugh out of him over that. "And do you have a lot of friends? It must be hard to maintain friendships if you're home so much."

"Yeah. They come and see me sometimes when I'm home. But once every week or two, or once a month… it's not enough to keep up on all of the gossip and what's going on with everyone. I miss out on a lot that way. But then… I don't have a lot of friends, either. Just two or three." She sighed. "Everyone at school thinks I'm a total dork. It's probably a good thing that I'm at home so much, because while a bully sticking out his foot to trip a normal person is just mean, doing the same thing to me could mean months in traction."

"Is that something that happened to you?"

"Yeah," Katt sighed. "People are stupid. They think it's funny when I have a stupid accident and get hurt. They're always trying to trip me up or push me around. You want to know why I have so many bruises…" Katt looked toward her legs, where the mottled bruises were covered by her blanket. "It's school more than home. Nobody pushes me around or tries to trip me up at home. At home, it's just my own clumsiness. At school, it's ten times worse because of the jerks."

"Doesn't your school have an anti-bullying policy?"

Katt looked at him. "Have you ever seen an anti-bullying program that actually works? As soon as you deal with one guy, the next is waiting in line. And anyone you try to get them to deal with… they're worse as soon as the teachers turn their backs."

Borden nodded sympathetically.

Katt went on. "When I was a kid, I used to always tell if someone was picking on me. But even the teachers told me not to tattle. And it only made things worse. So now… I try to just stay out of the way and keep quiet."

"Do you get bullied a lot?"

"I'm the dorky girl who's always having stupid accidents. What do you think?"

He scratched something into his little notebook. Katt hoped that he was noting to himself that maybe her injuries were because of school rather than parental abuse.

"Does your mother know about this?"

"Hmm…" Katt tried to figure out his angle. If she said that her mother didn't know, he'd say that she wasn't paying attention to Katt's needs. If she said that her mother did know, then he'd question why she hadn't done something about it. "She knows about some things, like when I hurt my chest," she touched her collarbone, "but all the day-to-day stuff… I try not to worry her. I can handle it myself."

"Unless you get tripped and end up in traction," he commented, quoting her own words back to her.

"I couldn't exactly keep that from her."

CHAPTER FOUR

Karina was shown into a small conference room to meet with her lawyer. A woman named Thyra Klassen had been assigned to her case by the public defender's office. The woman's wild spirals of reddish brown hair made her look particularly frazzled. She sat down and smoothed them, but they all just popped back up, wilder than ever, when she lifted her hand. She sighed and rubbed the fatigue lines around her eyes.

Karina was tired too. She hadn't slept in the jail cell she had finally landed in at the end of the long and stressful night. It was already morning by the time she'd been escorted to her cell. Not light out yet, but definitely morning.

"So, how are you doing?" Thyra asked.

"Not so good. I'm tired and sore, and my daughter has been taken away from me. She's in hospital, hurt, without me. I'm the person that she needs right now. Not some social worker or foster mom. Katt needs her mother."

"It must be very difficult for you," Thyra said, with no real warmth. "And difficult for her."

"That's the biggest understatement of the year."

Thyra's eyes dropped to her file, a neatly-lettered new file folder with several sheets of paper tucked into it. She opened it up and scanned the contents.

"So I have the basics here," she said. "Social Services states that Katt came to the ER with several bones in her foot broken. Her story didn't match the severity of the injury. On examination, the attending doctor noted that she had bruises on her extremities and on her back. Deep bruises. A full examination was not made, but they took x-rays of her body and found a large number of old breaks, some of which were never reported or treated. Her hospitalization history is extensive. Explanations given for broken bones or other injuries requiring treatment in the past often stretch the boundaries of belief."

She raised her eyes from the file and cocked an eyebrow at Karina. Her challenge was clear. Explain it all away.

"Katt has always been fragile," Karina said. "I have brought it up with doctor after doctor. None of them can give me any explanation. Some kids are just more accident-prone, they say. She's just clumsy and unlucky, and manages to fall awkwardly."

"Do you have records of these discussions?"

Karina stared at her. "What kind of records? Doctors don't keep records of the questions parents ask. I have journals. A medical history I keep of Katt's treatments. But who is going to believe anything that I bring forward?"

Thyra nodded, conceding the point. "They are going to have a lot of evidence," she warned. "They have the x-rays and her medical records. Today I'm sure they'll be doing a full examination of Katt, documenting every bruise and scar. They'll be calling up any of the doctors who have treated her, asking them if they ever considered the possibility that you might have been abusive. What doctor is going to say no? They would look like they were negligent. 'Yes, I considered it, I just didn't have enough evidence at the time...' "

Documenting every bruise and scar. Karina had a sick feeling in the pit of her stomach. It was one thing when she took Katt to the doctor, and they saw an arm or a leg and commented on a particularly bad bruise or scar. It would be a whole other story if they went through every single one. It would look like the girl had been tortured.

"Can't you file an injunction or something?" she suggested. "Say that they don't have enough evidence? That it's an invasion of privacy? All we did was go in to get a break set when Katt dropped something on her foot. All the rest of this... they just ambushed us. They didn't even ask me any questions. They didn't get permission to take those x-rays."

"The x-rays are questionable, but in light of the deep bruising, it is logical to go to the next step and make sure there are no other broken bones. I don't think we would have success in challenging the constitutionality of the x-rays, and it wouldn't dispose a judge toward us."

"What can we do, then?"

"What is your explanation for her injuries? Just that she's accident prone? That's an explanation commonly given by abusive parents."

"She's more than accident prone… it's more than that." Karina shook her head and swore softly. "If you only knew how hard I have tried to get her diagnosed. To figure out what exactly is wrong with her. But they just shrug and say there's nothing wrong. Do some physio to strengthen her joints. Get her into sports. Accept that she's just going to hurt herself more than most children."

Thyra tapped her pen on the table in a staccato rhythm. "When was her first hospitalization?"

"She was born premature. She was only a couple of pounds and they didn't think that she would survive. But she's a fighter, and she pulled through. She was in NICU for five months. I was in hospital myself for quite a while. Even though she was so tiny, I had a lot of tearing and bleeding and my hips went out of joint. And my back… has never been the same since. The doctors said don't get pregnant again. My body didn't handle it very well."

Thyra made a couple of notes. "So then she went home from the hospital. When was her next medical issue?"

"She cried all the time. Like she was in pain. I told the doctors that she was in pain, but they didn't believe me. They said it was just colic. She'd grow out of it. Ignore it, and let her cry it out. But I knew that she was hurting."

"And was she? What did you find out?"

"Nothing. It wasn't any good. They all just brushed me off. New mother. Preemie baby. Bound to overreact about everything. I thought maybe it was digestive. She was constipated all the time. I tried all different kinds of formulas, everything on the market. But nothing seemed to help. Between the spitting up and the constipation, we were both pretty miserable. When she got a little bit bigger, one doctor said that she had reflux, and gave her a prescription for that. It helped, but had other side effects as well. She's always had a sensitive stomach. We have to be careful what she eats… and how much… and what time of day. She can't have anything before bed, or she's just miserable. Then she can't sleep, and neither can I."

"So, no injuries until…?"

Karina shifted uncomfortably. It would be easy to say that she didn't remember. There had been so many doctor and hospital visits over the years that it might certainly have been obscured by more recent hospital visits. But that would be a lie.

"She suffered hip dislocations during diaper changes. The first time scared me so bad. She was still so small, and I felt it pop out when I lifted her to put a fresh diaper under her, and she started to scream like crazy. I didn't know if it had broken or what. I rushed her to the emergency room. They put it back into place and double-diapered her, and said that should keep it in position well enough. But that wasn't the last time. I had to be so careful, being sure to roll her gently from side to side when switching out diapers, not moving her legs too far apart, not letting her kick against me… I learned how to ease it back into position if she did pop one out. The doctors said that it would get better as she got older. Her ligaments would tighten up. Her muscles would get stronger and hold them in place. It was all nonsense. It didn't get better. I just got her potty trained so that we didn't have to worry about it so much. Even then, she would still pop one out while changing pants now and again."

Thyra scratched a few words out. She wasn't writing very much, considering how much Karina was talking. The narrative should have at least earned a full sentence.

"When was her first broken bone?"

"She climbed out of her crib when she was… I don't know… ten months old. Broke her leg."

"I see."

"I moved her to a bed after that, to make sure she could get in and out without getting hurt. Although it made it hard to keep her in bed at bedtime!"

"That must have been frustrating."

Karina saw Thyra's look and shook her head. "I never hurt her. I couldn't do that. Yes, sometimes she drove me crazy as a toddler when she kept getting hurt and wouldn't listen to me. Yes, I still get frustrated with her now as a teenager. But I've never hit her. Never."

"You can repeat that to a judge, but you can't prove it. The prosecutor is going to bring up each and every hospital or doctor's visit. Every one. And if you can't remember or explain what happened, they'll convict you. Even if you have a good explanation for each one, they'll convict you because they'll see the pattern. You need to plead this out. With her extensive medical history, there's no way to win."

Karina stared at the lawyer, all of the air leaving her lungs. She hadn't expected Thyra to be optimistic about the charges, but she had expected some kind of hope. There had to be some way for Karina to get off. An innocent person couldn't just be convicted of child abuse and sent to prison when she hadn't done anything. There was a hard, sick knot growing in Karina's stomach. After working so hard for so many years trying to get Katt diagnosed or treated properly. After everything she had done to see that Katt got the best care, that she kept up at school when she was hurt or sick, they couldn't just lock her up and throw away the key. There had to be some kind of hope.

"I didn't do it," she told Thyra. "I didn't abuse her. I can't plead guilty."

"We'll try to get them down to something reasonable. Child endangerment. Maybe some kind of suspended sentence, if you'll agree to treatment and a safety plan. Supervision. Things don't look good. You're not going to get off."

―――――

They brought her meals. They brought her pain medications. They even turned on the little TV and handed her the remote so that she would have something to occupy her time. But what Katt needed was her mother. There was no word from Social Services or the hospital staff as to her mother's fate, or who was supposed to be taking care of Katt when she was released from the hospital.

Katt was restless. It was just a broken foot, and it had been set, there was no reason she should have to stay there any longer. Hospitals were always places that Katt associated with pain and illness. She wanted to get out of there. To go home where she could sleep in her own bed and make her own sandwiches and not have to worry about penicillin-resistant staph infections.

She wanted so much just to go home. She could take care of herself until Karina got out of jail. Katt waited until the nurse came around to pick up her lunch plates.

"How are you doing?" the nurse asked as she cleared everything away.

"Tired," Katt said, affecting a yawn.

"Well, why don't you have a nap? You probably didn't get too much sleep last night."

"Yeah, I think I will," Katt agreed, pulling the blanket up to her chin and closing her eyes.

"Have a good nap."

Katt waited for ten minutes and then got quietly out of bed. It took a long time for her to get her own clothes back on, working around the cast and stopping every time she heard a noise. She gritted her teeth while she pulled out the IV, and she held a tissue over the IV hole until the bleeding slowed. Then she grabbed the nearby crutches and walked to the door. Looking down the hallway, she couldn't see any nurses or staff who would prevent her from leaving. As long as she behaved like she had the perfect right to be there, no one would stop her.

She swung down the hallway, going slowly to avoid tripping or wrenching her shoulders with the crutches.

"Hey, where are you going?"

Katt didn't look back. She kept walking, hoping that the voice was addressing someone else. They didn't have any reason to stop her. There was a murmur of voices, and for a moment, she thought that she was safe, and they were talking to someone else. She was almost to the elevator.

"Katt! You need to go back to bed. You can't be wandering the halls." It was a gruff voice. Katt kept going, while her detached brain tried to identify whether the voice was male or female. What were they going to do, tackle her?

"Security to unit three hundred," a different voice announced over the PA system. Was that her? What was security going to do about a patient wandering the halls? Katt glanced at the doorplate of the room nearest her. Three-oh-nine and three-ten. A double room. Security was being called to her unit.

There was a rapid footstep behind her.

Katt didn't look back. It was a nurse, she knew, not security. Security had big clunky shoes. The nurses wore comfortable sneakers.

She reached the elevator and pressed the down button, willing the elevator to already be on her floor. She could slip into the elevator, press the main floor and door close buttons, and she would be on her way. They might try to follow her, but it was a lot harder to chase after an elevator using the stairway in real life than it was on TV. If she got off on a floor before main, she might lose them altogether.

But Katt never did have very good luck. The elevator doors didn't open, and she stood there, heart thumping hard, as the footsteps approached her.

"Katt, what are you doing? Come back to your room!"

The nurse was puffing when she caught up to Katt.

"What do you think you're doing? Come on, now. Back to your room."

Katt still refused to look at her, waiting for the elevator to arrive. There was a firm hand on her left shoulder.

"Come on," the nurse repeated firmly. "Let's go."

"No. I'm going home," Katt insisted.

"You can't go home. You need to stay here until you're released, and then Social Services will look after you." The woman had big, capable hands, and her grip tightened on Katt's shoulder, insistent. "Now. Quit being so silly."

"I'm not being silly," Katt argued. "I'm going home."

The nurse tried to pull her, and Katt let her shoulder roll under her hand, slipping out of her grip. They were going to have to try a heck of a lot harder than that if they were going to force her back to her room.

The clomp of a security guard's clunky shoes moved down the hall toward them. Now it was two against one. Either one of them could take her physically. She wasn't big enough or strong enough to stand up to them.

Where was the stupid elevator?

"Help me get Miss Lindholm back to her room," the gruff nurse's voice called out to the guard.

"Come on, then, Miss."

Katt finally looked at the nurse. A hefty, red-faced woman. She had checked in on Katt a couple of times during the day, scowling while she recorded Katt's stats and then left again without a word of greeting. The guard caught up to them as well and stationed himself on Katt's other side. He wasn't massive, but he was bigger than Katt, his face determined.

"Let's go." His hand closed around Katt's arm. She whipped it away from him, slipping out of his grasp.

"Don't touch me! Leave me alone!"

"You don't want to fight me. Come back to your room quietly."

"No! I'm going home."

Finally, the elevator dinged and the doors slid open in front of Katt. She tried to step forward into it, but the nurse and the security guard each grabbed an arm and prevented her from moving forward.

"Let go of me! You can't touch me; I'll sue you!"

The nurse's grip loosened for a moment, then tightened again as the nurse decided to ignore her threat. They both pulled on her, trying to turn her around and force her to walk back to her room. Katt threw her elbows back and tried to hit them or squirm away. They were too strong for her and ignored her flailing around as if she were just a tantrumming toddler.

Katt threw the crutches down. "Leave me alone!"

The guard gave her arm a jerk. Katt could feel her shoulder separating and tried to grab it with the other hand, to protect it and keep it from pulling out of the joint. But the nurse wouldn't release her other arm.

"Ouch! You're hurting me, let go!"

"You had your chance to be cooperative and come along nicely," the guard growled at her.

"My shoulder!"

"Try to keep her off that foot," the nurse instructed. "The cast should protect it, but I don't want to take any chances."

Katt squirmed. The guard tried to lift and control her with his grip on her upper arm, and Katt's shoulder popped free of the joint.

The wave of pain it brought made Katt sway on her feet, black blotches growing in front of her eyes and threatening to completely block out her vision. The guard swore when Katt's arm went limp in his hand, and he knew that he'd done some kind of damage.

"I can't…" Katt tried to warn them that she was going to faint. But the guard figured it out on his own, and he grabbed her around the body, his arm crushing her ribcage, to support her and keep her from going down.

"What happened?" the nurse demanded.

"I don't know. Her arm."

The nurse released her hold on Katt's other arm. The guard tried to walk Katt down the hall a few steps, still holding her around her body, pressed against his side. Then deciding that wasn't working, he bent over and scooped Katt up, holding her cradled in his arms like a toddler.

"Which room?"

The nurse briskly walked him back to Katt's hospital room, and he laid her in the bed. Katt numbly reached over and levered her shoulder joint back into place. She sighed in relief, and some of the tension went out of her. But the rest of her body was hurting from the manhandling. Once her joint was back in place, her brain focused on the next most painful part. Her ribs. Katt probed them gently with her fingers and found the two that brought a sharp jerk of pain. She lay there, panting and trying to blink away the black spots. The guard and the nurse stared down at Katt, their eyes wide and worried.

"I think… you broke… my ribs," Katt puffed.

"It was your arm," the guard said blankly.

"Yeah. But… you grabbed me…" Katt was getting short of breath trying to breathe shallowly enough not to hurt her ribcage.

"I had to!" the guard protested, his voice angry. "What was I supposed to do?"

"You should not have been out of bed," the nurse threw in. But she was moving, approaching Katt's bedside and automatically feeling Katt's pulse while she considered the situation.

"I'll have to reinsert the IV. You shouldn't have pulled it out."

Katt saved her breath. The nurse pulled up her sleeve.

"You're bleeding." She pulled up the makeshift bandage and looked under it. "Sheesh! You just tore it out of there, didn't you? I'm going to have to use the other arm. This one's too ripped up."

She rebandaged Katt's arm, using a palm-sized dressing pressed firmly down over the tear caused by the IV.

"We're going to need to get you back into your johnny before we hook you up," the nurse advised. She picked up the blue gown that Katt had discarded earlier. "Shirt off."

Katt looked at the security guard. "No."

"No false modesty. He's not going to be looking at you."

"Don't… want to."

"You want painkillers; I need to put the IV back in. And if I put it in while you have your shirt on, you can't get back into the gown. Do you want something for your bruised ribs?"

Katt couldn't undress in front of the guard. She lay there, not moving. The nurse hovered over her, waiting.

"I'll turn around," the guard said. "But if you cause any trouble, I'm still right here."

He stared at her for a minute to make sure that she understood, then turned around, facing the wall instead of Katt. The nurse helped Katt to sit up, a slow and painful process, moving pillows behind Katt to prop her up so that the nurse could remove her shirt. The woman prodded Katt's shoulder for swelling, and poked at her ribs a bit, though it was obvious that she couldn't tell whether they were really broken or just bruised. She *tsked* over Katt's bruises.

"You want to go home when you're looking like this? Why would you want to go back to that kind of abuse? You need to take care of yourself; you're a big girl. Don't let anyone hit you."

Katt just breathed, holding her ribs. The nurse didn't have the grace or the sense to realize that *they* had just assaulted Katt, hurting her worse than any harm her mother had ever inflicted. And Katt didn't have the breath to explain it to her.

"Okay, on with the johnny," the nurse instructed, and she helped Katt to thread her arms through the hospital gown, then tied it behind her. "There. Lie down. I'll get the IV reinserted."

The guard turned around again and watched the proceedings.

"I'll have to get a doctor to issue orders for further x-rays on those ribs and your shoulder. You have a standing order for Demerol as needed, so I'll get that going. But you are going to need to stay in bed, do you understand?"

Katt nodded.

"I mean it. If I see you out of bed even to go to the toilet without permission, I'll order restraints. I don't think you want that."

"No," Katt whispered.

"Then you stay put. You're not going home. You're staying here where we can keep an eye on you, and then you're going to go wherever Social Services says you are. No more nonsense."

Katt swallowed, staring down at the white blanket that the nurse pulled up over her, still leaving her in her shoe and pants.

———

The Demerol dulled the pain enough that Katt drifted off to sleep again. She hadn't had enough sleep the night before; that much had been true. She roused slightly when they pushed her bed to x-ray, but Katt just closed her eyes again, allowing herself to drift. Even once she got to x-ray, it would likely still be an hour before they actually took the images. She didn't need to wake up until then.

She didn't know how long it was before they shook her awake. She felt like she had been asleep for a long time, dozing drowsily, shifting between waking and sleep a number of times. Normally, Karina would have been there to keep her company. Waking her up so that she didn't sleep all day. Getting Katt to help her with crossword clues or something else to keep her mind active.

"What time is it?" Katt asked thickly, though she had no idea what time it had been when she had gone to sleep. She had nothing to use as a reference point.

"It's four o'clock," the intern with his hand on her arm advised. "Can you get up and around on your own?"

Katt tested her shoulders, then used her arms to push herself up to a seated position. Her ribs throbbed briefly, but the Demerol was keeping the pain under control. And her foot was in a cast, so it wasn't going to bother her.

"Yeah... I think so."

"Good girl."

He put down the side of the gurney and gave her a steadying hand as she slid her feet to the floor. Katt stood there for a moment, waiting for her head to readjust to being upright so that the room would stop spinning. Then she gave a little nod.

"Okay."

The intern was looking down at Katt's shoe and pants.

"You going somewhere?"

"Well... I was."

He chuckled. "It's going to have to come off for x-rays. There's a change area in here," he gestured to the x-ray lab.

"Why? You're not doing my leg."

"Need everything off. Just the gown."

"You're not x-raying my legs," Katt repeated.

"The sooner you get changed, the sooner we can get started."

She tried to stare him down, but he just waited. Katt didn't have any crutches. She limped into the change area, and it took some time for her to get everything off. The x-ray tech smiled and had her stand against the wall.

"Which shoulder is the problem?" he asked, looking at his orders.

"A problem? Well… both."

"This says your right shoulder dislocated, is that right?"

"Yeah."

"That's the one we want to look at, then. For the first few pictures, I'm just going to have you stand still there, in a natural position, and I'll show you what position I want you to hold your hand in."

Katt nodded and followed his instructions the best that she could. While the different positions gave her shoulder a few twinges, they didn't cause any problems. But then he had her raising her arm and holding it in several different positions. Katt put her left hand over it, trying to give it a rest and keep it in the proper position.

"You need to put your other hand down."

"This is hurting."

"Only a few minutes longer. Put your left hand down, and hold your right arm up…"

Katt released it slowly, biting her lip. Not only was the muscle burning from having to hold her arm in so many unnatural positions, but she knew that unstable feeling that preceded a dislocation. As long as she could hold it steady, and not let it drop, it would be okay.

"A bit higher," the tech encouraged. "You're dropping it."

"It's too hard. It's going to pop out."

"You'll be fine," he assured her. "We're just about done. I just need a couple more shots. Then we'll look at your ribs. They'll be a lot quicker. Raise it about an inch."

Katt shook her head. "I can't."

With a huff of exasperation, he left his position behind the x-ray machine and marched up to her.

"One more inch. Like this." He gave her arm a little lift. And then he was holding the weight of her arm, a look of shock on his face. He swore, his eyes wide. He let it go, and her arm fell limply to her side. It didn't hurt too badly, with the level of Demerol she was already on. Katt just looked at it, and then at the x-ray tech. He caught her arm again. "I… should… we'll have to call emergency to get it back in place."

"No," Katt said, shaking her head. She used her other hand to manipulate it, but it was harder than usual to get back into place. "Hold my wrist," she told him. "Pull it straight out."

He seemed squeamish about touching the dislocated limb. But with encouragement, he stretched it out, and Katt was able to turn her body and push with her fingers to get it into place. She stretched and rotated it gently.

"No more," she told him.

The tech nodded, his face white. "Okay," he agreed.

She was glad he was listening to her now, but not so happy about having to have her shoulder dislocate again before he took her seriously.

"Let's get some films of those ribs," he said.

The rib x-rays were simple and straightforward. Katt breathed a sigh of relief when they were done. But not too hard.

—————

When Katt was returned to her hospital room, there was finally a social worker there. Katt blinked as the woman introduced herself as Brooke Wicker.

"So where is my mom?" she asked. "I told that other social worker and the police that she didn't do anything to hurt me. I need her to sit with me."

Brooke pulled a visitor chair over and sat down with a sigh. She had curly blond hair, cropped short around her broad face. And she wore pink.

"Your mom has been arrested, honey. Weren't you told that?"

"I know, but what happened then? They can't keep her in jail when she didn't do anything. I'll tell a judge. I'll tell whoever. She never did anything to hurt me."

"She's in jail right now, as far as I know. She hasn't had a hearing yet to see whether she can get bail. Maybe she will, but there will be conditions. Like not being able to visit you. Not without supervision."

"Did the nurse tell you that they broke two of my ribs? And dislocated my shoulder? Twice? Maybe you should go arrest them!"

Brooke studied her, her blue-eyeshadowed lids closed halfway.

"I hear you saying that you want your mom back," she said. "But that's not going to happen in the near future. We need to evaluate the situation. See how you do when she doesn't have access to you. Review the evidence. Interview witnesses. Those things take time. Weeks, not hours."

"Weeks?" Katt demanded. None of the other Social Services investigations had ever lasted more than a couple of hours. They were always satisfied once they talked to Karina and Katt. They understood that it was illness, not abuse, that kept sending Katt to the hospital.

"Yes. At least. Once we get you stabilized here, you'll be going to a foster home. I'm reviewing who would be able to take you now. In a few days, we'll have something lined up, and you won't have to bounce from one place to another."

"I don't want to go to a foster home. I want to go to my mom."

"That's not an option right now. We need you to take a holiday from your mom so that we can get a reading on how many of your *medical issues* are… related… to her."

"What does that mean?"

Brooke just raised her eyebrows and smiled. "Don't you worry about it. That's my job."

"Well, you'd better investigate all the doctors too, because they're the ones who should have figured out some way to help me years ago."

"Is there anything that I can get you, Katt? I realize that you are here without any of your belongings, other than what you were wearing when you arrived here. Is there anything you need?"

Katt shook her head. She didn't need the social worker doing anything for her. She could manage all on her own. The medical staff would take care of her food and care as long as she was at the hospital, and then she was going to go home and she would have all of her stuff. In the meantime, she had her phone and a few of her graphic novels.

Brooke glanced around the hospital room. "It's nice that you have a room to yourself. That doesn't happen very often, hey? How about your phone? You need that charged for you?"

"No. I always bring my charger to the hospital."

"You're a pro at this, huh?"

Katt cleared her throat, angry at the reference to her being a frequent visitor at the hospital. "If you're going to be waiting in the ER for hours, your phone runs down," she said simply. She turned her head away from the social worker. She'd been waiting for someone to update her on what was going on all day, but now that Brooke was here, Katt just wanted her to go away.

"I'm going to go back to sleep," she said. "Pain and Demerol make me tired."

"Okay, Katt." Brooke stood up and patted Katt's arm before leaving. "You take care. I'll be by to see you again sometime tomorrow. And we'll get a good family lined up for you right away."

CHAPTER FIVE

Katt had barely eaten since getting to the hospital. She had been sure to eat before going to the ER, so she hadn't needed anything the night she was admitted. And the Demerol took away her appetite, so she only picked at her meals when they were brought to her.

A doctor came around to look at her chart. Not Dr. George, but whoever was attending in ward three hundred. Katt didn't catch his name and didn't remember seeing him before. Blond-haired, blue-eyed, young but with an abrupt manner.

"I'm going to dial you back to Tylenol," he said. "I don't think you need opiates now that your foot has been set. Tylenol should take care of the pain for the next few days."

"I have broken ribs too," Katt pointed out. Even with the Demerol, she could still feel the ribs when she moved the wrong way or breathed too deeply. Tylenol wasn't going to cover it.

He looked at her chart for a bit longer, flipping back and forth between pages. "You're going to need to be weaned off," he said. "You won't be sent home with a prescription for opiates. We'll lower the dose over a period of days, but you're going to be off it before you leave."

"So you don't care how much pain I'm in?"

"You'll be able to manage it with this prescription."

He scribbled instructions on the chart. "How about eating?"

"What?"

"You need to start eating. Full meals. The nursing staff has concerns."

"I'm not hungry."

"You need to eat. I'll be expecting a better report when I check in tomorrow."

Katt didn't promise to eat more. She just waited for him to leave again.

After he was gone, supper was brought around. Katt sat and looked at it, trying to will herself to be hungry. Roast beef and mashed potatoes with gravy. Green peas in butter. A cup of milk. A jello cup for dessert.

She started with the jello cup, hoping that it would whet her appetite. It didn't. The sugar killed any fraction of appetite that she had had before starting. Katt forced herself to take a few bites of the greasy vegetables, tough meat, and bland instant potatoes. If someone had bought her a cheeseburger, she might have been able to eat some of it. But the institutional food was awful. She looked forward to going home. Or wherever else she could get good food. At least a foster home would have better food.

After eating, she leaned back in her bed, the head still raised and pillows behind her, and tried to go back to sleep. There was nothing else to do to pass the time. She could read, watch TV, or play games on her phone, but she didn't have the attention span.

As she lay there, her stomach started to churn. Acid burned her stomach and esophagus. She belched a few times to try to let out the air, but the pain in her stomach just kept getting worse. Katt held her stomach and rolled back and forth, trying to find a comfortable position.

Finally, she pressed the call button. She should have pressed it earlier and allowed for the time it would take the nurses to notice her page and come and check on her. It always took a long time for them to answer a call. Katt could hear them gossiping out by the nursing station, ignoring the call. It wasn't until a doctor came by to see a patient that they giggled and broke up their hen session. A few minutes later, one of the nurses, not the broad-faced one who had stopped her from running away, arrived to see what she wanted.

"Done eating?" she asked, collecting Katt's tray and looking as though she was just going to turn around and leave without finding out what Katt had called about. Maybe she hadn't even responded to the call; maybe she was just collecting dishes and no one had bothered to respond to Katt's call for help yet.

"My stomach is really bothering. Can you give me something for it?"

"What's wrong with your tummy, hon'?"

"Acid indigestion. I'm on a prescription for acid inhibitors. It should be on my chart."

"We don't usually distribute them without a reason. A lot of patients need to wean off of them."

"My stomach is really hurting. I'm going to throw up if I don't get something."

"Uh-huh." The nurse touched Katt's forehead, then put her stethoscope on Katt's stomach for a few seconds. "Well, listen to it going to beat the band," she observed. Katt belched again. The nurse made a face.

"Sorry," Katt apologized, her face getting hot with embarrassment.

"All right, I'll get you a pill. Eat more slowly next time. Drink lots of water between meals. I'll put you on a bland diet and see if that helps."

"That wasn't bland?" Katt asked, gesturing at her half-empty tray.

The nurse chuckled. "No dear. You haven't had that pleasure yet."

———

Katt watched the IV drip, waiting for the pain to come back. She knew they were weaning her off of the Demerol and she knew that the Tylenol wouldn't be enough to calm the pain of her ribs.

She alternated between watching the IV waiting for the pain, and watching the door in the expectation that Brooke the social worker would be coming back to check on her. She probably wouldn't be released from the hospital for a few more days, but if Brooke showed up and said that she had decided on a foster family for Katt… Katt didn't know what she would do.

She was still holding out the hope that they would see that Karina wasn't guilty of anything, and her mother would be back at her side. Everything would go back to normal.

Her heart was pounding hard like she'd been running. Of course, Katt never actually ran, it was too dangerous for her. When they said to run in phys ed at school, she walked faster and swung her arms, but she didn't actually run.

Maybe she was going through withdrawal from the Demerol. Had she been on it for long enough to get addicted? Her doctors always talked about opiates like Katt would get addicted to them if she was on them for one day longer than she had to be. But she'd been on them for longer before, and hadn't gone through withdrawals. So it couldn't be the Demerol.

On top of her rapidly beating heart and the shortness of breath that went along with it, Katt's stomach was just as bad as it had been the previous day. Maybe more so. She was keeping a bedpan close, worried she was going to throw up. The nurses who were on shift said that she didn't need acid reducers, since she was on a bland diet and barely eating any of it anyway. But the acid burning Katt's throat said differently.

Karina said that when Katt was a baby, she had thrown up all the time. Karina would get one bottle of formula into her and then end up wearing half of it. Katt gained weight so slowly because she couldn't keep anything down. Katt was glad that it wasn't that bad anymore, but she wished that it would settle down and she could just eat anything and feel fine like a normal teen.

Her thoughts shifted to school. How was she going to get to school if she were in a different home? What if the home they put her in were not even in bussing distance of the school? She would have to start at a new school. Totally new, with people who hadn't ever met her before. While she entertained the thought for thirty seconds that if no one knew who she was, they wouldn't know she was so dorky and clumsy, and she could have friends and be more popular, but she immediately shook her head at her own naivety. Of course, they would know that she was clumsy and dorky, they would see it the first time she tripped down the hallway and fell on her face.

A new school, with new bullies and teachers she didn't know, and no Karina. It was going to be hell.

A boy walking down the hospital hallway turned abruptly into Katt's room, interrupting her escalating panic. He was wearing a gray hoodie, with the hood pulled up over his head. He was thin and serious-looking, and despite the hoodie, she could see that he had short dark hair.

"Hi, there," he greeted, throwing a smile in Katt's direction.

Katt caught her breath. He was talking to her. She had no idea who he was or why he was there, but it was so nice to have someone other than a nurse or a social worker talk to her. Even if he had just turned into the wrong room.

"Uh—hi."

He took a quick glance over his shoulder into the hallway, then walked up to the bed. His manner was casual, but he moved in an oddly deliberate way.

"Who are you?" Katt asked.

"Katt Lindholm," he read the name on her chart. "I like the name Katt."

"Yeah, thanks. And you…"

"Is it short for Katherine? Or is it just Katt?"

"Just Katt."

He nodded, smiling. He looked around her small room, studying the curtain on a railing around the bed, and the narrow little closet in the corner. He looked at the other door.

"You don't mind if I use your restroom, do you?" He headed toward it without waiting for a response. And what was Katt going to say? No, you can't use it? Go find another one? She was glad for the company, even of a stranger.

Clapper, the nurse who had chased Katt down when she had attempted escape, stood in the doorway and looked around the room carefully. She looked at Katt with some suspicion.

"Everything okay?" she asked.

Katt was sure that wasn't what she had been planning to say. She had something else on her mind. She didn't care a bit how Katt was feeling.

"Yeah, fine," Katt snapped.

The woman stood there for a moment longer, her dark, beady eyes staring into Katt's soul, and then she withdrew and went on. What was her problem? Clapper didn't like Katt, and Katt didn't like Clapper, but they weren't there to be best friends. Katt usually got along with nurses. Nurses were attracted to vulnerability. But occasionally, she ran into one like Clapper, who just couldn't seem to stand her. Katt didn't know whether it was because she had tried to escape, or because she had fought back against Clapper, or because Katt had ended up getting hurt and Clapper now thought she was weak and a loser. But Clapper did not like her.

The bathroom door opened, and the mysterious boy came out. Katt rubbed her eyes. It was easier to get distracted when her anxiety was so high. With the Demerol being withdrawn, she was no longer feeling languid and dopey. Her thoughts were racing, and she jumped from one idea to another, without allowing any time to evaluate and ponder any one thing.

"Thanks," the boy said.

"Yeah. No problem. Who are you again?"

He shrugged as if names were unimportant. "I heard them talking about you," he commented. "You're the one whose mom is in jail?"

"She didn't do anything wrong!" Katt protested hotly.

"I didn't say she did. Sometimes Social Services makes mistakes. And the doctors. And the police. It sucks that you're here all by yourself."

He picked up her clipboard and frowned, studying it. He flipped from one page to another. He was a young man, maybe a year or two older than she was. A darkening shadow of facial hair around his jaw.

"That's private," Katt said. "You can't read that."

"I can't read most of it anyway," he chuckled. "Doctors and their handwriting! The only things that are clear are the prescriptions, and those are in pharmacy code."

"Put it back."

He slowly deposited the clipboard back onto its hook at the end of the bed.

"They think your mother has Munchausen by Proxy? That she hurts you or makes you sick for medical attention?"

Katt stared at him. "What are you talking about?"

"You've heard of it before, haven't you?"

"Yeah… mothers poisoning their babies and stuff. But my mom doesn't do anything like that. She takes good care of me."

"She doesn't give you anything to eat that makes you sick? Or hurts you and says you did it yourself?"

"No! Who the hell are you, and where do you get off accusing my mom of abuse? You've never even met her!"

He raised his hands in a calming gesture. "I didn't say she did. I said that's what the doctors and social workers are thinking. I just asked whether she did anything. If she doesn't, that's good… but not good that they arrested her."

"You should go now."

He glanced toward the door but didn't move. "There are people who can help," he said in a low voice. "Just keep that in mind." He took a cautious step toward the door and stuck his head out to look up and down the corridor for an instant. "You're not alone."

And then he was gone. Katt stared after him for a long time. Was he for real? Maybe he was an escapee from the psych ward. Or maybe she was having hallucinations with the withdrawal of the Demerol, and he didn't even exist. Munchausen by Proxy? *You are not alone?* Could she have just dreamed that up?

Now that he was gone, Katt's heart started to race again. She hadn't noticed how the panicky rhythm had slowed while he had been there. He had acted like he believed her. Like he believed that her mom hadn't hurt her. *There are people who can help.* Who could help her? She was alone, at the mercy of the medical staff and social worker. There wasn't anyone who could do anything to help.

———

"Time to change your bandage," Nurse McKenna said cheerfully.

Katt liked the young male nurse. He was always happy, with real, sincere smiles, and upbeat. He was professional and efficient. She just liked being around him.

He carefully unstuck the dressing from her arm, where the original IV line had been inserted. Her skin had torn badly when Katt had removed the IV and when it wouldn't stop seeping blood and scab over, they had decided to put a few stitches in it to close it up and allow it to clot and scab properly.

Katt had asked them not to do it. Stitches never seemed to work out right for her. But they didn't understand what she meant when she said that the stitches would just make it worse, or they didn't believe her.

"Let's have a look," he said, peeling the dressing away from the wound. He frowned.

Katt sighed. She knew what was coming.

"The stitches pulled out, didn't they?"

He dabbed at the wound with the bandage. It was obviously still oozy and not scabbed over.

"You've had this happen before?"

"I told them not to stitch it. But they wouldn't believe me!"

"Well… this is a mess. That's not usually what happens when you stitch a wound."

"It's what happens to me. I told them."

He nodded. "You didn't pull them out intentionally, did you…?"

"No!"

"So what usually helps? This is just getting wider and more messy."

"Sometimes it helps to use tape," she said, "but if it pulls... it still doesn't work."

"Can you avoid moving it around?"

"I've already been trying that. I didn't exactly want it to tear!"

"No. We might have to splint you to keep it straight for a while and let it start to mend."

Katt nodded. "And tape."

"And tape," he agreed. "Okay, let me gather supplies, and we'll see what we can do."

Katt looked at the hole in her arm. "It's not infected, is it? If it gets infected, it will be really bad."

"No, it's clean. We'll be careful to keep it sterile."

———

She hit the call button again. Katt was soaked in sweat. She would be tossing and turning, except that every movement hurt, and she couldn't lie on either her sides or her stomach. Only flat on her back. But she squirmed and moved her arms uncomfortably. Even that wasn't easy, with one arm in a splint. She had already pressed the button several times, and she wouldn't think at night the nurses would have had that much to do. They just didn't think there was anything to be concerned about and were taking their own sweet time getting to Katt.

One of the night nurses finally came in. Katt wasn't as familiar with them as she was with the day shift. She had been sleeping at night until they withdrew the Demerol.

"Having trouble sleeping?" the woman asked, her shoes whispering over the tile as she approached the bed.

"I need pain pills," Katt said, trying to keep the tears out of her voice. No nurse liked dealing with a whiny patient. The more Katt complained, the less helpful the nurse would be.

"Well, let's have a look..." The nurse was an older woman. She had gotten into nursing later in life, or had been working as a nurse for twenty years already. She took a look at Katt's chart. "You have a full dose of Tylenol before bed. You're not due for another dose yet."

"Then something else," Katt urged. "More Demerol."

"No Demerol. What's your pain at now, on a scale of one to ten?"

Katt wiped at a tear with her unsplinted hand. "I don't know… eight."

"Eight?" The nurse rolled her eyes and shook her head. "What's hurting? Your foot?"

"My ribs. And my arm." Katt indicated her immobilized arm. "Everything. Please, I need something for it."

"I think you're exaggerating. You've gotten yourself worked up. The Tylenol should still be holding."

The nurse felt Katt's forehead, then brought out an electronic thermometer. She jabbed it into Katt's ear.

"You've got a slight temperature."

She felt Katt's pulse. "Hmm. We'll try some Ibuprofen and see if that helps.

"Demerol would be better."

The nurse wrote something on Katt's chart, her mouth in a pronounced frown.

"Ibuprofen," she repeated.

———

It might have been a dream. Katt had been closing her eyes, her mind wandering, then had heard a movement in the room. She rubbed her eyes and looked around. It was the boy in the hoodie again. He was still in the same hoodie. Was he a patient at the hospital? Some homeless guy wandering around where he shouldn't be? He didn't look dirty or smell bad, but she wondered.

"You're not looking so good," he said. He touched her throat with the backs of his fingers. His touch felt real enough. "You're hot and flushed."

"I have a fever," Katt agreed.

"You gotta get out of here before they end up killing you. Every time they touch you they screw up."

"Already tried to get out of here. They broke my ribs."

He shook his head. "There are people who can help," he said in a low voice. "Have you ever heard of medical kidnap?"

Katt shook her head. "They kidnap people from hospitals?"

He chuckled. "No. Not exactly. They use Social Services and the medical profession to take kids with medical issues away from their parents."

"Why would they do that?"

Katt's head was muzzy. She pushed herself up, trying to force focus.

"To allow them to do medical research. To get grant money. To get money for kids in foster care."

"What money?"

The boy stroked her hair, an intimate gesture for someone who didn't even know her. "You're so out of it right now; I don't think you could understand even if I had time to explain it. What you need to know is that there's an underground railway. A way to get out, to get somewhere safe. Do you understand?"

Katt nodded. The movement made him bounce up and down in front of her eyes, making her dizzy.

"How do I get on this… railway?"

"Wait. You'll be contacted. But I have to be sure that you aren't really being abused. That it is a medical kidnap case."

"My mom never hurt me. I just have… accidents. It's true!" She gestured at herself, shaking her head. "When I was admitted, all I had was a broken foot. My mom hasn't been here at all. And now I have broken ribs, this laceration," she indicated her splinted arm, "and they've dislocated my shoulder twice. They won't give me anything for my stomach, or any Demerol even if I tell them the pain is an eight or nine. And now… I have a fever too!"

"Which means an infection," the boy agreed, nodding. "I'll be in contact. Or someone else will be. Okay? Do you know where you're going yet?"

Katt closed her eyes and shook her head. "No. Foster family."

"You don't know who you're going to?"

"No."

"Okay. Hang in there, all right? We'll figure something out."

Katt sighed. He couldn't do anything for her any more than the doctors or Karina could. Just wait there while the hospital staff tried to kill her.

"You have a phone number?" she mumbled to him, suppressing a yawn. "A business card maybe?"

"No. Too dangerous. I'll be in touch. Promise."

"Okay."

Katt closed her eyes again and drifted off to sleep before he was gone.

CHAPTER SIX

The doctor confirmed that Katt's lacerated arm was infected, a fact that she had already guessed at, and they put strong antibiotics directly into her IV, promising that the swelling and fever should be gone by the end of the day. She'd have to be on oral antibiotics after that, but would be able to be released and go home to her family.

Except that they weren't really her family.

She was informed that she was going to the Foegels, a family who were used to dealing with medical cases and would do just fine taking care of her. Katt doubted they had ever had to deal with anyone like her. They might think that they were experienced, but they hadn't seen anything yet.

Katt had a boring and restless day. She watched for the mysterious young man, but he didn't show up again. Her fever and swelling subsided, and as the evening drew on and it was dark outside the window, Brooke Wicker made her appearance.

"I'll bet you're ready to get out of here!" she exclaimed, making a motion that took in all the hospital equipment and noise around them. "You'll probably get your first sound sleep in a week."

Katt just eyed her and didn't respond to that.

"Why don't you start getting changed into your clothes? I will talk to one of the nurses about getting you released," Brooke suggested.

"I can't get changed yet."

"Why not?"

"They have to take the IV out first. And… I'm going to need help because I can't bend this arm."

"What happened to that arm? Is that the side that you hurt your shoulder on?"

"Well… yes, but that's not why it's splinted. If it was for the shoulder, they'd have to put my arm in a sling, or strapped to my body."

"Oh. So why is it splinted?"

"Because of the damage left by the IV, when it was in this arm."

"Ah." Brooke nodded as if she remembered this detail. If she'd ever known in the first place. "Well then, I guess we need a nurse to take out your IV and get you changed."

Katt nodded. Brooke went out to find a nurse to help. Katt looked around the room. It was her last day there. While she'd hated every minute of it, she was anxious about leaving. She didn't know what was going to happen next. At least she was familiar with the hospital and knew how everything worked. But she didn't know foster families. She didn't know the environment or the rules, or how things worked. It was a big, black hole.

While waiting for Brooke and the nurse to return, Katt got out her clothes and put them on the bed. She unplugged her phone charger, but couldn't wrap it up with only one hand, so she left it on the bed beside the clothes. Moving around was hurting her ribs. Bad. She stood for a few minutes, just breathing. Her body wasn't taking kindly to standing up. It was good for her stomach, but bad for her ribs. And her sore arm was starting to throb.

Eventually, Brooke brought back one of the nurses, who went without a word to Katt's IV and untaped it.

"We'll get this one taken out properly," she said. "Avoid getting all ripped up like the other one."

Katt gritted her teeth and looked down at it, hoping that the nurse was right. Katt had been careful in taking the IV out, but it wasn't as easy for her to take it out by herself. The nurse inched the IV straight out and smiled at Katt.

"There, you see, just like that." She pressed a piece of folded gauze over the hole left by the IV. "Hold that tight for a couple of minutes."

Katt sat there holding it.

"May as well take a look at the other one while we're waiting," the nurse commented. She moved to Katt's other arm and peeled the dressing back. She dabbed at the wound. Katt could see that it was weeping fluid. Not bleeding, but a light-colored liquid. The nurse patted it with the dry section of the dressing, examining it closely. "The inflammation has definitely gone down. But it doesn't look like you're out of the woods yet. You're going to have to watch this very carefully. If the fluid and the swelling don't go down more, you'll need to come back to get it taken care of."

"Okay."

The woman redressed Katt's arm and then nodded to the other one. "That should be fine now. Let's put a bandage on it."

Katt lifted the gauze slowly, peeking underneath carefully to see if it had stopped bleeding. She shook her head. "Still bleeding."

"No, it isn't! Let me have a look."

Katt lifted the gauze farther and watched blood well up from the hole.

"Do you have a bleeding problem? A clotting disorder?"

"It always takes me longer to clot," Katt admitted. "But they can't tell me why."

"Well, let's tape that down so that we can at least get you into your clothes. You can apply pressure after that."

"Okay."

Katt looked at Brooke, waiting for her to leave. Brooke stood there for a moment as if she didn't understand, then she chuckled a little and stepped out of the room, pulling the door behind her. "Don't be long."

Katt moved slowly and stiffly as the nurse got the hospital johnny off and helped her get her pants and shirt on over the cast and splint. The nurse put a sock and shoe on Katt's uninjured foot and looked at the other shoe and sock.

"I'll get you a bag to carry that in."

Katt nodded.

"Put pressure on that dressing now. I'll be back in a minute."

Katt sat on the bed again as she waited. Brooke returned to the room and hovered impatiently, obviously wanting to be out of there. But hospitals moved at their own pace. Katt had long ago learned not to expect speed. Even in an emergency, hospitals moved on their own timetable. You couldn't hurry them.

Katt wondered how many patients the nurse had to stop and help before she could return to Katt's room. Katt was almost falling asleep sitting up, even with the level of pain.

"Here we go," the nurse called out. She put Katt's extra clothing and phone charger in the bag. She threw some Ibuprofen and Tylenol sample packets on top. "Those will tide you over until you can get your prescriptions filled. Let's check that bandage one more time before you go."

Katt let the nurse take it off, feeling too exhausted to be bothered. The nurse was silent for a minute, and Katt finally looked at her arm to see what the problem was. The wound was still welling up with blood. Not very fast. Katt knew it would eventually stop. It had definitely slowed already. But the nurse was shaking her head as she examined the hole left by the IV.

"What did you do to it? How did it get so big?"

Katt shrugged with the opposite shoulder.

"It just does that," she said. "Any time I get cut or something, it leaves a big, wide scar."

"It shouldn't be pulling apart like that." The nurse bit her lip, looking at it. "I'd suggest a couple of stitches to hold it closed, but I know how that turned out last time. I'll put a couple of suture tapes across it and hope that holds."

"Yeah, okay."

The nurse fixed Katt's arm up the best she could. "Maybe we should splint the other arm too, so it doesn't tear open like this one."

Katt pictured herself completely immobilized in casts and splints.

"Uh—no. Thanks. I think I'll pass on that one."

———

At last, they were on their way to the foster home. Katt didn't know whether to be relieved to have left the hospital or anxious about how she was going to do at the foster home. She stared out the window at the dark sky, wondering what Karina was doing at that moment. Was she in prison, staring at a blank wall or prison bars? Was she by herself or with someone else? Another prisoner might bully her. They always joked that Katt came by her clumsiness and freak accidents naturally; Karina was not nearly as bad, but she did have her share of funny accidents and bizarre injuries. She was fragile too and Katt worried about what might happen to her while she was incarcerated.

"Do they have other kids?" she asked Brooke.

"What's that?"

"The Foegels. Do they have other kids?"

"Yes, of course. Not their own, if that's what you mean. They only foster. But they always have a full house. They are one of the families that can deal with more severe medical issues, so they're always in demand."

"Are there that many kids in foster care that have medical issues?" Katt asked, thinking about the hooded boy and his mention of medical kidnap. Taking kids away from their parents so that they could be put into research programs or foster care.

"Actually, a lot more than you would guess," Brooke said, nodding vigorously. "I guess a lot of parents abuse or neglect their children, leading to medical issues that cause them to be removed."

"So the other kids the Foegels have, they were abused?"

"Yes. Right."

"How many are there?"

"I think… four others right now. They've had more than that before, but we try not to overload them too much. Especially when they're dealing with kids with such high needs."

"Are they going to have trouble taking care of me?"

"Oh, no. Not at all. I think you'll be just fine there. You can help supervise the younger children! Lend a hand if you can."

Katt nodded. Not agreeing that she would help, just acknowledging what Brooke had said.

"Are they far away?"

"We're just about there."

Katt watched out the window. Lots of suburbs. Street after street of family homes. They all blurred together after a while. Like rows of cages housing mice in a lab. Square box upon square box.

The house that they pulled up in front of was not square, it was put together like a child's Lego set, wings and additions jutting out here and there. Katt was eager to get out and stretch her stiff legs, but as soon as she stood up and put her crutches under her armpits, she regretted it.

They had taken her to the car in a wheelchair, so Katt hadn't yet tried walking with the crutches. Fitting them under her arms was excruciating. They caused a stretch in her ribs that burned like fire and continued to throb even when she eased the pressure. And the splinted arm and trying to avoid bending her other arm made her movements so awkward she could barely hobble along.

"Are you okay?" Brooke asked, giving her a quizzical smile.

"Uh. No. This really hurts."

"What hurts?"

Katt moved slowly, taking tiny steps and trying not to put her weight on the crutches, just to use them to balance herself and provide a bit more stability. It was easier to walk on the cast than it was to use the crutches. Except that she was so weak and unstable.

Brooke marched past Katt and up to the door, and she and Mrs. Foegel stood in the doorway chatting while Katt made her way up the long sidewalk. Katt stopped to rest, studying Mrs. Foegel from halfway up the walk. She was a brunette. Shorter than Karina. Not so long and willowy. She had darker skin. Not ethnic, just tanned. Spending time in her garden, which Katt admired in the moonlight as she walked up the walkway, looking at her feet and the flowered border. As Katt got nearer, Mrs. Foegel looked concerned. She stepped out of the house and took a few steps toward Katt.

"Are you okay? What can I do?"

Katt shook her head. "Nothing. I can make it."

"Are you sure? You look like you're in a lot of pain."

"It's pretty bad," Katt admitted. But she kept moving. She didn't want to have to hang onto Mrs. Foegels' arm. She could get there under her own power, and the woman would just be in the way if she tried to help.

But Mrs. Foegel didn't continue to fuss at Katt. She gave Katt space and continued the conversation with Brooke.

"Follow-up care?" she was asking.

"She has a couple of prescriptions for painkillers, but she's got enough for tonight, you don't have to rush out and get anything. No stitches to be taken out. Have to keep an eye on the infected arm and make sure the other one doesn't get infected too. She has oral antibiotics. Other than that, just follow up on the cast in a couple of weeks and keep an eye on any other injuries to make sure she's healing up okay."

"Okay." Mrs. Foegel smiled at Katt as she made it up to the front door, where there was one step to go up, and then got her feet up and over the doorstep into the house. Katt gritted her teeth and put her weight on the crutches to get up those last two steps.

With the pain and awkwardness of using the crutches with her injuries, it was bound to happen. Katt tripped and toppled facedown in the entryway.

"Whoops! Are you okay? Let me help you," Mrs. Foegel leaned over her and took her arm to lift her up.

Katt resisted. "Don't pull. Just let me…"

Mrs. Foegel backed off, letting Katt get herself up. Katt carefully rolled to her side, tears running down her cheeks. She sniffled and tried not to breathe while she was finding her arms and gradually levering herself back up. Mrs. Foegel was ready to hand her one of the crutches when she got partway up. Katt was slow, but managed to get herself upright. She leaned against the wall for support.

"Your nose is bleeding," Mrs. Foegel said. "You must have hit it."

Katt touched her nose with the back of her wrist and confirmed the fact. "Can you get me some tissues?"

"Sure, of course. Come on over to the couch and sit down, you look ready to pass out."

"I don't want to bleed on it. Or the rug."

"Don't worry about that. I'm good at stains. Come on, please."

Katt maneuvered herself around to the couch and lowered herself into it. She sighed, wiping at her tears with one hand before pinching her nostrils shut. Mrs. Foegel left to get tissues, leaving Katt alone with Brooke.

"Well, Mrs. Foegel will get you settled. She has my number if there's anything you need."

"When can I see my mom?"

Brooke blinked. "Your mom? You can't see her."

"Can't I have a supervised visit? I want to see her. The other social worker at the hospital said that there would be supervised visits."

"Right now she's in jail. You can't see her there—"

"They don't allow visitors at the jail?"

"I'll… have to look into it. I don't know… we want you to have a chance to recover from your injuries."

"I want to see her."

"We'll have to see," Brooke said, shaking her head.

Mrs. Foegel returned with a wad of tissues. "Pinch tight and tip your head forward," she said. "You don't want the blood running down your throat. It should stop pretty quickly; I don't think you broke it."

Katt nodded.

"Are you okay?"

"Uh-huh."

Katt was focused on stopping her nose from bleeding, but she looked up at Mrs. Foegel and saw the concern in her eyes. It probably shouldn't have come as a surprise. In order for her to take on children with medical issues, Mrs. Foegel had to have compassion. She couldn't just be in it for the money like some foster parents were. Though maybe she got more for more challenging cases.

Mrs. Foegel touched her lightly on the back, making small circles, her touch as light as a feather.

"Can I get you anything else?"

"Ice," Katt suggested. "It will stop faster."

"Of course. I'll just be a moment." Mrs. Foegel stood up and looked at Brooke. "Do you need anything else, or are we done?"

Brooke considered for a moment, then shrugged. "You know how to reach me if you have any more questions. Mostly, she just needs a place to recover from her injuries."

"Sure. I'll call you if I need anything."

Brooke took it as her dismissal and left without even saying goodbye to Katt. Mrs. Foegel was just a couple of minutes down the hall in the kitchen, where Katt listened to her opening and closing the freezer and smashing ice into smaller pieces. She returned with a bag of crushed ice that was tucked into a light fabric packet like a pillowcase. It had penguins in ice skates on it. Katt placed it on the back of her neck and just sat there hunched over for a while. She started to hear the other noises of the house. A TV played somewhere. There was a TV in the living room, but there must have also been one in a family or playroom somewhere, or in a child's bedroom. There were occasional voices lifted over the din of the TV. A man's voice off to the right wing of the house. A young boy's. The sing-song voice of a girl, babbling nonsense.

The front door opened with a bang, making Katt jump. There had been no knock or ringing doorbell to warn her. Mrs. Foegel touched Katt's shoulder for an instant, a warm, reassuring smile on her face, and turned her eyes to the new arrival.

"Collin. How was your game?"

He grunted something that made Katt think that his team probably hadn't won whatever game they were playing. She could hear him kicking off his shoes.

"New girl?" he observed.

"Collin, this is Katt. She just got here a few minutes ago. Katt, this is Collin, our oldest foster child."

Katt turned her head far enough to see him out of one eye. A big guy. Halfback on his school football team, maybe. He was examining her with bright interest.

"Just got here and she's already bleeding. Not a good sign."

Mrs. Foegel laughed. "Well, it was quite the entrance. But it's just a nosebleed. It will stop in a few minutes."

Collin grunted something else, and he tramped off down one of the hallways. Katt heard him dump his sports equipment in his bedroom. He walked past again on his way to the kitchen.

"Did you want anything to eat?" Mrs. Foegel said suddenly, realizing that she hadn't offered Katt anything.

"No. Had something at the hospital. Not feeling great."

"Oh, I'm sorry. Do you have any allergies I need to know about?"

"I have reflux," Katt drew the tissues back from her nose slightly to see if it was still bleeding and to allow her to speak more clearly for a moment. "I have to be careful of spicy or acidic foods. And I need acid reducers. They didn't give me acid reducers at the hospital. I have a prescription."

"They didn't give me that one. Was it prescribed by the hospital, or another doctor?"

"My old doctor."

"Oh, okay. I'll check with Social Services, and if it's okay, we'll take you to our doctor and get a new prescription."

Katt's nose was still bleeding. She pinched it tight again.

"Why wouldn't it be okay?"

"A lot of the kids that they bring me are demedicalizing. Getting off of multiple prescriptions, to see which ones they really need and which ones are causing worse symptoms. I just need to make sure it's okay for me to get you back on your old prescription."

Katt shook her head slightly. "That's stupid."

"Sorry. Those are the rules we live by around here. How about something that might help settle your stomach? A piece of toast or some tea?"

"No. Thanks."

Katt shifted the ice bag to the front of her face, just over the bridge of her nose. Usually, ice helped. If she didn't ice, her nose might bleed for a couple of hours. But with ice, it would usually slow within twenty minutes or so. In the meantime, she had a headache, and her ribs were pounding in time with her pulse.

———

Eventually, her nose stopped bleeding and Mrs. Foegel took Katt to introduce her to the rest of the family. First stop was Mr. Foegels' home office. He was taller than Mrs. Foegel, and his hair was turning gray. He took off his glasses and rubbed the bridge of his nose.

"Katt, it's good to meet you. I'm Matt. You can let me know if there's anything you need, okay? I may not know my way around here quite as well as Heather, but I can usually figure something out."

Katt nodded, smiling at him uncertainly. It was going to be weird living with a man in the house. It had always just been her and Karina. No other kids. No men. Just the two of them.

"Will you put Iris and Alvah to bed soon?" Mrs. Foegel asked him.

"Yeah, sure." Matt was already looking down at his work and his voice was far away.

"Let me rephrase that," Mrs. Foegel said. "I'm going to shut off the TV and tell them to get ready. I want you to make sure they're in bed by nine."

He nodded. "Nine," he echoed.

But Katt wondered if he would. Heather Foegel shook her head at Katt ruefully. "We'll see."

Katt laughed.

They went to the darkened family room where the TV was playing. Two children lolled in beanbag chairs. They were about seven or eight years old, black, a boy and a girl.

"TV off now," Mrs. Foegel sang out.

"No! Not yet!" protested the boy.

The girl groaned. Mrs. Foegel turned it off herself.

"Alvah, Iris, this is the new girl. This is Katt."

They gazed at her. She could see the whites of their eyes reflecting in the dimness of the room.

"Now it's time to get off to bed. I want you brushed and in your beds in ten minutes. Matt will come in for lights-out."

"Heather…" the boy protested. "We're not tired."

"Iris is already yawning. Off you go. School day tomorrow."

They continued to grumble and groan. Heather touched Katt's arm and guided her back out of the room. They went down the hall and around a corner. Katt was completely turned around by the crazy additions to the house. She hoped that she wouldn't get lost too much before she learned her way around. They went into a girls' bedroom. There was a lamp on, but not the overhead light. Heather showed Katt first to the white crib, where a fat blond toddler was sleeping soundly.

"This is Alex," she whispered. "I don't know why I'm being so quiet, because nothing will wake her up once she's out."

They turned around, and Katt studied the other girl sitting on the bed, toys strewn around her. Maybe nine or ten, but frail-looking so she seemed younger.

"And this is Luce."

Luce was the one who had been singing the nonsense sounds. She didn't look at Katt or Heather, but continued to play with her toys, holding them up over her head at various angles, spinning wheels, and humming to herself.

"Luce, this is your new foster sister, Katt," Heather said. "You know, like a kitty cat?"

"Only it's not spelled that way," Katt pointed out.

"No. But she won't be reading or spelling it. I just want to give her a way to remember it."

Katt looked at Luce doubtfully. The girl hadn't even looked at Katt. Hadn't acknowledged Heather's words in any way.

"Does she talk?" Katt asked.

"No, not really. She echoes sometimes, and occasionally she'll try to tell me something. She only uses a few words appropriately. The rest is just noise to her, I think. But we don't know how much she really understands about what we say and the world around her. She may be taking it all in."

Katt looked at Luce's unfocused gaze as she manipulated the toys with long, slender fingers. It was a little creepy imagining that there might be an intellect behind those blank eyes. A real personality, recording and analyzing everything and having independent thoughts that she never shared with anyone.

"Hi, Luce," Katt said.

The girl still didn't look at her.

"She'll fall asleep at some point," Heather said. "Sometimes not until after Matt and I are in bed. But she stays put and doesn't get into mischief. There's an alarm on the door just in case."

As she and Katt exited the room, Heather reached over and pushed the red button mounted outside the bedroom door, and a flashing green light went on. Heather pulled the door shut.

"Now, what do you need? You're not hungry?"

"No."

"Pajamas?"

Katt shook her head. "I don't… I don't have anything. I just went to the hospital to have my foot set, and they *took* me." She couldn't keep her voice from breaking as she explained. "I haven't been home. I don't have any of my stuff. Not even a toothbrush."

"Don't you worry about it," Heather soothed. "I always have extra toiletries and clothing. We've been foster parents for a long time. It comes with the territory."

But that wasn't what was bothering Katt. It was hard to realize that she had nothing now. No possessions other than her phone and a couple of books and the clothes she was wearing. No home. No family. It was something else. Thinking about what they had done to her. They had just taken her, with no proof that anything was wrong. They had just exercised power and control over her life as if she didn't have any will of her own. They just plucked her up from her life and her family and deposited her somewhere else. Like she was nothing more than an object.

Katt cleared her throat, trying to keep the hot tears at bay. She had nothing to complain about. She had a safe place to sleep. Heather would provide her with a toothbrush and pajamas. Deodorant. A comb. All those little things. Katt would just have to forget about everything else.

"Thanks."

Heather gave her a quick rub on the back. "It will be okay. I'm sorry this happened to you. But we'll take care of you and help you to get better."

She led Katt to another bedroom. When she opened the door, Katt got the feeling that the room hadn't been used for a while. The walls were green so that it could be used for a boys' room or a girls' room. The furniture was similarly unisex, blocky, unadorned wood pieces. But the bed had been made with a pretty coverlet with tiny flowers and with lace around the edge.

"This will be your room. Please make yourself comfortable. The bathroom is just between you and Luce, so you don't have to go wandering looking for it during the night. I'll get you some clothes and other things." Heather's eyes went over Katt, estimating her measurements. "We can buy a few things for you tomorrow, but we've got plenty to get you through the night."

Katt nodded. She put down the plastic bag with her things in it and sat on the bed. It was firm, but soft enough to still be comfortable. The coverlet was soft and cool, and she lay down carefully, relieved to be flat on her back again, the position that caused the least amount of pain for her. Her ribs still burned, and her arms were now throbbing in unison. There hadn't been enough time for her newly bandaged arm to get infected, so Katt wasn't sure why both were throbbing. She closed her eyes, trying to relax every muscle and ligament in her body completely.

She was asleep before Heather got back with the pajamas.

CHAPTER SEVEN

Katt awoke in the morning as the sun started to creep in her window. There were closed blinds in front of the window, but she was still getting light from outside. For a while, Katt just lay still, trying to remember everything that had happened and to keep her various pains from flaring up again.

But she needed to use the bathroom, and as soon as she moved a muscle, everything seemed to be sore. Katt pushed herself to her feet and reached for the crutches. It was probably better if she didn't even use the crutches, it hurt so much to put them under her arms. The cast should be strong enough to walk on. Particularly just around the house. Katt rested the crutches back against the wall again, and stood still, waiting for a wave of dizziness to resolve so that she could walk.

In the bathroom, she could hear singing. Luce again. Katt assumed that Luce had gone to sleep the night before, and had awakened early. Katt must have been asleep for a long time.

She washed her face and combed her hair with a comb lying beside the sink. She looked at the shower stall longingly. She could really use a nice hot shower. Or bath. Surely there was a bathtub in another bathroom in the big house. A nice, big bathtub with jets. That would be wonderful. But they'd have to get her cast covered up and keep it out of the water so that she wouldn't damage it. That would take collaboration with Mrs. Foegel. Heather, Katt corrected herself. They went by their first names.

She removed the toothbrush lying on the counter from its package and brushed her teeth carefully. She kept her arms as low as she could to avoid hurting her shoulder. The splint made it impossible to brush with her dominant hand, and she was clumsy using the other arm. The toothpaste made her feel better. Wider awake. Clean and fresh. Katt splashed water on her face and went to find Heather and something for breakfast. And painkillers. She hadn't had anything all night, and her body was protesting.

She found Heather in the kitchen, cleaning up the breakfast dishes the other children had left. Katt was glad that Heather hadn't woken her up to send her to school. It was too soon for her to go back. She was still too sore, and she wasn't ready to face all those strangers.

"Hi, Katt. How are you feeling this morning?"

Katt eased herself into one of the kitchen chairs and leaned back, trying to reduce the pain in her ribs. "Need painkillers."

Heather nodded. "You slept all the way through the night, or I would have gotten you something. You want the Tylenol or the Ibuprofen? You haven't eaten, so I suppose it's Tylenol."

"Yeah. Sure."

Heather popped a couple of pills out of the blister packs and brought them to Katt with a glass of water. Katt drank them down and closed her eyes, swimming in the pain and waiting for them to take effect.

"You really conked out. You get enough sleep?"

"I don't know. Been sleeping a lot lately."

"Your body is trying to heal," Heather said. "It needs extra strength."

"Uh-huh."

"What would you like? Toast? Cereal? Leftovers?"

"I don't know. Toast, I guess. Do you have honey?"

"Sure."

Katt listened to Heather popping bread into the toaster and moving around the kitchen opening various drawers and cupboards.

"So why don't you tell me about your injuries?" Heather suggested. "I only have a list from Social Services. That doesn't tell me much."

Katt took a slow breath in and blew it out again. Her ribs burned with every breath.

"When I went to the hospital, all I had was a broken foot. I dropped a full jug of milk on it. The rest all happened at the hospital."

"Really? What happened?"

Katt told her the story of her hospital stay. Heather listened without interruption, buttering Katt's toast and slathering it with honey. She placed it in front of Katt, shaking her head at the narrative. She sat down for the rest of the story. Katt finished and looked down at her toast.

"I'll be right back," Heather said, and left the room. She came back a couple of minutes later with the little one. Alex. The girl's face was round and rosy, and now topped with a thick pair of glasses that wrapped around her head, held in place by an elastic. Heather strapped Alex into a high chair with an extra chest strap to hold her upright and sat down next to her with a jar of baby food.

"You really had some bad luck at the hospital," Heather observed, getting back to Katt's story. "I'm glad you got out of there!"

"If I stayed too much longer, I probably wouldn't be alive," Katt said.

"No kidding. I understand an accident or two, even a misdiagnosis or incorrect medication, but mistake after mistake like that," Heather shook her head. "It's crazy. You probably *were* wondering how you were ever going to survive."

"I'm used to having accidents. But other people trying to interfere… just makes it worse."

Heather nodded. She spooned baby food into Alex's mouth, a long, tedious process as the little girl kept spitting it back out and trying to grab the spoon.

"Isn't she too old for baby food?" Katt asked.

"For a normally developing child, yes. But we just barely got her off of tube feeding. She needs to learn how to swallow properly and to tolerate new textures. So it takes a long time, but it's good progress."

"Wow. I had lots of stomach problems when I was little. I was only tube fed when I was a tiny baby, though. I was a preemie, and that's how they fed me."

"Preemies often have problems even when they get older," Heather acknowledged. "They can do a lot for preemies now, but they can't prevent all of the problems."

"Do you think I'm clumsy because I was a preemie?" Katt had wondered before if her difficult birth had ended up causing any of her other issues.

"I don't know. It's possible. A lot of preemies have brain bleeds or strokes that could cause permanent problems with balance or movement. Or cerebral palsy that wasn't severe enough to be diagnosed. You don't seem like you have any cognitive problems, but there could be any number of nervous system issues."

"My doctors always just said I was clumsy."

Heather rolled her eyes. "Doctors don't always dig deeply enough to find the truth. Did they ever do an MRI or any kind of brain imaging to see what was going on?"

"No… I don't think so. Not that I remember."

"So they don't know."

Katt nibbled at her toast, thinking about it. The butter and honey had melted down into the bread, so it was a little soggy and leaky, but it was sweet and a welcome change from the hospital food. She licked her fingers.

"They always just say, 'take your time' and 'think before you take a step,' like it's my fault."

"Some people are impulsive. But it doesn't sound like you're particularly reckless."

"I don't think so," Katt agreed. She took a drink of her milk, leaving fingerprints on the glass.

Heather continued to feed Alex, incredibly patient and persistent. Inserting a spoonful into Alex's mouth, collecting what she spat back out and putting it back in, sometimes two or three times before Alex managed to swallow it all. Katt supposed all the other children were at school.

"So Social Services said that you had lots of bruises and scars," Heather said.

"I just have fair skin. It bruises whenever I bump into something. Sometimes even something like my backpack bouncing against my back or shoulders. It doesn't hurt at the time, so I don't realize until later. I have bruises all the time and I don't know what they're from."

"And scars? You can't blame that on fair skin."

"I don't know. It takes forever for cuts to heal, and they leave big wide scars even when it's just a paper cut. Look at the holes I got just from the IV," Katt indicated the wide bandages and splint. "That's just from one poke; they didn't even have to jab me extra times."

Heather was frowning, a wrinkle between her eyebrows. She wiped her face when a particularly explosive burble from Alex showered her with strained carrots. Katt laughed at Heather's expression as she wiped up with a paper towel.

"You silly girl," Heather told Alex, patting her hair and tickling her chin.

"Social Services thinks my mom hit me to give me those bruises and scars," Katt said. "But she didn't! You'd know that if you met her."

"Things aren't always what they seem. Social Services generally gets them sorted out in the end, but sometimes they do make mistakes. It's less dangerous if they make mistakes being overcautious. Better that they remove a child from a potentially dangerous situation than that they don't take a child out because there's not enough proof, and let them continue to be abused."

"But they shouldn't be able to take a kid away just because they have a medical condition."

"No. Of course not. But if it looks like a child is being abused… sometimes a child with brittle bones or another disease gets taken away when there isn't abuse… but those cases are few and far between."

"I don't have a bone disease. They've checked."

"That's good. But it is still strange…" Heather shook her head, frowning again. "You shouldn't get broken ribs or dislocated joints just from being restrained. Not unless they were being a lot more heavy-handed then they needed to be."

Katt shrugged and didn't point out that she shouldn't get a broken ankle from stepping down from a trampoline either. She was used to people telling her that she shouldn't have been injured.

———

The first few days, everything was pretty routine. Katt slept a lot and took her antibiotics and pain pills. Social Services said she didn't need a prescription for her stomach trouble, so Katt continued to battle heartburn and indigestion, trying to control her symptoms with diet, which never worked.

Heather started talking about getting her registered for school and starting on some independent work. Katt remained noncommittal, hoping to delay as long as possible. Saturday morning, Katt ended up in the family room with all the other kids, wrapped up in blankets eating fruity loops and watching kids' cartoons on TV. It was fun; kind of like a sleepover, but with little kids. Collin was off to some football camp, but everybody else, even Luce, was jumbled together on the couch and beanbag chairs like sleepy puppies, zoned out on sugar and the hypnotic effect of too much TV. Alex burbled in a bouncy seat positioned so she could see the TV and the other children.

An episode of Scooby Doo came on, and Iris and Alvah jumped up and started dancing around and vaulting over the couch, back and forth. Luce perked up suddenly and jumped to her feet, waving her arms and stomping her feet wildly. She laughed out loud, the first time Katt had seen her react to what the other children were doing. She started dancing around, her knees lifting up high. Her voice followed the ups and downs of the music, even though she wasn't saying the words.

Before Katt saw it coming, Luce leaped at her, vaulting into the beanbag chair Katt was in. She tried to catch Luce and keep her from either hurting herself or landing on Katt's ribs. But Katt's usual gracelessness took over, and she took a knee to the chin before actually catching Luce. In trying to prevent Luce from vaulting right over Katt and landing on her head, Katt managed to pull Luce directly on top of herself, feet landing on Katt's ribs.

Katt screamed. Luce pulled away from her and scrabbled off. The other children stopped laughing and horsing around, looking at each other with wide eyes. Luce hid behind the couch where Katt couldn't see her, howling.

It wasn't long before Heather was there. "What's going on? What happened?"

She went first to Luce to see if she was okay. Then she followed Iris and Alvah's eyes to Katt. Katt held her ribs, crying; the pain so bad she thought she would throw up.

"Katt, are you okay? What happened?"

She knelt down by Katt, reaching out to touch Katt's chin, pulling her hand away bloody.

"That's pretty bad. We might need to get stitches."

Katt shook her head. She touched the wound with careful fingers. "No, no stitches."

"What on earth happened? How did you cut it?"

Trying to stifle tears, Katt held her hand over her screaming ribs. "She landed… on my ribs."

"The ones you broke? Oh, Katt, I'm sorry. Are you okay? What can I do?"

Katt blinked, the tears continuing to stream. "Ice pack... more painkillers."

"Okay. I will get them, right away. And what about your chin? I don't know what happened here, how did you cut it?"

"Didn't. Luce's knee hit it. Split the skin."

"Maybe it isn't too deep, then. If I bandage it...?"

Katt could feel the warm, slick blood running down her chin and neck. But she didn't care about bloodstains on her shirt. What she cared about was the pain of her ribs.

"Please..."

"Okay. Hang in there. I'll be right back."

Iris and Alvah sat back down on the couch, darting worried glances at Katt. Luce was still hiding, making small whimpering sounds. Katt supposed she should comfort Luce and try to make everyone feel better, but she wasn't up to it. She closed her eyes, breathing shallowly and waiting for Heather to return.

"Katt...? Here's the ice..."

Katt opened her eyes and took it from her, positioning it carefully over her ribs and hoping it would numb the heat and pain quickly. Heather then offered her a couple of pills, which Katt washed down with the rest of her breakfast milk.

"Can we take a look at that chin now?"

Katt shook her head. "Not yet..." The world was flickering and gray.

Heather hovered. "Should I take you to emergency? Do you think... more ribs are broken, or they've punctured your lungs?"

"They can't splint ribs."

"Are you breathing okay?"

"Fine."

She was breathing. Shallowly and painfully, but her lung wasn't collapsed. The doctors couldn't do anything other than give her painkillers, and after her recent stint at the hospital, she knew they wouldn't even do that for long. Not the good stuff. They wouldn't even believe how much pain she was in.

Heather gave her some space, going over to coax Luce from her hiding place and get her sitting down on the other beanbag chair again. Luce continued to moan. Heather draped a blanket over her, and Luce pulled it around herself and snuggled down. Heather handed her a toy and Luce quieted, occupying herself.

"So what happened?" Heather asked Iris and Alvah.

They explained what had happened, obviously feeling guilty because they had started the dancing and roughhousing. There were sniffles and apologies. Heather rubbed both their heads and went back to Katt.

"Any better?"

"Little."

"If you can stand it, I'd like to look at your chin now."

Katt gave a small nod.

Heather was gentle. She had brought her first aid supplies with her and washed away the blood first, then cleaned the split skin with a disinfectant wipe. "Don't want another infection, do we?"

"Uh-uh." Katt held her jaw still while Heather worked on her.

"I'm worried about just patching this together. I think we should see about stitches."

"Stitches will tear it. Just tape."

"I should tape the sides together?"

"Suture tape," Katt said through gritted teeth, not wanting Heather to try duct tape.

"Right," Heather laughed. "I have strips."

"Okay."

Heather worked carefully on the cut, laying suture strips across the split in the skin. Then she put a large dressing over it.

"There. I think that's the best we can do for now. We'll see if it seals up."

"Yeah." Katt shifted the ice pack on her ribs.

"Is the painkiller working?"

"Not great."

"Do you want to go to your bed and lie down? A beanbag chair doesn't give you good support."

"No. Can't get up yet."

"Do you want me to do anything else? Do you just want to keep watching TV?"

"Yeah."

Heather stood there for a moment, looking at Katt with pursed lips. Then she finally shrugged and turned to leave. "Just give me a shout if you need something. Or ask Iris. She's good at helping."

"I'm good at helping too," Alvah protested.

"Alvah too," Heather said, but she rolled her eyes at Katt.

———

Katt picked at her supper, not really hungry, but a little nauseated from having nothing but fruity loops and painkillers all day. She knew that she had to get something in her stomach, even if she didn't have any appetite. Collin didn't get in from his football camp until halfway through supper. He dropped his equipment in his bedroom and then made his way to the empty spot at the table, which was set and waiting for him.

"Wash up, please," Heather told him.

Collin rolled his eyes and scowled. But he didn't voice his complaint. He got up from the table, went over to the sink and splashed water over his hands, then returned to his seat, wiping them dry on his jeans. He started dishing up without any greeting or comment to the family.

Once he started eating, his eyes went around the table. He studied Katt for a moment.

"What'd you do now?"

Katt's face got hot. Collin, the jock, was the kind of boy who normally wouldn't even talk to her unless it were to make fun of her or trip her or play some other prank. She looked down at her plate and didn't answer.

"Luce and Katt had a collision," Heather said. "Poor Katt has had a pretty rough day."

He shook his head, suppressing a grin. Katt didn't have to imagine what he would have said if he'd been in front of his friends instead of his foster parents. She'd heard it all before. All the name calling and belittling. Sometimes even pretending to be friendly, just to build her up more before knocking her down.

"So, what's wrong with you?" Collin asked, digging into his mound of mashed potatoes.

"Nothing," Katt mumbled, still not looking at his face.

"Must be something wrong with you. You're a medical case, aren't you? And every time I see you, you're bleeding."

"Katt hasn't been diagnosed," Heather told him, making a downward motion with her hands to encourage him to tone down the questioning.

"We're going to have to make some doctors' visits to figure out what's going on."

Collin grunted. He put a big piece of meat in his mouth and chewed on it. "Glad I'm not a medical case," he said around it. "This body's the only asset I got."

CHAPTER EIGHT

I think you'll like Dr. Meyers," Heather said. "He's one of the best doctors we've had, and he's good at ferreting out the details that can lead to diagnosis."

"You think that I have some disease?" Katt asked. "You don't think it's just clumsiness or bad luck?"

Heather shook her head. "No, I don't," she said. "I think that's a lot of nonsense. Someone should have looked seriously at it before this."

"My mom was always trying to get answers."

"But they thought she was just a worrier?" Heather guessed.

"Yeah."

Katt looked out the window, thinking about it. The emergency room doctors never had the time to do any research to figure out what was going on with her. And medical clinic doctors were almost worse, with dozens of colds and flus in the waiting room and doctors seeing ten patients in an hour. They just brushed Karina off, checking on casts or braces and telling Katt to take it easy and look before she leaped. Like she ever leaped

"Did they tell you anything about my mom? Do you know where she is?"

"I was told she was incarcerated; I'm afraid I don't know any more than that."

"They don't want me to see her, not even supervised."

"Try to be patient. It can take a while to set up visits sometimes. Let's worry about treating you first."

"What's she going to do? Beat me in front of a social worker or guard? That's just stupid."

Heather shrugged. "Some kids do get reinjured even on supervised visits."

Katt looked for an argument to that, but couldn't find one. Did they really think that her mom would hit her in front of a social worker?

Did that really happen?

———

Dr. Meyers was a pleasant-looking man in his sixties. He was completely bald, but he looked more baby-faced than like an old man. He didn't use glasses and he greeted Katt with a smile instead of acting rushed or stressed.

"So, what do we have here?" He asked, looking Katt over and noting the cast, splint, and various bandages.

"I'm hoping you can tell us, doctor," Heather said. "Katt has a knack for getting injured. Social Services thinks she was being abused, but after what I've seen and heard… I think there's something else going on."

"Oh-ho," Meyers said, eyes sparkling with interest. "You're hoping I'll put on my deerstalker hat and chase down the real culprit?"

Katt blinked at him, not quite getting his meaning.

"Your diagnostic skills are legendary," Heather said. "Everybody else has said that Katt's just clumsy or unlucky. Or they suspect her mother. I want someone with a brain to see if they can give me a better answer."

Meyers chuckled. "Where do you want me to start?" he asked Katt. "Shall we go from most recent backward?"

"Most recent…?"

"That would be her chin," Heather said. "She—"

"Don't give me any details yet. Let me make my examination and draw what conclusions I can without being tainted."

He peeled back the bandage on Katt's chin and looked at the long split in the skin.

"This is very recent," he observed. "It hasn't sealed up or started to form a scab yet. Did this happen today?"

"No," Katt said, "It was—"

"Not yet. The tape is doing its job and holding the wound together, and there isn't a lot of inflammation, so I don't think I'll touch it."

He rifled through a drawer and came up with an eyepiece that he used to study the wound.

"It's bruised and I don't see evidence of a cutting edge. Looks more like an impact injury, like a split lip. Am I right? Or was it cut?"

"It split," Katt confirmed.

"Good. But not today?"

"No."

Meyers looked at Heather.

"Three days," she advised.

"Three? Goodness. Slow healing. Okay. Before that?"

Katt touched her bandaged arm. Meyer unwrapped it.

"This wound is starting to heal. So older than three days. An IV access. A large hole, like the skin has stretched it wider. A stitch or two might have been a good idea, but the tape has done its job."

"Stitches—" Katt started, then stopped, remembering not to tell him anything until he asked. He nodded.

Meyer ran his thumb over a similar scar on Katt's arm, long healed but of a similar size and position. He studied her arm, with several other wide scars.

"You don't heal well, do you?"

"No."

On a spot on the back of her arm, away from the IV hole, he pinched her arm and drew the skin back, stretching it out and then letting it go.

"Other arm?" he suggested.

Katt nodded. He unwrapped the splint and then removed the bandage.

"And this is why you don't want stitches," he said, observing the shredded flesh. "Pulled right out of there, didn't they?"

"Yeah."

"This one is older, but I don't see any more healing there than in the other arm. Very slow. And the foot is last?"

Katt hesitated. "No… my ribs and my shoulder."

"Oh, ribs and shoulder," he looked intrigued. "And what did you do to them?"

"Broken ribs and dislocated shoulder," Heather supplied. "But the shoulder is okay. It's not hurting anymore, right Katt?"

"Yeah. That's right."

"May I? Which shoulder?"

Katt gestured. He touched it with gentle fingers, feeling for tender places and moving it around gently.

"Can you hold it straight out to the side? Or does that hurt?"

Katt extended it.

"You see this joint?" Dr. Meyer said, indicating her elbow. "You see how it has been extended past straight, to start bending farther, in the wrong direction? This is called hyperflexion."

He again felt for any sore or swollen places in the shoulder joint, and then let Katt lower her arm again.

"And ribs? You had an accident, in which you broke your ribs. A freak accident. Something unusual."

"Yeah."

"We'll come back to the cause in the end. I can see you don't want me to touch them. They are very tender still. Your breathing is fast and shallow."

He *was* good. Katt nodded. "All they'd give me is Tylenol or Ibuprofen."

She wasn't sure what he was going to do about her broken foot. He couldn't see or manipulate it or look at her x-rays. But Meyers still looked at her other leg and foot, his eyes sharp and discerning.

"Deep contusions," he said. "Do you walk into things a lot?"

"No. I trip or fall down. Or sometimes, I don't know where the bruises come from."

"You said trip *or* fall down. Not trip and fall down. Do you fall down without tripping over something? Just drop or collapse unexpectedly?"

"Yes, sometimes my—"

"Shh. Can you stand for me for a moment?"

He helped her down from the examination table. Katt stood for him, conscious of her posture. She tried to stand in a straight, balanced stance.

"You see," Meyer said, tapping the side of one of Katt's knees. "There is that hyperflexion again. Can you touch your toes?"

That one would have been easy, normally. "Yes… but not with my ribs."

"Would you be able to put your palms flat on the floor?"

Katt liked to show off her flexibility. The only physical prowess she could claim. If she hadn't been so awkward, she would have made a good gymnast or dancer.

"Yeah, easy," she told him.

"Wow," Heather said. "That's amazing."

"Can you do this?" Meyer pulled his thumb toward his forearm. He wasn't able to get it closer than a couple of inches. Katt mimicked the maneuver, able to get her thumbs touching her forearms on both sides.

"Have a seat up here again."

Katt climbed back up.

"You have broken bones before?" Meyers suggested.

Katt laughed. "Yes!"

"You bruise and scar easily."

"Yes."

"Have you been tested for osteoporosis? Brittle bones?"

"Yeah. They said it's all fine."

"Tell me about how you broke your foot and your ribs."

Katt described both injuries.

"How often do your bones go out of joint?"

"I don't know… a lot."

"More than, say, once a year?"

Katt laughed. "Oh, yeah! Even my mom pops joints out more than once a year. Me… more than once a week… maybe not every day, but sometimes more than once in a day."

"You sound like you have an idea," Heather said to the doctor.

"Your mother has had some of these things too?" Meyer asked, ignoring Heather's question.

"Not like me, but… sometimes. She needs to keep a brace on her wrist. The physiotherapist says it's very bad to do that, because by immobilizing it, it doesn't get as much exercise and gets weaker. But she has to, or she can't function."

"How was her pregnancy with you? Complications?"

"She had to go on bed rest. I was born premature. She had lots of back and hip problems. And tearing and bleeding, even though I was tiny."

Meyers grabbed a form from one of the wall pockets and removed the cap of the pen he pulled from his pocket by biting it and keeping it clenched in his teeth.

"I'm going to order a muscle biopsy," he said around it. "If I'm right, it's going to be positive for something called Ehlers-Danlos Syndrome. It's genetic. You got it from your mom. But she has a milder form than you do."

Katt shook her head. "What's that? Mom was never diagnosed with anything."

"It's not well-known. Milder cases often go undiagnosed until there is a member of the family tree who has a more serious presentation. All of these things go along with it. Fragile, stretchy skin. Hypermobile joints. Bone breaks. Wounds that are slow to clot and heal." He folded his arms and looked at Katt, smiling. "What do you think of that?"

"I… I don't know. No one ever thought it was anything. But if you can prove I have this…" she looked at Heather. "Then we can get my mom out, right? You can prove that I wasn't being abused, I just have this disease."

"I hope so," Heather said. "Don't expect anything to happen immediately. Social Services will still want to make sure that there isn't this syndrome *and* abuse. One doesn't exclude the other. Parents dealing with mysterious diseases can get very frustrated and take it out on the child. But it will sure help your mom's case."

"I told them I wasn't being abused. I told them that right from the start."

"I know, Katt. But the same is true for most abused kids. And the system moves slowly. We'll get the diagnosis confirmed and then we'll see if we can get Brooke to review your situation."

"I can't believe it… everyone just said I was clumsy."

Meyer shook his head. "Let's give them joints that go wonky without provocation and drop them on the ground and see if *they're* clumsy."

Katt laughed. She wished she *could* inflict Ehlers-Danlos on all the doctors who had brushed off her case for the last fifteen years. Why hadn't a single one of them clued in? They acted like she was stupid and careless, like all she had to do was think ahead, and she could avoid injury. But she couldn't plan every footstep and every movement and anticipate whenever her joints were going to hyperextend, give way, or pop out. It was an impossible feat.

"What's the treatment?" she asked. "I've done physio, but it's never really helped. Is there a medication?"

"No… there's no cure for EDS. All we can do is treat the symptoms, take care of injuries in the best way possible and try to stay ahead of some of the more serious conditions."

Katt didn't like the sound of that. There was something more serious than tripping and breaking a leg to worry about? Did he just mean not stitching up lacerations? It didn't sound like it.

"Like what?"

"Like rupturing your aorta. Once we get the muscle biopsy back, we'll need to book you for some testing to see what condition your heart is in. There are different subtypes of EDS, and those with the vascular type run a high risk of rupturing a major blood vessel. While the risk is less for those with other subtypes, we still have to watch for any problems."

Katt's heart raced. There was pain in her chest just at the thought. Her heart beat so fast that she thought it could rupture any time. She must have the vascular type. She could die on the spot. Suddenly, she wasn't so excited about having a diagnosis.

"We'll take it one step at a time," Meyer said soothingly, putting a hand on her arm. "One step at a time, dear. Your heart is probably just fine. It's just precautionary."

———

Katt was silent most of the drive home, trying to sort through all the feelings that came with Dr. Meyers' diagnosis. She was excited that it would help to clear her mother and for them to get back together again. She was vindicated before all the doctors who had called her clumsy or awkward and who had missed the real reason for her injuries. And she was scared to death of dying suddenly. Dr. Meyers hadn't been able to tell her what things might cause a rupture. What if someone scared her? Or she got hit in the chest? What if she fell and broke a rib? What if she got too hot and her heart beat too fast?

"Are you going to call Brooke as soon as we get home?" Katt asked.

"I'll give her a ring. I don't know if we'll be able to light a fire under her before the results of the muscle biopsy are in, but I'll start her thinking about it." Heather tapped her fingers on the steering wheel as she drove. "You have to be so careful about how you approach these things. You don't want to step on anyone's toes or make anyone feel like you're accusing them of incompetence. You don't want to make someone look bad in front of their boss. We need to take each step carefully to avoid ruffling any feathers."

"That's stupid. All you should have to do is tell them that my injuries are caused by this disease, and they should reverse their decision and send me back to my mom. Right away. And what about the police? Are Social Services going to call the police and tell them that there was no reason to arrest my mom? Or are you going to do that?"

"I'm not. They won't listen to me. We need to go through channels. I know you're impatient to see your mom and get back to her as soon as you can. But this isn't going to happen in a day. You need to keep your head down and not aggravate Brooke or call the police. You don't want them thinking that you're a troublemaker and that you're going to run. You have to play along."

Katt looked at Heather. She frowned, thinking about it. "Play along? It isn't a game; it's my life."

"I know. But I've seen what happens when teens are disruptive and get on the wrong side of their social worker or a judge. You don't want to be that kid."

They were up to the house before Katt spoke again. "Have you ever heard of medical kidnap?"

Heather didn't say anything. Katt turned from the window to look Heather in the face. Heather was pale, her eyes wide.

"I've heard the term before," she said finally. "But I don't think we should be talking about it."

"Why not?"

"Social workers around here do not respond well to accusations of medical kidnap. It's a really good way to get yourself put into a secure facility. I mean it when I say not to make waves, Katt. If you start spouting off with accusations about medical kidnap, no one is going to take you seriously. Social workers make mistakes, yes. Sometimes they see caretaker abuse and neglect when the child really has a medical condition that throws up red flags. But when that happens… we have to just work within the system to get changes made. It's the only way."

Heather waited until after Katt had gone to lie down for a nap and to make the initial call to Brooke. She didn't want Katt to overhear the call and to interfere with it. She knew how difficult it was to manage social workers, especially when they might be in the wrong. Bruised egos could result in repercussions for Katt, Heather, and all of the foster children in the home. They did not need a social worker going ballistic and shutting her down as a foster parent. Her kids needed to be where they were, not to be rehomed in anger.

"Brooke Wicker." Brooke apparently took a second to notice Heather's caller ID. "Oh, Heather. Hi. What's up?"

"How are you doing?" Heather asked, putting off the topic of conversation for a few minutes so she could feel Brooke out. "You sound busy."

"I'm always busy, Heather. You know how it is. I've got investigations to work on, kids to catch up with, two that need new homes, and I don't know how many forms piled up in my inbox. It's a crazy job. We need about a hundred more social workers, but I don't think it's in the budget!"

"I don't think so," Heather agreed. "You'd be lucky to get a couple of interns or phone operators."

"Uh-huh."

There was a rustle of papers. "So, you didn't call to discuss my likelihood of having an aneurysm today. What's going on?"

"I have some new information for you about Katt."

"Katt Lindholm…" Heather could hear her tapping computer keys, and waited for the go-ahead. "How's she settling in?"

"She's just fine. No problems. Other than the accident with Luce. I already told you about that."

"Kids will be kids. You can't stop them from playing games. We got it down under incident reports, no need to worry about it. No permanent damage."

"It's pretty ugly. But she'll heal, eventually."

"What's your news?"

"I took her to the doctor today. To look at her chin and see how everything else was coming along."

"Uh-huh."

"You know Dr. Meyers? I've used him for years. He's a great doctor."

"What did he say? Did he identify any injuries that we hadn't seen before?"

"He's ordered a muscle biopsy."

Brooke's keys continued to clack for a few seconds, then stopped. "A muscle biopsy for what? Cancer?"

"No. Nothing like that—"

"We have to watch the bottom line. They keep tightening the purse strings on us. Unless it's a program that brings in extra research dollars…"

Heather ignored the warning. "Dr. Meyers says she has something called Ehlers-Danlos Syndrome."

"He says she has it? Or he wants to run tests?"

"The test is just to confirm his diagnosis. It all fits; her odd accidents and bones that break easily, the bruises and the scars, even her problems as a baby."

Brooke was silent. Heather waited for her to consider the facts and understand where they were headed.

"Say that again." Brooke's voice was cold.

"This EDS, it makes her connective tissues very fragile. So she gets bruises easily. Cuts don't heal well and leave big scars. Her joints can cause her to drop things or fall down without any provocation, and her bones are more fragile…"

"Where did the doctor come up with this hooey?"

"I asked him to evaluate Katt. To see if she might have a medical condition that was causing all of these injuries."

"Let me get this straight… you asked him to come up with something to exonerate the mother?"

"No, no." Heather bit her lip and tried to figure out where she had made a wrong turn in the conversation. "I felt like there was something else that was going on with Katt. She keeps having these bizarre accidents, even here and at the hospital when her mother was not around. Things just didn't add up. It didn't make sense that it was just her mother hurting her when it kept happening while her mother was out of the picture."

"And you didn't think that maybe this was something you should discuss with me?"

"Not without any evidence. I'm calling you now since Dr. Meyers has suggested a possible explanation. Before that, all I had were my doubts. Now we have a solid hypothesis to explore."

"You should have talked to me before taking her to the doctor. This is not at all helpful to the situation. And I suppose that the doctor told Katt that she has this disease, so now the girl's all worked up, thinking she's going to go home."

"I explained to her that nothing would happen until all the results had been reviewed and the investigation into her mother was complete… She understands. She knows that nothing is going to happen right away."

"Nothing is going to happen at all," Brooke snapped. "This doesn't change anything. The doctor and the hospital social worker both swore statements that point directly to the mother. She is incarcerated and under active investigation. Nothing has been put to bed. We are still in the beginning stages."

"But I'm sure you will take this new information into account. Knowing that there may be a medical explanation for the injuries that the hospital was seeing…"

"We'll put forward the diagnosis when it is confirmed. But it doesn't change anything. Syndrome or not, that girl needs to be protected. We can't let her come to further harm."

"No," Heather agreed. "Of course not."

____

CHAPTER NINE

____

Heather looked across the table at Katt. It had been a couple of weeks, and Katt was settling in. But today she was sitting there stirring her cereal, not eating.

"Are you okay?"

Katt startled and raised her eyes to Heather. "Oh… I dunno, I'm not feeling great today."

"Are you coming down with something?"

"Maybe."

Heather got up and went around the table to Katt. She leaned over and felt Katt's forehead.

"You're warm. You don't have an infection, do you? One of those arms? Or your chin?"

Katt made a face, working her jaw to check the pain level of the cut under the big white bandage around her chin.

"No… I don't think so."

"So what's not feeling good? Your stomach?"

Katt nodded. Heather went back to her own seat. Alex was making noise and banging her table, angry at her interrupted breakfast. Heather inserted another spoonful of food into her mouth.

"Maybe I'm just hungry," Katt said. "Sometimes I feel a little sick when my stomach is just hungry."

But she didn't take another bite, so Heather doubted it. Katt was normally so pale it was hard to tell anything from her complexion, but Heather didn't think she was just hungry.

"You don't have to eat if you're not hungry."

At that, Katt shoveled in a couple of bites. "No, it's nothing. I can eat."

Eventually, she ended up throwing out most of her breakfast, apologizing the whole time and assuring Heather that the food was not the problem. Heather laughed at this.

"My cooking prowess is not exactly offended if you didn't finish a bowl of cereal. It's okay. Why don't you go lay down for a while, see if you feel any better?"

Katt nodded, and dragged herself down the hall to her bed, looking way too exhausted for someone who had just had a full night's sleep. When Heather checked on Katt ten minutes later, the girl had pulled the quilt over herself and was asleep. Hoping that was all she needed, Heather left her alone and went to get Alex dressed for the day.

Half an hour later, she heard Katt moving around again. Up and straight to the bathroom. Heather hoped the short nap had done Katt some good, and she was ready for a shower and to be up and around, but the toilet lid clinked against the tank and Katt was throwing up.

"Darn it," Heather murmured. She waited what she hoped was an appropriate interval, until the heaving stopped. "Are you okay, Katt? I guess you weren't just hungry."

Heather stood in the doorway. Katt knelt in front of the toilet; her head bowed with fatigue. She looked wiped out and faintly green.

"Uh-huh." Katt grabbed a wad of toilet paper and wiped the slime from her mouth and nose. "I'm okay. Feeling a little bit better now, actually." She doubled up the toilet paper and blew her nose, scrunching up her face and looking dubiously at the contents before flushing it away. "But I hate throwing up."

"I know. Not much fun, is it?"

Katt got to her feet. She washed her face and rinsed her mouth. Heather walked her back to bed. Katt's gait was wobbly.

"I'll get you a bucket in case you're not done yet. Try to rest."

———

Katt lay in bed, her brain clouded with fatigue. She had woken up feeling icky, but that had rapidly dissolved into nauseated and exhausted. Her joints ached. Her bones ached. Her head ached. The pain in her stomach had faded when she threw up, but it was building up again, and pretty soon she anticipated another session hunched over the toilet while her body tried to rid itself of the invading virus.

Why did she have to be sick when she was just starting to recover from her injuries? The pain in her ribs was only just starting to dull, and throwing up did them no good at all. She couldn't swallow any painkillers because she would throw them back up before they could dissolve and do their job.

It wasn't fair. Katt wanted her mother. She wanted Karina, who had always taken care of her through her illnesses. Why did Social Services have to take her away? Heather was kind and sympathetic, but a poor stand-in for Katt's own mother.

The pain and nausea built, and Katt tried to decide whether to stay in bed and use the bucket or to stagger her way into the bathroom to throw up in the toilet. Neither one was a particularly attractive option.

She decided to go back to the bathroom.

At first, she had hoped that since there was nothing left in her stomach, she wouldn't throw up again. But then she hoped that she would throw up so that the pain would go away again. But she wished there were something in her stomach to throw up because she hated the dry heaves.

She carried her bucket, not sure she was going to be able to make it to the bathroom.

She did make it to the toilet in time. The first few heaves were nothing but yellow bile. Her body strained and strained, but there was nothing else in her stomach. Katt rested for a few minutes but didn't dare go back to her bed. She sensed that her body wasn't yet finished. So she hung over the toilet, eyes closed, waiting for the next cycle.

Her ribs were burning. Agonized. She was so tired she thought she might fall asleep right there with her forehead on the porcelain. Except that the pain and the nausea were too much. She couldn't find sleep again until they settled once more.

Another wave of vomiting. This time more than just bile. Katt was surprised to find that there was still more to throw up. No longer on acid reducer tablets, maybe her stomach was producing stomach juices at an accelerated rate.

It burned her throat, mouth, and nose. The taste in her mouth was foul, worse than the bile. Katt kept her eyes screwed shut tightly, the pain in her ribs like a knife twisting in her side. When the wave passed, she kept her eyes closed at first, giving her muscles a chance to relax and waiting for the worst of the pain to subside. She opened her eyes and reached over to flush the toilet.

———

"Heather!"

Heather looked up at the urgency in Katt's tone. She put down the laundry she was folding and hurried into the bathroom. "Katt, what's wrong?"

Katt gestured at the toilet, her eyes wide. Heather looked over and saw blood. Not just a few streaks of blood from the force of the heaves, but what Heather would estimate was a cup or more. Katt turned from looking at the toilet to look at Heather's face. She hadn't wiped her face, and blood mixed with thick saliva ran in a streak from her nose and mouth down to the bandage on her chin.

"I'll take you to emergency," Heather said in a calm, even tone. "Wash up, and take your bucket with you. Slip on some shoes. I just need to grab Alex."

Katt's face was so white; Heather thought that she was going to pass out.

"Katt? Can you do that? Or do I need to get an ambulance?"

"I can," Katt whispered.

"Okay." Heather didn't wait to see if Katt would get herself ready but hurried to get Alex, her mind running through what else she needed to do. The other children would be home from school early in the afternoon. Heather might need to be at the hospital for most of the day. She packed extra food and a book. She called Matt on her cell while she hefted the baby and the backpack.

"Matt, I've got to take Katt to emergency. I'll get someone to watch the kids as they get home from school. But I'll need you to get off when you can and make supper. I'm not sure if they'll admit Katt or if we'll be back in the afternoon."

"What's wrong with Katt? Did she fall again?"

"No. She's throwing up blood. I thought she just had the stomach flu, but I'm worried she's ruptured something. I'll update you later, okay?"

"Yes. Are you driving? Be careful."

"I will."

She tapped the connection off and headed for the door.

"Where are you, Katt? Are you okay?"

Katt shuffled toward her from the adjoining hallway. Her face was damp, and she held the bucket in front of her in her non-splinted hand like she was afraid she might drop it. She hobbled along, hampered by the cast.

"Doing good, kiddo. I'm going to run ahead to get Alex settled. Just pull the door shut behind you."

"Okay."

When Heather looked up after fastening Alex into place and dropping her backpack on the back seat, she saw Katt struggling to pick up her bucket without toppling over. She'd had to put it down to pull the door shut since she only had one usable hand. Heather reached in through the driver's door to get the car started, and then hurried up the front walk to reach Katt and walk her to the car. Katt looked relieved.

"I'm getting a little lightheaded," she confessed.

"Let's just focus on one step at a time."

Katt nodded and held onto Heather's arm as they walked to the car. She didn't sway or fall, but Heather was relieved nonetheless when they got to the car. She was having second thoughts about taking Katt by car instead of calling an ambulance. But they were on their way; it would only take ten minutes to get there. She hurried back around to the driver's side and climbed in.

"Okay. We're on our way."

"Should I buckle?" Katt asked uncertainly, reaching for her seatbelt and then stopping.

"Uh… let's not tighten anything around your belly. It will only take us a few minutes to get there."

Katt nodded and didn't buckle it. She leaned back her head and closed her eyes.

"Stay awake and talk to me. I'm sort of worried about you."

"Why? I don't have a concussion."

"I know. But just… don't go to sleep. How are you feeling?"

"Crappy."

"Are you in a lot of pain?"

"My ribs, mostly."

"Still nauseated?"

"No, but it will come back."

"Hang in there."

Heather had to stop for a red light. She glanced over at Katt, then away, trying not to make her self-conscious.

"Have you done this before?"

"Gone to the ER?"

"No." Heather gave a short laugh. "I know you've been to the ER before! I mean throwing up blood."

"No… I don't think so. Not that much. A little, sometimes."

Heather drove on in silence. It seemed like it took forever to make it to the hospital. Every slow car or stop light was excruciating. But when she checked the time, they had made it to the hospital in eight minutes. That was actually pretty good.

"Stay put. I'm going to get you a wheelchair."

"I can walk."

"No. Wheelchair. I don't want you passing out, and they'll see you faster if you're not on your feet. This way I can convince them that you are more critical."

Katt gave a shrug. Heather fetched a wheelchair and pushed it back out to the car. She got Katt transferred into it and picked up the baby and the backpack. It wasn't easy pushing the chair with the baby carrier, but Heather persevered until an orderly came over to take over.

"She's throwing up blood," Heather told him. "A lot of blood."

He nodded and pushed Katt to the front of the triage line, cutting off several patients who had arrived there earlier, and went up to the window to talk to the admitting nurse for a moment, eventually getting permission to have Katt evaluated next.

Heather stood at the counter, putting down the baby carrier and facing the stern-looking nurse. She opened up the backpack to get out Katt's medical card, while Katt started to answer the nurse's rapid fire questions. It was obvious that the nurse didn't think much of their concerns. Probably people came to the ER all the time for microscopic streaks of blood in their vomit.

Katt's answers were getting slower, with more pauses as she searched for words. She opened her mouth to answer another question, and then hunched over her bucket, spewing dark red fluid. The nurse hurried out from behind her glassed-in enclosure, looking down at the contents of the bucket and putting her fingers over Katt's wrist. She started calling out instructions to the other nurses in the fishbowl and grabbed the handles of Katt's wheelchair, pushing her quickly to the treatment area.

Heather grabbed her bag and baby and followed on her heels.

The nurse ignored her, rushing on ahead. She and an intern transferred Katt from the wheelchair up onto a gurney. There were doctors and nurses coming from everywhere, rushing to help get an IV into Katt's arm and a monitor on her. Katt had stopped throwing up and was breathing shallowly, her hand over her broken ribs.

"She has broken ribs," Heather told the doctors. "I don't know when the last time she had a painkiller was."

"How do you know she has broken ribs? Why didn't you bring her in sooner?" one of them snapped.

"She was in hospital when it happened. She was released."

"What started her bleeding today? Did she get hit in the ribs? Was she in some kind of accident?"

"No, I don't know what happened. She was feverish and not feeling well this morning. I thought it was just a tummy bug."

"Has she thrown up blood every time? How many times?" The doctor looked into the bucket and tipped it, estimating the amount of blood. "Hang a unit. Do you know her blood type?"

Heather had managed to find Katt's card just before chasing after them to the treatment area. She looked down at it.

"O positive."

"Hang a unit O positive. What's her name?"

"Katt."

"Katt, how are you doing there?" he asked the teen in a loud voice. "Are you in a lot of pain?"

Katt nodded. "Yes."

"Point with your finger where it hurts the most."

Katt pointed to her broken ribs. The doctor didn't touch them but probed her belly. "How about this? Does it hurt when I touch you?"

"Yeah, some."

He continued to probe, watching her face and feeling for a reaction.

Heather wondered what his sensitive fingers were able to find, just feeling like that.

"How many times have you thrown up today?"

"Three."

"Was there blood every time?"

"No. Not the first time."

"None at all?"

"No… didn't see any."

"But yes, when you threw up the second time?"

"Not at first… just… toward the end."

"Lots, like this?" He indicated the bucket.

"Yeah. I was really scared, so I called Heather."

"Well, you did the right thing to come here right away." The doctor grabbed the card out of Heather's hand and pushed it on one of the nurses. "Run off her chart for me. Are there any medical conditions?" He turned to Heather. "You are her guardian? Do you have her medical history?"

"Just an outline. She was just recently diagnosed with Ehlers-Danlos Syndrome."

He was scribbling down Katt's vitals and didn't look up from the clipboard. "What's that?"

"You don't know?"

"I can't know everything about every disease. Fill me in."

Heather had been doing research on it, hoping that if she could tie all Katt's injuries to EDS, they could make decisions on her case more quickly.

"I'm just her foster mother, and this is all new to both of us."

The doctor nodded impatiently. "Understood."

"It's a connective tissue disorder. A problem with the collagen. So it affects skin, bones, blood vessels, everything. Makes them more fragile. That's why her ribs got broken, and she bruises and scars easily. Her skin tears or splits really easily. You'll have to watch that IV hole to make sure it doesn't turn into a big open wound. One of her other ones got infected when she was here last."

"So this would make the lining of her stomach more prone to tearing?"

Heather shrugged, moving her hands in a wide, uncertain gesture. "Your guess is as good as mine. I would assume so."

"I want her into CT as soon as possible," the doctor was no longer talking to her, but giving orders to the various medical workers gathered around Katt's bed. "Let's get a look at what's going on, where the bleed is. It's fresh, so it's either stomach or upper intestine. Order an upper endo as well, we may or may not do it, depending on what we can see on the CT. But get it booked in anyway. I want a consult with someone familiar with this Ehlers-Danlos Syndrome. Rheumatology, I assume? But it has to be someone who really knows about it. Who has seen actual patients."

The various professionals broke off to complete the assignments that he had made. The doctor watched Katt's vitals on the monitor beside the bed.

"Let's push some painkillers. Codeine. What has she been taking?" He turned back to Heather and shot this question at her.

"Tylenol and Ibuprofen."

"Nothing stronger? How much ibuprofen?"

"The big ones," Heather held out her fingers to show him the size. "I think… five hundred milligrams."

"One or two? How often? And for how long?"

"I don't know. Pretty regularly. For a couple of weeks now."

"Any history of ulcers?"

"I… don't know. Katt? What about ulcers. Have you ever had one?"

Katt opened her eyes. "No. Reflux, though."

"What are you taking for that?" the doctor asked.

"Nothing. They took away my acid reducers."

"Who did?"

"The hospital. Social Services. They said I didn't need them."

"Is it because they didn't give her acid reducers?" Heather asked. "Was that what triggered the bleeding?"

"We won't know anything until we get a look inside."

"Okay… how long will that take?"

"I hope to have her in CT within the hour. This is a significant amount of bleeding."

———

The timeline was muddy for Katt. She couldn't keep track of when she had been awake and when she had been asleep, and what order everything happened in. She wasn't sure whether she had finished all of the tests that had been scheduled, when the last time she threw up was, and whether they had said they were going to do surgery or not. It was all a muddy muddle.

"Are you awake, Katt?" It was a man's voice and fingers, prodding her gently and encouraging her to wake up. She wasn't sure why they wanted her to wake up. She was dopey and just wanted to sleep, and hopefully to feel better when she woke up again on her own.

"Mmm," she groaned. She pushed his fingers away. Why did she have to wake up? Couldn't they bother her later? Or tell her mom what was going on, and Karina could tell Katt when she was awake next.

"Come on, wake up," the man encouraged again, shaking her more insistently.

Katt opened her eyes and rubbed them sleepily. "What?"

"Why don't we sit you up a bit, then you'll have an easier time waking up."

"I'm awake."

"Good. Stay with us." He pushed the button that raised the head of the bed.

It was one of the doctors. He had probably introduced himself, but Katt couldn't remember his name. He tapped keys on a nearby keyboard, bringing a series of images up on the digital screen on the wall.

"Here are your films. First ones are the CT scans. The arrows you see point to gastric ulcers. Thinning or holes in the lining of your stomach. That's where the bleeding was coming from. The ulcers were there already, probably not bleeding, or only bleeding a small amount. The vomiting tore one of them open and produced a really good bleed." He switched to another picture, this one focused in on the bright spot that Katt could only assume was the bleeding ulcer.

"Do you need to operate?" Heather asked.

Katt blinked at her, remembering in a sort of slow-motion that it was Heather at the hospital with her. Her foster mother. Not Karina.

"Usually, we prefer a wait-and-see approach," the doctor said. "See if the bleeding will stop on its own. I've talked to a specialist on EDS, and he suggests going non-surgical whenever possible. Because of the complications that can develop with EDS. We could end up with a bigger bleed and complications from opening her abdominal cavity, instead of doing any good. So for now… we watch and wait, knowing that she will take longer to stop bleeding than the normal patient. We'll keep giving her blood as long as she's bleeding. Some extra platelets to help things along."

Katt let her eyes close. It didn't sound like there was anything she needed to stay awake for.

"Is this because they took her off of the acid reducers?" Heather asked.

"It could be a contributing factor. As could the ibuprofen. But it might have happened anyway, just because of violent vomiting with Ehlers-Danlos. Impossible to tell. No more ibuprofen for the time being. We'll prescribe something less risky. And we'll put her back on acid blockers."

CHAPTER TEN

Ow are things progressing on Katt's case?" Heather asked, carefully keeping her tone casual and non-demanding.

"She's safe where she is right now," Brooke pointed out. "We're not in any great rush to change anything."

"But the investigation of her mother, in light of the Ehlers-Danlos diagnosis…"

"Her lawyer has applied to have her case reviewed," Brooke's tone was disapproving. "See if they'll grant bail now that some question has been thrown on the origin of Katt's bruises and scars. But there's still no proof that Karina *wasn't* abusive. When you take into account her finances, single parenthood, having to deal with a demanding special-needs child… there are a lot of risk factors. She doesn't have a strong support network. She's trying to do it all on her own. And that hasn't been working."

"You can't assume just because she's a single mom that she's abusive."

"No, but we can note it as a risk factor. And her finances are going to make it difficult to afford medications. She's had to apply for help with medical bills before. That's a very high stressor and may make her more prone to avoid medical treatment in the future when it is needed. She's going to be leery of taking Katt to hospital at all since being arrested. What guarantee do we have that she's going to take Katt to the hospital when she's critically ill?"

"Her mother will still take her to the hospital."

"You don't know that. You don't know her at all. We've seen things during the investigation. Red flags. Can you imagine how you would feel if you were instrumental in returning Katt to her mother and then the girl died from medical neglect?"

"That would be terrible," Heather agreed. And it would. "But does that mean… you'd never consider returning Katt to her mother? Even if the police dropped the abuse charges or she was found not guilty?"

"We can't play fast and loose with Katt's life. How is it going to hurt her to be in foster care for a couple of years? If we can keep the investigation going, she'll age out before her mother can get her hands on her. We can save her."

Heather hung up slowly when the conversation was over.

———

Heather thought about Katt's situation while she fed Alex, cleaned the house, and ran errands. Katt certainly wasn't the first child whose social worker she disagreed with, and she wouldn't be the last. In fact, Heather seemed to be running into a lot more situations where that was the case. Especially the medical cases.

There were cases where they were certainly justified in keeping children away from their parents. A lot of the medical cases were precipitated by abuse, and Heather didn't want her kids ever seeing their parents again, let alone going back to live with them. But the cases like Katt's, where the child had a medical condition that had been mistaken for abuse, were growing more and more common. Unsubstantiated claims of abuse, medical neglect, and Munchausen by Proxy used to be few and far between, but they had become a regular occurrence. They were on the TV and in the paper. She heard them discussed in lowered voices in support groups. Medical kidnap was becoming part of the vocabulary.

Heather knew better than to make waves. Claiming that Brooke was doing something wrong in her protection of Katt would only end up getting Heather in trouble. She didn't want to lose her kids. But she also hated to see Katt sick and in hospital, pining for her mother's comforting hand, when it was obvious that her injuries were the result of Ehlers-Danlos Syndrome rather than abuse.

Somebody should be on Katt's side, trying to get her reunited with her mother.

———

After visiting with Katt and making sure that her needs were being taken care of, Heather made a decision. She would go visit Renata. Katt was on the mend and would soon be released to go back home, and there had been developments in her case. Heather would have liked to have talked with Gabriel about it, but Gabriel wasn't reachable. Not by Heather, anyway.

It took a while to persuade the hospital to let her see Renata.

"She's in secure psychiatric," the woman at the computer said.

"I know she is. She has been for months. But she is allowed to have visitors."

"It's secure psychiatric."

"Does it say there that she's not allowed to have visitors?"

The administrator looked dubiously at the screen. "No."

"They can block visitors for a few days while they evaluate her, but she's been there for ages. They can't isolate her from friends and family for months on end."

"I don't think you understand what 'secure' means."

"I don't think you understand the law," Heather said. "Even if she were in prison, you wouldn't be able to keep her from having visitors for that long. It's unlawful imprisonment. It's cruel and unusual punishment. Do you want me to call her lawyer?"

"Her lawyer couldn't do anything about it."

"Oh, I wouldn't be so sure. Maybe we should ask him."

The woman's face was a stubborn grimace. "You can't just come in here and break all the rules and upset all of the protocols."

"What is the protocol for visiting Renata?"

"There isn't one; she is in secure—"

Heather pulled out her phone and started tapping the screen.

"What are you doing?"

Heather didn't answer.

"Wait. Let me talk to someone," the woman ordered. She didn't want to end up in trouble, or getting the hospital in some kind of legal trouble. "Just wait here and don't do anything."

Heather raised an eyebrow and lowered her phone reluctantly. The administrator got up and used her card to let herself past the glass that separated them from secure psych. Heather could still see her as she spoke to one of the nurses, and then a man who might have been a doctor or another nurse, and then they all made a call on the phone, standing around it. It was too bad that Heather couldn't hear what was being said on the speakerphone. She was sure it would have been entertaining.

Eventually, the sour woman came back out to her desk and sat down. She pulled a plastic tub out from under her desk and set it on top.

"Put all of your personal items and the contents of your pockets in there," she ordered, a bite to her voice.

Heather obeyed without a word.

"Your name?"

"Heather Foegel."

"You got ID?"

Heather retrieved her wallet from the tub and pulled out her driver's license. The woman barely glanced at it.

"Your reason for visiting Renata?"

"Personal."

"Your reason?"

"I don't think I'm required to tell you my reasons. It's a personal visit."

A security guard approached them. The woman flapped a hand, directing Heather's attention to him. He held up a metal detector wand.

"Legs apart, arms held out to the sides," he instructed.

Heather obeyed and the guard ran his wand around her, ignoring its squawks.

"Remove your belt and leave it in the tub."

Heather didn't argue. She removed it and waited. The woman handed her a security badge with her name and the big bolded word *Visitor* across it. Heather attached it to her shirt.

"Follow me," the guard snapped.

Heather was escorted into the psych unit. Inside, once past the nursing station, it didn't look that different from any other hospital ward. There wasn't a huge security presence. Most of the hospital room doors sat open and patients walked from one place to another without escorts or supervision. The guard led her to Renata's room. He didn't go in, just nodded to the open door and watched Heather enter.

Renata was sitting up in bed. She was a pretty girl. Part Hispanic, very slim, her eyes danced with mischief even when she was too exhausted to get into any trouble. Heather had visited her only sporadically, but she always left feeling amazed at Renata's persistence and strength of will. She was an amazing person even in the face of incredible adversity.

Renata was holding a bag of white fluid, a tube snaking into the inside of her gown. She looked at Heather and gave her a smile.

"Sorry, lunchtime," she said, giving the bag a little wiggle.

"No problem," Heather said. "At least you won't be talking with your mouth full."

Renata grinned. "How's *your* little tube-feeder?"

"She's doing really well. We've actually started her on feeding by mouth. It's slow going, but she's making progress."

"Good for her! What I wouldn't give to be able to eat real food sometimes! But…" She shrugged philosophically. "When it's either tube-feeding or die, I prefer the tube."

"I would too," Heather agreed. "At least… I think so."

Renata chuckled. "That would mean no chocolate," she teased.

"Well, then…"

They both laughed.

Heather looked around Renata's room. In spite of the fact that Renata had been there for months, there were no personal touches. Nothing to indicate that anyone else visited her, bringing flowers or magazines of interest. No family pictures. No letters on the bedside table. It was all as sterile as if Renata had been there only a day or two. She seemed small and vulnerable in the bed, but Heather knew she was incredibly tough mentally.

"So what brings you by, Mrs. Foegel?" Renata prompted.

"Heather. That's what my kids call me; you may as well too."

Renata just raised her brows and waited.

"I thought someone should check in on you. I know you don't get many visitors."

"I have a social worker. She and the nurses keep me company."

"That's not much of a support system. No friends…? Do any of your friends come by to visit? Gabriel…?"

"You know Gabriel couldn't show up here, or he'd be in trouble. I don't really get visitors. Was it easy for you to get in?"

Heather shook her head, giving a grimace.

"I think Fort Knox would be easier. Are they that afraid that you're going to escape?"

"I have before," Renata said with a smile. She turned her attention to her formula, tipping the bag to make sure that she got all of it down the tube.

"How about phone calls?" Heather asked. "Do they let you talk on the phone?"

"Sometimes." Renata's eyes narrowed. "Why?"

"Just wondered," Heather said, letting it go. She couldn't risk setting Renata's paranoia off. Hopefully, Renata would get the message. She pulled the visitor chair over and sat down. "You'd be interested in one of the kids I have right now," she offered. "I can't share names, of course, but she's been diagnosed with a rare disease called Ehlers-Danlos Syndrome. Have you ever heard of it?"

Renata considered. "Might have heard of it. But I don't know much about it. It's a genetic thing, right? I remember something about two sisters who had it. One was in a wheelchair."

Heather nodded. "It's a connective tissue disorder, so it can result in spontaneous dislocations, broken bones, skin that tears and bruises easily, but doesn't heal well."

Renata's quick eyes showed that she understood this immediately. "So you got a kid with lots of accidents, with unexplained bruises and scars. Presto, abuse case. Remove them."

"Right. She wasn't diagnosed before she came to us, and now that she is… Social Services is resisting making any reassessment. The charges against the mother have been dropped, and she has just been released from jail. But… they say mom doesn't have sufficient resources to take care of her properly. She could snap under the strain. Maybe she has before."

"How old is the girl?"

"Teenager."

"So mom already took care of her for fifteen years, or whatever. What's the difference now?"

Heather shrugged. "Now she's in foster care and they'd rather not take the chance. They'd rather just leave her in foster care until she ages out."

Renata rolled her eyes and shook her head. Unselfconsciously, she pushed her gown aside to disconnect her tubing and discarded the empty formula bag.

"Since when did 'it's easier' become an argument for keeping kids from their parents?" She swore, then apologized. "Sorry, you know how much this crap bugs me."

"I do. I just thought it was an interesting case, with her being diagnosed, but Social Services refusing to consider returning her."

Renata studied Heather for a moment, then looked at the empty door to the hallway. "Yeah. Interesting," she agreed. She gave Heather a thumbs-up so fleetingly that Heather almost thought she had imagined it.

———

Renata watched Heather go, her brain working hard on the new project. When she had first met Heather Foegel, the woman had been the enemy. She had been nice to Gabriel, but had enforced Social Services' rules, which meant that he was stuck in the mito program, getting sicker and skinnier, with no chance of seeing his mother again. They were lucky that, in the wake of Gabriel running away with Renata, they hadn't turned her into an enemy. She had softened over the ensuing months, occasionally stopping to check in on Renata, never asking where Gabriel was or why they had run like they had.

And now she'd brought them a new case. They would have to do some research first. Find out who this new girl was. What all of the circumstances of the case were. Assuming Mrs. Foegel was telling the truth. It could all be fake. A sting. Give them a new kid to rescue, dangle it in front of them, and then be waiting for them to swoop in. Maybe there was a teenager with Ehlers-Danlos, who was being unfairly kept from her mother, and maybe there wasn't.

Renata wasn't about to trust appearances. She had to be wily if she wanted to avoid getting locked up. She snorted to herself. Avoid getting locked up? Like she hadn't already been locked up for months, waiting for the chance to get out of secure psych? But it wasn't the same as prison. If they decided to try to pursue kidnapping charges against her, she could be in prison instead of hospital. And then her chances at escape would be much slimmer. Chances were, she wouldn't survive for long on the inside.

———

Gabriel couldn't help but feel a little guilt when he borrowed a phone. Renata always laughed at him and teased him for being such a goody-two-shoes. They were fighting for justice, and whatever they had to do was right. But Gabriel didn't feel that way. And he didn't think that the mom with the diaper bag would think so if she saw the skinny black teen using her phone. But if he was careful, she wouldn't. She was occupied with feeding her children and keeping them corralled in one place. Very distracted. She had hardly taken a bite of her own burger, giving instructions and grabbing busy hands to redirect the kids. Gabriel put the phone to his ear and spoke quietly. Hopefully, it would be a good day, and they wouldn't take long to get Renata for him.

"Can I talk to Renata Vega?" he asked politely.

"Who is this?"

"Is she available, please?"

"Who shall I tell her is calling?"

Every few weeks, Social Services or the police would remind the psych unit that they were trying to track Gabriel down, and encourage the hospital to do their part in trying to track Gabriel down. Then the hospital would make it harder for him to reach Renata. Maybe try to notify the police whenever he called so that they could trace his phone, or to talk him into revealing something. After a few days, they would get frustrated with the games and just let Gabriel talk to Renata when he called. It figured that they had cycled back around to giving him a hard time.

"It's her brother," he said.

They knew very well that Renata didn't have a brother, but they let it go. It was a few minutes before they connected him. Gabriel watched the mother with the children anxiously, worried that she would reach for her phone and notice its absence.

He could hear the nurse as she handed the phone to Renata. "Your brother."

"Hi," Renata greeted.

"It's Gabriel," he told her, though he was sure she would already know that.

She didn't say anything for a minute, waiting for the nurse to leave.

"My brother?" Renata asked with a laugh.

"They were demanding to know who it was. I wasn't about to tell them."

"No," she agreed.

"So… how are you doing?"

She sounded good. He could usually tell right away what her frame of mind was. Her physical health was trickier. And she might or might not tell him the truth.

"About the same," she said. "I've been pretty stable, so you'd think they'd be letting me out of here before long. They can't keep me here forever."

"But to where?"

"Yeah. I dunno. I doubt they'd put me in a foster home. Maybe a group home or residential. Hopefully no lockdown."

"Yeah. It would be nice if I could see you again."

"No kidding," Renata agreed. "It would be nice to see the sky again."

"I'll bet."

"I had an interesting visitor the other day."

"Yeah? Who?" Gabriel tried to think of who would be going to see Renata other than her social worker. A psychologist? Some other new doctor? What would make a visitor interesting?

"Mrs. Foegel."

Gabriel hadn't been expecting that. "Heather? Why?"

"She was telling me about a kid she's got right now. You're going to need to go check her out."

"Check Heather out? What are you talking about?"

"She came to tell me about a kid she's got. A girl with a rare disease that makes her break bones and bruise easily. So she looks like she's abused. They've just dropped the charges and released the mom, but they still won't consider reuniting them."

"Uh… okay…"

"She wants us to put her on the underground railway," Renata insisted. "Get her out of there and back to her mom."

"No… Heather would never do that. There's no way."

"Then why did she come here and tell me?"

"It was just a conversation. Telling you what's going on with them."

"No, it wasn't. If it was just talk, she would have talked to me about the other kids. She wouldn't have shared that kind of information with me. Information about the girl's mom and how Social Services was screwing around."

Gabriel had to admit it was out of character. It seemed like a long time since he had lived with Heather. When he had been there, she had been careful not to share anything with him about his own case that Social Services wouldn't want her to. And she never shared private information with him about the other kids in the house. She had always toed the line with Social Services, even when he knew that she disagreed with them. Like the way that she had insisted he follow the experimental med protocol at the mito clinic. She didn't get to choose how to handle it. She just did what she was told. What was she doing going to Renata and talking about the details of one of her kids?

"Tell me about the child she was talking about," Gabriel said.

It was always possible that Renata had imagined the whole thing. Or that Heather had gone to see her, but the conversation itself was imagined. Gabriel would have to check it out very carefully. Be sure before they took any steps.

"A girl, teenager. She said that Social Services just wants her to age out, so she's probably sixteen or seventeen. The disease she's got is Ehlers… Ehlers-Danlos? I think that's it. And like I said, it means she gets broken bones and bruises and other injuries more easily."

"Okay. I'll poke around. See what I can find out. She didn't tell you the girl's name?"

"She said she couldn't give me any confidential information. But it should be enough. I doubt she has more than one teenage girl with broken bones."

"Yeah. I'll check it out."

"Great." Renata sighed. "So how are you, Gabe?"

Gabriel stretched, considering. "Been trying to take it easy the last week. Got too exhausted on the last transfer."

"You gotta be careful. Aren't going to help anyone if you crash."

"I know. But I can't drop things in the middle of a transfer, either. People depend on me."

"Get help. There are other people who want to help."

"The more people I get involved—"

There was a nurse's voice in the background, but Gabriel couldn't tell what she was saying.

"I'm still talking," Renata snapped.

"Give me the phone." That, Gabriel heard clearly.

"I'm not done my call!"

There was a commotion as they wrestled for the phone, but Gabriel knew who would win. Renata was strong when she had a psychotic break, but she had been stable for a few weeks, and the mito meant that she didn't have a lot of energy. If she used it all up wrestling for the phone, she would crash and wouldn't be able to do anything else for several days. Gabriel held his breath. He was hoping that she would just let it go and conserve her energy. But it wasn't in Renata's makeup to cooperate.

"Give me that!" Renata yelled. "You can't take my phone!"

"It's not *your* phone," the nurse snapped. "And you've been talking for long enough. You should be resting."

"Give it back!"

"Renata—"

There was another crash and the line went dead. Gabriel looked at the phone in his own hand. He knew he wouldn't be able to get her back. He just hoped that she would be okay.

The mother with the children was starting to pack up her things, throwing the children's leftovers in the garbage and trying to herd them all to the door. Gabriel quickly tapped and swiped the phone to delete his call from the log, and waved at the woman.

"Excuse me! Ma'am…"

She looked at him anxiously. Gabriel flourished the phone.

"You left your phone, ma'am."

"Oh!" Her face relaxed. "How stupid of me. Thank you so much! I would have been really upset when I didn't have it!"

Gabriel handed it to her. She headed out the door with the noisy children. Gabriel breathed out, relaxing for the first time since he had picked up her phone. He watched through the window as she got into her car. If the police traced the phone call to Renata, the woman might have some explaining to do. But she didn't know anything. Chances were, she wouldn't even remember the young black man who had handed her back her phone at the restaurant. Gabriel was still safe, and he hadn't had to use a burner phone.

———

Renata dove at the nurse, howling with rage.

She got a phone call once every week or two and that was her only contact with the outside world. The only lifeline she had to friends outside of psych. For the staff to terminate one of those calls early was unforgivable. Gabriel was gone now and she wouldn't be able to get him back.

Nurse Piper took a quick step back from Renata's bed, avoiding a collision. Renata landed in the space between them, managing to catch herself on her hands and knees rather than ending up flat on her face. She quickly pushed herself up and grabbed the railing of the bed to help pull herself to her feet. She grabbed at the phone that Piper still held in her hand, even though she knew that it was too late and she wouldn't be able to get Gabriel back. Piper knew that too, and she let Renata tear the phone away from her, which enraged Renata all that much more. Piper knew what she had done and that it was pointless to fight over the phone now. That had been her intention the whole time. Renata threw the phone on the floor, but it didn't bust into pieces as she had hoped.

"You can't do that!" she yelled at Piper. "I have rights! I'll call my lawyer and sue you!" She shoved Piper. "You can't do that!"

Nurse Piper wasn't a small woman. And she wasn't easy to push around. Renata looked for something to use as a weapon. The hospital room was bare for just that reason. Renata scooped up the discarded wireless phone and threw it at Piper. The nurse sidestepped it and grabbed Renata by the wrists.

Others could hear the commotion and there were rushing feet in the hallway outside. A couple more of the nurses and an orderly ran in. Renata squirmed to get out of Piper's grip to face the new threat. Piper didn't let Renata break free. Renata aimed a head smash for Piper's nose. See if a broken nose would teach that cow to leave Renata alone when she was on a call. Nurse Piper avoided the blow, swinging Renata to the side and throwing her off balance.

"Will you chill out, Renata?" she growled, pushing Renata into the grip of George, the orderly, whose job it was to handle problems like this. Renata screamed as his fingers closed around her and he pulled her hands around, pressing them together behind her back so that she couldn't move. There was no way to hit him or throw anything at him. She tried a backward kick but couldn't land the blow. Renata writhed, trying to break away from him.

"You're going to hurt yourself," George warned. "You want to break your arm or dislocate your shoulder?"

"I don't care!" Renata raged, still struggling to escape.

"You want the quiet room or restraints?"

"No! Just let me go! Let go of me and I'll settle down!"

She felt his grip loosen slightly and ripped her hands away from him.

"Don't—" Piper warned.

Renata tried a kick to the groin, but George avoided it, grabbed her again, and twirled her around to again pin her hands together behind her back.

"I even gave you a chance," he said. "Now, was that very nice?"

"Let me go!"

"We already tried that, remember?"

"Let go!"

Renata was at the end of her strength. She pretended she didn't feel it, trying to jerk away from George one last time, but he could feel it draining from her as well and was ready to catch her as her knees buckled so she never hit the floor. He held her body tightly against his for a few moments, making sure she wasn't just faking. Not hard enough to break her ribs, but still hard enough to restrain her, especially since she couldn't even hold her head up anymore and it lolled to the side like a broken puppet.

George bent down and scooped her up, transferring her back to her bed. Renata could feel the restraints being done up around her wrists and ankles, but couldn't fight back. She watched Piper through half-closed eyes as the nurse took Renata's pulse.

"Just had to explode, didn't you?" Piper said irritably. "How are we supposed to get you out of here when you keep doing things like that?"

Renata didn't have the strength to argue that it was their job to get her meds right so that she didn't lose it. And that if they didn't do things like cutting her off in the middle of a phone call, she wouldn't have anything to explode about in the first place.

"What was that all about?" George asked. It would fall to him to fill out an incident report and Renata knew how much he hated the paperwork.

"She was upset over being taken off the phone."

He looked at the phone on the floor. "Why was she taken off the phone?"

"She'd been on for long enough. And you know she's not supposed to be talking to that boy."

"I know the police want to catch him, but Renata talking to him doesn't keep them from doing their job. What's she going to do to help him?"

Piper shrugged. She bent down and picked up the phone. She examined it.

"You broke the phone," she said to Renata. "I guess that means no more phone privileges for you."

Renata tried to object but only got out a weak groan. George glowered at Piper. He turned his head and looked at Renata before leaving. He met her eyes and Renata knew that his incident report was going to point a finger at Nurse Piper. George knew that she was just being vindictive and had no reason to take the phone away from Renata mid-call, other than to provoke a meltdown.

Renata closed her eyes the rest of the way. Darkness was washing through her body and she wouldn't be conscious much longer. Her body started to shiver. Nurse Nancy, one of those who had come running in at the sounds of the scuffle, noticed immediately.

"She's hypo." Grabbing an armful of blankets from the skinny closet, she spoke over her shoulder to Piper. "Get her glucose. Don't worry about an IV; it can go into her feeding tube. And let's put a monitor on her. I want to keep track of her vitals."

Renata breathed out slowly and let the darkness that filled her blot out her consciousness.

CHAPTER ELEVEN

It was strange being back at the Foegels' house. Gabriel had only been there for a short time, and he'd been very sick while he'd been there. It wasn't home, but it had been the last place that he'd had a bed of his own. In the time since then, he'd been sleeping rough, with the occasional stay at a cheap hotel or shelter. Everything he owned was in his backpack or a rented locker.

It wasn't easy to be invisible watching a house in the middle of a residential neighborhood. Not like it was when he was downtown, and all he had to do was sit on the sidewalk with his hat or cup out, and people would studiously ignore him. He couldn't just stand or sit in one place in front of Heather's house. Someone would take notice and maybe even get suspicious and report him to the police. Being black in a predominantly white neighborhood didn't help matters.

But he'd honed his skills over the past year. He moved from one place to another, keeping an eye on the house without appearing to look at it. He saw Collin come out of the house, walking at a quick clip toward the school. Gabriel waited. If there were a teen girl, she should also be headed to school. But none came. Heather saw the younger children off on their various buses.

Had the whole conversation between Renata and Heather been a hallucination?

Gabriel paced anxiously. He didn't like to be so exposed, especially if there weren't a valid reason for it. He would put himself at risk for a child, but if the girl that Renata had been talking about wasn't even real, what was he doing hanging around there?

He had contacts now. Other parents and foster parents who supported the cause. Even some social workers and judges, most of them working anonymously, not wanting to risk disclosure and disciplinary action. He could find out through one of them whether Heather really had another child in her care that answered to Renata's description.

But Gabriel couldn't just walk away. He couldn't just leave.

A boy in a dark hoodie walked down the other side of the street, on his way to school. He stopped in front of the house for a moment, looking around, and then continued on. One of Collin's friends, most likely. He would be late for school if he didn't pick up his pace.

Once the boy had turned the corner and was out of sight, Gabriel crossed the street. He knew it was dangerous for him to be so close to the house, but he had to get a closer look. He looked at his watch before approaching. All the kids should be on their way to school. It should only be Heather and any little ones left in the house.

With one more look around, Gabriel walked across the front yard to the gate and let himself through into the back yard. The meandering shape of the house meant that the back yard was small and had lots of dark corners. Gabriel slunk around the house, looking in windows and trying to remember the layout of the house. Matt's home office. The playroom. Collin's room, which had been Gabriel's during the time he had stayed there. The master bedroom and bath. More children's rooms. He looked in each one carefully, trying to identify by the furniture and whatever else he could see what the age and gender of the occupants were. He saw a crib and a small girl's bed. He had seen Luce leave on her bus and suspected that was her room. Another child's room. A room storing unused furniture and bags of clothes, neatly stacked and labeled. He hadn't really been conscious when he lived there of how big the house was, with bedrooms tucked everywhere.

Another bedroom. Gabriel took a long look. It was green. Not decorated, so whoever was there hadn't been there for long enough to start putting up posters or other personal touches. An older child, he had to assume a girl from the frilly bedspread. Was this the teenage girl's room? And if so, where was she?

Gabriel barely had time to think the question when the back door opened and he could hear Heather's voice.

"I'm sure everything is fine," she was saying. "But we need to follow up to make sure that you are healing properly. We don't want you getting worse."

Gabriel ducked into a shadowy corner, crouching down to take cover behind a bush and an outdoor chair. He peeked through the leaves, trying to get a good look at them.

Heather was carrying Alex in a baby seat. The toddler was way too big for it and must have weighed a ton, considering how fat she was. Heather set the seat down to unlock the garage. The girl who followed behind her was slim and willowy. Blonde. A teenager.

"Bingo," Gabriel whispered, too low for them to hear him.

The girl hobbled on a cast but wasn't using any crutches. The side door was on a spring to keep it from sitting open and letting cats or vermin in. The girl held it open so Heather didn't have to shoulder it open as she walked through with the baby seat.

"Thanks, Katt."

A name. Gabriel watched them disappear into the garage without finding anything else out. He listened to the garage door open and the car drive away. He went to the back door.

When he had left the Foegels, he had a key in his possession. While he hadn't ever thought to be back or use it again, he hadn't been able to throw it away. He had too few possessions to consider getting rid of anything. But surely they would have changed the locks? Gabriel pulled out his key and tried it in the door. It turned easily. He stood there for a moment without opening the door. Was he breaking and entering? The Foegels had given him the key, but they hadn't expected him to use it a year later. Shrugging off the uneasiness he always felt at breaking the law, Gabriel pushed the door open and stood listening for a moment to make sure that the house was empty.

The only thing he could hear was his own breathing. He couldn't sense any other presence in the house. Gabriel took off his shoes and walked silently through the kitchen and into one of the branching hallways that led to the bedrooms. He turned the wrong way looking for Katt's bedroom, disoriented from looking at the rooms from outside the house. But then he found it. He stood there looking around, trying to learn anything he could about her.

There was a pile of comic books and graphic novels beside the bed. A sketch pad with some of her own drawings and panels in it, mostly just in graphite pencil but some with color added with markers or pencil crayons. The drawings looked good. He wasn't sure how talented she was; he didn't have a lot of teenage art to compare it to. Certainly she was better at drawing than Gabriel would ever be. He flipped through the sketch pad, but there were no clues there about her sickness or her family situation. No pictures of children in hospital or being rescued from abusive parents.

He checked the drawers of the nightstand, taking note of the medications that she was taking to look up later. There were some drawing implements there; no journal or letters to her mom. Gabriel poked through everything else, but couldn't find anything of note. She was a foster child; she hadn't had time to accumulate any possessions. He did note the phone charger in the wall. Any secrets were probably password protected, the phone in her pocket.

Gabriel was careful to leave everything as he had found it, and walked back out of the room. He went next to Heather's room. Unlike Matt, she didn't have a dedicated office space. There was a writing desk in the kitchen area, but she never used it. Mostly she just threw bills there as she sorted the mail, to be taken care of later. But she had a lap desk that she used as she sat on her bed, and a file cabinet in the closet with Matt's shirts hanging over it.

Gabriel found a well-used notebook on the lap desk, sitting beside the bed. He paged through it carefully. Notes on each of the children. Dated at the top of each page. Things to discuss with their social workers. Notes for doctors. Logs of how much Alex was eating. Gabriel looked for Katt's name and flipped the pages back one at a time. She hadn't been there for long. Though Gabriel knew from experience how long it probably felt. She had been at the hospital before coming to the Foegels, just as Gabriel had. Gabriel was lucky; his mother had never been arrested, though they had talked about it. With him, they had mostly claimed medical neglect, not actual abuse like with Katt.

Gabriel read through the brief notes about Katt's condition and how she was faring each day. What was healing and what ways she had injured herself. He found the page documenting the day that she had been diagnosed with Ehlers-Danlos Syndrome. Heather had obviously done some internet research when she got home from the doctor's appointment, and there were notes about collagen and the different types of Ehlers-Danlos Syndrome and how it affected the patients.

Gabriel's eyes stopped on Ehlers-Danlos Vascular type. Possible arterial or organ rupture. Death before forty.

That was grim. There was no indication of which type of EDS Katt had. He thought about taking her away from Heather to get her back to her mother. They would be on the run, avoiding the authorities and getting her out of the area to where she and her mother could be safe. Was he really ready to take charge of someone who was so delicate? What if she tripped and fell? What if they were chased by the police or arrested? What if they ran into homeless youth or adults who decided to beat them up? What if an artery or organ just spontaneously ruptured? He was used to dealing with sickness and with kids who were high risk. But he wasn't sure about taking responsibility for a kid who could just keel over dead on his watch.

After checking through the log book for anything else of help, Gabriel returned it to its resting place on Heather's lap desk. He looked for anything else of interest on the dresser or in the drawers immediately beside Heather's bed. An odds and ends drawer. Big bottle of Tylenol. Underwear. He closed the drawers quickly and went to the filing cabinet in the closet.

Bending over the drawers while he sorted through the files one at a time was not good for Gabriel's body. His legs and back quickly got sore, and he knew he wasn't going to be able to stay on his feet for long. It wouldn't be good if he collapsed and was unable to get out of the house before Heather's return. Though if they were gone to the doctor's office, Gabriel should at least have a couple of hours to complete his investigation. He knelt down and continued going through the top drawer. He stopped at a file with his name on it, neatly printed with a handheld label printer like all the rest.

Gabriel pulled it out and sat down, stretching his legs out and leaning against the wall to rest.

There were newspaper clippings reporting on Gabriel's and Renata's appearance on TV, breaking the story of medical kidnap in the mainstream media. And the dark days that had followed the TV show airing, when Gabriel and Renata had been on the run. Nick had been killed. Ray disappeared. And a doctor from the mito clinic had attempted to murder Renata in hospital, right in front of Gabriel.

They had escaped unharmed. But in the weeks that followed, Renata had become more and more unstable, until one of the shelters had called the hospital and had her admitted. That was the last time that Gabriel had seen her in person. They had communicated by phone in the months that followed, but Gabriel longed to see her face-to-face again.

There were other bits of paper. Printouts of emails from other foster parents in the networks Heather was a part of. Other foster parents discussing medical kidnap, the underground railway Gabriel was running to get kids away from doctors and foster families and back to their bio parents. Sometimes giving news of a sighting of Gabriel or gossip about where he was and what runaways he had been involved in. Some of the incidents Gabriel remembered. Others were just hogwash. Taking kids to states or countries that he'd never even been to. Taunting the police. Calling in favors from judges. That would be the day.

Gabriel slid the file back where it had come from, and continued to go through what was there. As he had expected, he found a research file on EDS, just like the one on mito. Both were pretty thick. He didn't spend any time going through the one on mito. He knew first-hand more than she could have researched. It couldn't even compare to the hours and years of research that Gabriel's mother had done.

But he did stop to skim through the research she had done on EDS. It would save him having to do the same thing at the library or another public computer. He skimmed through the file as quickly as he could, keeping an ear cocked for the sound of the garage door opening. He knew that he needed to get out of there before too long. Maybe they would run other errands, but he couldn't count on it. With Katt crippled by her broken foot and still-painful ribs, she wasn't going to want to be walking around the mall. With blood-loss from her still-bleeding ulcer, she would probably want a nap too. The bleeding was slow now, Heather's journal recorded. The doctor said that it would stop on its own sooner or later. In the meantime, Katt was taking iron along with her other medications and would get a blood transfusion any time her heme level got too low. Gabriel hoped that their trip to the doctor would bring good news. He couldn't take Katt anywhere in that condition.

Heather had highlighted and made notes throughout the printed research papers, which helped Gabriel, allowing him to shortcut to the bits that applied to Katt. Joint dislocations, broken bones, bruises, and scars. Just like Renata had said. He was glad that she had been lucid and that it hadn't all been a dream. Bad news for Katt, but good for Renata. There were a few stories about other patients with EDS and how it affected their lives. Gabriel tried to imagine dealing with dozens of joint dislocations in a week, brought on by the most basic activities. He remembered when Renata's ribs had been broken in the hospital, how much it had hurt her and the way that they had punctured her lung. At least Katt didn't have a punctured lung. But Gabriel worried. That didn't mean it couldn't happen. If it were going to happen to anyone, it would be to Katt.

There were even a couple of other cases of children who had been taken away from their parents for abuse, only to have EDS diagnosed later. He couldn't see any examples of children being returned in fewer than sixteen months. Katt was already fifteen. In sixteen months, she would be sixteen or even seventeen, depending on her birthday. It was no wonder Social Services was suggesting Katt just be left in care until she aged out. If they did all the work to get Katt back to her mother, she would be seventeen. If they just didn't do anything, she would be eighteen. No big difference in their minds, and in the meantime, they'd have the extra funding. Greed and laziness suggested the path of least resistance. And if Katt ever had been injured by her mother's neglect or abuse, no one could accuse them of returning her to an abusive home.

Gabriel put the file back into the filing cabinet and looked for anything else of interest. That was all he could see. He went back over to Heather's bed and picked up the journal. He'd seen her use similar notebooks when he had lived there. He should have known better than to stop when he reached the last entry, with the previous day's date. Because he knew that while she started the journal at the front, she started the reference material at the back. Doctors' phone numbers, social workers, medication schedules, school holidays, all the stuff that she needed to look up as she ran the household.

Other people might have stored that information on their phone or computer, but Heather only trusted a hard copy. With each new notebook she started, she would copy any needed reference material from the old notebook to the new one so that she always had the current information close at hand. It was lucky Heather hadn't taken the notebook with her to the doctor's appointment. That told Gabriel that she had probably only planned a quick trip to the doctor's and back. If she'd had a long list of things to do or might need other reference material with her, she would have taken the book.

Gabriel took out a notepad of his own. Switching phones as often as he did, going from one burner to another and borrowing other people's cells as often as possible, he couldn't trust his reference material to a phone either. His notebook was a pocket-sized one, much smaller than Heather's. Pulling the stub of a pencil out of the coil of the book, he opened it and started jotting down numbers that Heather had noted. Katt's doctors, social worker, and judge. Her court case number. Her medication schedule. There was no number for her mother and no school schedule. When Gabriel had lived with the Foegels, he had done his schooling online, but he couldn't find a login for Katt. Maybe she was still too sick to do anything.

Gabriel was reluctant to leave. He wanted to stay and dig out more information. But more than that—the Foegels' house had been his home, for however short a time, and he had an overwhelming urge to go back to his old bed and stretch out and just sleep. Take himself back in time to when he had a home and a place to sleep again.

The more the ennui set in, the more he knew he had to go. He was digging in his heels, looking for excuses to stay. Other bits of information that he needed to look for. Other things he could do if he stayed there. Washing his clothes in the machine instead of in a restroom sink. Getting himself a glass of milk. He needed to keep up his energy level. Seeing if there was also a file on Renata in the drawer. He hadn't seen one the first time, but maybe he hadn't been paying close enough attention.

Gabriel forced himself to straighten up and leave the master bedroom. There was no time to search the rest of the house. He had the information he needed. He had to get out of there before Katt and Heather returned. His legs were tired, but he made himself put his shoes back on and leave the house. He heard the garage door just as he stepped out onto the back step. He darted to the side, finding new energy reserves. He secreted himself as he had before, behind a bush where he could see them, but hopefully, they wouldn't see him. Katt led the way to the house. When she reached the door, she turned the handle and let herself in.

Heather frowned. "Did we leave that unlocked?"

Katt looked back, her hand on the door.

"Um… I guess. I don't remember locking it."

"I don't either. But I never leave it unlocked; it's just something I do automatically."

Katt shrugged. "I guess you forgot. Maybe you got distracted by Alex."

"Maybe," Heather said doubtfully. She looked around the yard.

Gabriel froze where he was. If he moved, she might see him. As long as he was still, he didn't think that she could see him through the leaves of the bush. But Heather didn't just glance around quickly. She took a slow and careful look around.

Alex started to fuss and wave her arms around. Heather's attention was distracted, and she looked down.

"What's up with you, Miss Fuss-budget?" she asked in a high, silly voice.

Alex gurgled and waved some more.

"She's probably getting hungry," Katt suggested. "You said she didn't eat much at breakfast."

"That's true." Heather walked the rest of the way up the walk and into the house, not worrying any further about the door having been left unlocked.

Gabriel waited a long time before leaving the yard. He didn't want to walk across the kitchen windows. If Heather were going to feed Alex, then she or Katt might sit where they could see him. He sat down on the ground, where it was cold, but he'd gotten accustomed over the past year to sitting on the ground no matter how uncomfortable it was. He might as well take the opportunity to rest and get his energy back. His heart slowed, and Gabriel closed his eyes and rested.

He didn't know how much time had passed. When he next became aware, the sun was high in the sky, and sunlight was shining down on him from above instead of filtering through the bushes. Gabriel stretched and rose to his feet. He rubbed his sore joints and sneaked as quietly as he could up to the kitchen windows. He stood with his head right beside them, out of view, and listened. He couldn't hear any voices. He waited, concentrating hard. If there was one thing he had learned in the time since leaving the Foegels, it was not to hurry. Don't rush things. Wait for it.

There were no sounds from the kitchen. Gabriel peeked in through the window. There was no one at the table. No one at the sink. He ducked down and slipped past the windows as unobtrusively as he could manage. Five more minutes, and he was away from the house, waiting at the bus stop that he and Renata had used when they had left the Foegels' house a year ago.

———

Gabriel was at a payphone the next time he called Renata. There weren't a lot of pay phones around, but every now and then he came across one. It was always a surprise when they worked. Gabriel leaned against the wall, holding it to his ear. The cord wasn't long enough for him to sit down with it, so he would have to keep the call short.

It took longer than usual for the nurses to answer it.

"Hi. Renata, please."

He tried to use a different greeting each time he called. Never asking her for the same way twice in a row. Using a different tone of voice or accent.

It was silly. He knew that he wasn't fooling anyone. They knew exactly who it was every time.

"Renata's not available," the nurse said in a smug tone.

Gabriel considered. "Is she okay? She's not hurt or sick, is she?"

"This is a hospital, what do you think?"

"No, I just mean… is she worse? Did she have a… problem? Or is she just off at therapy?"

"Her phone privileges have been revoked."

"Oh. For how long?"

"Until we decide that she can handle the privilege. She will have to choose to be cooperative if she wants to talk to anyone."

Whatever Renata had done, she'd ticked off at least one nurse. That wasn't unusual. Renata had a way of getting under people's skin.

"So… next week?" Gabriel suggested.

"I wouldn't count on it," the woman said nastily.

"You can't keep her from the phone for longer than that," Gabriel said. "She'll be screaming human rights violations."

"She can scream all she likes; she won't be getting the phone."

Gabriel hated the way that they tried to control Renata. He remembered how they had bullied him in the hospital, especially in the psych unit. If they didn't get the behavior they wanted, they would find a way to get it. And pushing around frail, isolated teenagers was easy.

He hung up the phone without any further discussion or saying good-bye. He dialed up Wilkes, Renata's lawyer instead. The man was court appointed, but he was pretty good about taking action when Renata needed something. Gabriel had his direct line so he didn't have to go through a secretary or gatekeeper to talk to him. He didn't bother introducing himself. An officer of the court, Wilkes would be required to report any contact with a fugitive who wasn't his client. Wilkes couldn't help but know who Gabriel was, but if neither of them ever confirmed it, the man still had plausible deniability.

"Renata needs you," Gabriel told him.

"Renata? What's wrong?"

"They're denying her phone privileges. The nurse said they're going to hold them back for weeks, until she behaves. They can't do that."

"No," Wilkes agreed. "She has to have some way of communicating with the outside world. I'll take a run over there later today and have a talk with them."

"Maybe get her social worker involved too. She's Renata's guardian; she's supposed to be making sure that kind of thing doesn't happen."

"I'll see what I can do. Any message you want me to pass on to Renata?"

Gabriel hummed while he thought about it. "Ummm… yeah. If you can tell her that I have confirmation of the diagnosis. Uh… I still need to do more research before taking action."

"Hang on, let me write that down." There was silence from the lawyer for a minute. "Okay. I'll let her know. Keep out of trouble."

Gabriel laughed and hung up.

CHAPTER TWELVE

The information in Heather's files had included printed out emails from foster parents who were in Katt's home neighborhood who vouched for the fact that Katt and her mother were known, and they didn't think that there was any abuse. Gabriel had written down all the clues to where Katt had lived. Street and school names gave him a starting point. He looked like he fit in at the school, even if no one knew him there, and with a few casual conversations, he managed to elicit Katt's last name and the street she lived on. He rang doorbells along the street until a woman answered one door. Gabriel put on a bewildered expression.

"I was looking for Katt," he said, looking past the woman as if Katt might be hiding behind her, "isn't this her address?"

"Your cat?" the woman said blankly.

"No—no, Katt Lindholm. Did I write down the wrong house number? I thought it said—" he took a quick look at her house number, "sixty-five."

"No, there's no Katt here."

Gabriel wasn't sure whether she was still saying cat, or if she had understood him.

"And you don't know where she lives? A slim, blonde girl and her mom…?"

The woman frowned for a moment, then pointed to a house across the street. "That pink one, I think. With the fence."

"Oh, great. Thanks so much!"

She closed her door, and Gabriel crossed the street but didn't go directly to the house that he'd been directed too. He rang the bell of one of the neighbors' houses and got an answer the first time. The woman who answered was younger than the first. She smiled at Gabriel and looked curious. Maybe she thought he was selling something, but she seemed friendly enough.

"Is this Katt Lindholm's house?" Gabriel asked.

"Oh, no. You're a couple of houses off. It's that one there. The pink one."

"Oh, okay!" He smiled at her. "Do you know them? I heard Katt was hurt again…"

She picked at a nail, not looking at him. "I don't know anything. They haven't been around for a while. But I saw her mother back a few days ago."

"It seems like she gets hurt a lot," Gabriel suggested. "You don't think… her mom hurts her, do you?"

"No, no." She frowned and shook her head adamantly. "Her mom is very nice. We talk all the time. It's just that Katt is a little… well… awkward. She hurts herself."

"On purpose?"

"No! She doesn't cut herself or anything like that. She just… well, she falls down a lot, for one thing. I've seen it happen myself. She'll be walking along the street on the way home from school, her backpack on, and then she just goes down in the middle of the street." She shook her head again. "Awkward. Just… really… awkward."

"Oh." Gabriel tried to show relief at her words. "So you don't think she's abused. She's always got bruises, and her scars…"

"No. If you know her, you must have seen how she runs into things, falls down. I'm not just repeating things they've said. I've seen it myself."

"Yeah, I guess you're right," he said. "I was just worried. I wouldn't want my friend to be hurt… you can't turn a blind eye, right?"

She smiled approvingly. "You're a good boy," she said, touching him briefly on the arm. "You're looking out for your friend. You don't need to worry. Really. Ask her yourself."

"Yeah. I will. Thanks for your help!"

She nodded, and Gabriel walked away, back down to the city sidewalk. She kept watching him. Gabriel wasn't quite ready to talk to the mother, but the neighbor kept watching, so he was forced to go to Katt's house and ring the doorbell. It would look pretty suspicious if he asked for Katt's house and then went somewhere else.

He hoped there would be no answer, but it was only a minute before the door opened. The woman looked similar to Katt. He hadn't gotten a really close look at the girl, but her mother had the same general body shape and hair, though hers was darker. She looked tired, but she summoned up an inquiring smile.

"Can I help you?"

"Are you Katt's mom?"

"Yes. But she's not here."

"Could I come in?"

She looked like she would say no. But after a pause of several seconds, she nodded. "Yes, of course. Come in."

She opened the door farther and motioned him into the house. Gabriel stepped in and looked around, trying to compose his approach in his mind. Karina Lindholm sat down and looked at Gabriel.

"So… are you a friend of Katt's?"

"Sort of," Gabriel said. He tried to find the right words, looking away from her and pretending to study the pictures on the side table. "I'm here to find out if I can help you and Katt."

"Help us… how?"

Gabriel looked back toward her. He noticed that she had a brace on her wrist. It was a genetic condition, he remembered, so Katt's mother or father had EDS as well. There was no hint in the room that her father was in the picture. He literally wasn't in any of the pictures on display.

"Have you ever heard of medical kidnap?"

She shook her head. "I hadn't… until the last few days."

Gabriel wasn't sure what to say to that.

"Katt and I don't need any help," Karina said. "I was released. They dropped the charges and released me."

"Did they say they're going to reunite the two of you?"

Karina looked at Gabriel, pursing her lips and looking at him with narrowed eyes.

"No, but they have to. Now that they know I didn't hurt her, they will bring her back."

"They won't."

"Of course they will."

"Did they tell you that?"

"They will."

"They won't," Gabriel told her. "EDS kids taken into care take at least a year and a half to get returned to their families, if they ever are. And right now, Social Services says they're just going to let her age out in foster care. They don't plan to return her to you at all."

"How do you know that?"

Gabriel shrugged. "I heard it through the foster family."

"Who are you? How would you know any of this?" Karina shook her head. "Who are you?" she repeated.

Gabriel didn't answer her directly. "There is an underground organization that helps get kids reunited with their parents. Outside... outside Social Services."

"What do you mean? How can you do something like that outside Social Services?"

Gabriel shrugged. "It's underground. If you want us to help get Katt to you, you would need to be willing to take on a new name and identity. You wouldn't be able to stay here; you'd need to move out of state. Somewhere they couldn't find you."

"I can't do that," Karina said blankly. "How could I do that?"

"We would help you. But you would have to understand that what you were doing was... outside the law."

"Illegal?"

"Yes."

"I don't think I could do that."

Gabriel stood up. "That's fine. It's your decision. You'll need time to think it through and decide if that's what you really want. But you have to understand... they're not going to send her back. Just because they've dropped the charges against you, that doesn't mean that they believe you. And even if they do believe you and don't think that you hurt Katt... there's still more money in it for them if Katt stays in foster care. They'd rather not take the risk."

"I don't believe that."

"Talk to the social worker. See if she tells you she will return Katt. And if you think she's telling the truth."

Karina shook her head and walked Gabriel back to the door. She didn't offer to shake his hand; she just showed him out of the house.

"If you decide that you do want to go through with it," Gabriel said, "you'll need a way to get into contact with us." He handed her a small white paper. "Send a postcard to that address. Say you wish you could see the ocean again."

"What?"

"If you want us to try to reunite you with Katt. Send a postcard to that address and say that you wish you could see the ocean again. It will have to be in the next month or so. We don't keep the same address for long." He gave her a long, measuring look. "Do you understand?"

Karina nodded mutely. Gabriel walked out, and she shut the door behind him.

———

Wilkes showed his business card at the security desk and was also required to show his driver's license and his bar membership card before they would agree to allow him into secure psych to see Renata. But they knew they couldn't keep a lawyer away from his client, so after running him through the metal detector, they finally let him in.

He knew the way to Renata's room and didn't need to be escorted, so he ignored the guard that walked a couple of steps behind him. He stepped into Renata's room and his blood pressure immediately went up a few notches.

"Why is she restrained?" he demanded.

The guard stopped in the doorway and looked reluctant to engage. "I don't have anything to do with that," he objected.

"You're a security guard here, and you don't know why she's in restraints?"

"I wasn't the one who put her into restraints. I don't know what has been going on."

"Renata?" Wilkes shook Renata's arm gently. "Renata, are you okay?"

Her eyes opened a crack so that he could see the glistening of her eyes, but she didn't wake enough to talk to him. Wilkes prodded her harder.

"How long has she been tied up? And what's she doped up on?"

The guard held his hands up defensively. "Not my department," he insisted. "I didn't have anything to do with it."

Wilkes pressed the call button for a nurse, but he didn't wait to see how long it would take one to appear. He walked back out of the room to the nursing station.

"What's going on with Renata? Why is she restrained?"

The nurse that faced him, Piper according to her name tag, gave him a smile that was all bared teeth.

"Who are you? Renata isn't allowed any visitors right now."

"I'm her lawyer. You have to allow me to see her. Why is she in restraints?"

"She has been acting up. Violent. She attacked me. So she's in restraints for her own safety and the safety of those around her."

"Ridiculous. I demand that she be released now. And what have you drugged her up with?"

"She's not on any drugs." The woman shook her head. "No new meds. She's just tired herself out fighting. She'll be fine once she relaxes and just accepts the situation. If she'll behave herself and quit fighting back, everything will be fine."

"How long have you had her in restraints?"

She measured him with her eyes, trying to predict his reaction. "Two days."

"Two days," Wilkes repeated. "You can't keep her tied up twenty-four hours a day. You can't keep her in restraints continually for two days."

"She's had breaks."

"She's been up and walking around?"

"Not walking around, no. But she's been out of the restraints for a while."

"You think that's reasonable? You want me calling judges to order you to discontinue restraints?"

She tried to stare him down, but Wilkes didn't flinch. Eventually, Piper dropped her eyes, shuffling papers on the nursing station desk.

"I'll have to get it approved. It's not up to me to restrain or release her."

"You weren't the one who had her put into restraints?"

Piper held her head up. "No."

"Well, you'd better talk to whoever is in charge around here and get her released pronto. Because I'm not leaving until she is. Otherwise, I'll be getting a court order and laying charges for false imprisonment. Do you understand that?"

"I'll talk to someone," she agreed sullenly. "You'll have to wait. If you want to, you can go sit with her."

Wilkes could continue to stand there and glare at Piper, but decided against it. She would just continue to be sullen and dig in her heels harder. If we wanted to get action, he would have to give her a little space to get it set right again. He went back into the hospital room and pulled the visitor chair up close to Renata's bed, where he'd be able to see her face if she woke up.

———

He'd had to cancel his appointments for the rest of the day. As the evening drew on, Renata started to get restless. Eventually, her eyes opened, and she started pulling against the restraints.

"Renata."

She stopped and turned her head toward Wilkes. "Oh. What are you doing here?"

"Came to see if you needed my services."

"By services, do you mean untying me?"

"Well, I came to see about getting your phone privileges restored, but found out that there was a little more than just phones to worry about."

Renata nodded. She pulled on one wrist restraint. "So untie me."

"I'm still waiting for the staff to get it approved."

"You don't need their approval to untie me."

"Well, I sort of do. I can't go around treating patients myself, and that includes untying those that have been restrained."

Renata jerked on both her hands and feet, grinding her teeth.

"Just take it easy," Wilkes soothed. "I'm sure they'll be in any minute to get those off. They've already been delaying for a few hours. There's bound to be a reprieve soon."

Renata snorted. "Don't count on it. I've been working on it for three days already."

"Three days? They said two."

"Yeah? They're fudging. It's been two full days and pretty far into a third."

Wilkes shook his head. "Why don't you tell me what happened?"

She blew her breath out and stretched her hands and feet before answering. She told him about the call with Gabriel that had been interrupted and all that followed. She was about to the end of her narrative when two nurses and a guard came into the room, approaching Renata's bed with caution.

"You gonna take these off?" Renata demanded. "I'd like to knock some sense into—"

"Renata," Wilkes warned.

"What? You think it's okay that they tie me up like this? Leave me there for days at a time?"

"Certainly not. That's why I'm here to make sure they are removed. But you threatening the staff isn't going to do you any good. You need to behave yourself."

"That's what we've been telling her all along," one of the nurses agreed.

Wilkes noted that Piper was not one of those who had come in.

"I thought the other nurse said that Renata had been out of restraints during the last couple days," he challenged. "That doesn't match Renata's story."

"Renata lies," one of the nurses offered. "She's delusional. That's one of the reasons that she's here. You should know that by now and know that you can't believe anything she has to say."

"Has she been out of the restraints?" he challenged.

The nurses looked at each other.

"She has been. But not while she's been conscious. She won't behave when she's conscious, but we have released her and taken care of her while she was asleep."

Wilkes raised his eyebrows and didn't comment. The nurse shrugged and looked away.

"Are you going to let me go?" Renata demanded, bringing their attention back to the restraints on her wrists and ankles.

"Are you going to behave yourself, or start fighting again?"

Renata pulled on them. "Just let me free, will you?"

The nurses and guard looked at each other and cast glances at Wilkes.

"You'd better at least give it a try," Wilkes advised.

There was no movement for a few seconds, and then one of the nurses finally moved to Renata's feet and undid the straps around her ankles. Renata wiggled her toes and bent her knees, easing her cramped legs. The nurse eyed Renata's feet warily and made a wide circle around her to her hands. She paused after releasing the first wrist. Renata made a fist with the released hand, but didn't move.

"Are you going to behave?" the nurse demanded.

Renata swallowed, not moving. They released Renata's second hand. The two nurses and the guard exited quickly, leaving Renata alone with Wilkes. Renata kicked, drumming her heels on the mattress, then flipped over and beat her pillow with her fists.

"Arggh!" she growled. "Please let me knock her teeth out!"

Wilkes chuckled. "You showed great restraint," he said.

"Great *restraint?*" Renata repeated. "Did you say that on purpose?"

They both laughed.

"Feel better?" Wilkes asked.

Renata rubbed her wrists. Wilkes leaned over and looked at them. "Those look pretty painful."

"Yeah."

"Is that from the restraints being too tight?"

"No. From fighting against them."

"Maybe you shouldn't fight them, then."

"I can't help it."

"When you fight, they keep you restrained for longer. If you didn't struggle and get so upset, they would let you go sooner. Or not tie you up in the first place."

Renata shook her head. "Really—I can't help it. You telling me you wouldn't fight if they tied you up?"

Wilkes thought about it. "I don't know. I haven't ever been tied up. I guess I might want to."

"You would," Renata assured him.

"Well," Wilkes looked at his watch. "I've been here quite a while and I need to be getting on my way." He stood up, patting Renata's shoulder. "Oh… I have a message for you. That's how this whole thing got started. I was told that your phone privileges had been revoked."

"Yeah… what was the message?"

"Let me make sure I get it right. The diagnosis is right and the caller is doing some more research."

Renata smiled for the first time. "Yeah? That's great. I hope it all works out."

———

Getting in touch with Katt was not easy. She wasn't going to school, and with her injuries, she wasn't doing much walking or spending much time outside the Foegels' home.

He kept an eye on the house, watching for his opportunity. He couldn't spend a lot of time on the street where he might be observed, so it was a few days before he could make another move.

Heather left the house with Alex during the day, when all the other kids were at school. That left Katt at home alone. Gabriel wasn't sure whether to go up to the house and ring the doorbell, or approach the house another way. Would Katt even consider answering the door when she was home alone? Even if she came to the door and looked through the peep-hole, would she open it to a black teenage boy she didn't know?

He went to the back door like he had on the previous occasion, using his key to unlock the door. Gabriel walked in, his heart pumping hard. How was she going to react to an intruder in the house? He listened for the sound of a TV, and not hearing one, he walked to Katt's room. She was sitting on her bed, drawing in her sketch pad. Gabriel knocked on the open door.

Katt's head jerked up, and she looked at him with wide eyes. She didn't panic, just stared at him.

"Who are you?"

Maybe she assumed that he was another foster child or someone else who had a reason to be there. He had needed a key to get into the house. He hadn't broken in, and he wasn't threatening her in any way. Maybe she didn't consider the skinny boy before her any danger at all. Just another sick kid, like herself.

"My name is Gabriel."

"Like the angel?" The corner of her mouth quirked up. "If you're my guardian angel, you've kinda been falling down on the job."

Gabriel had to laugh at that. "Well, you're right there. You've had a lot of bad luck, haven't you?"

She nodded. Gabriel walked in and sat down on the other bed in the room, unoccupied.

"So who are you? Did you used to be a foster kid here?"

Gabriel wondered how she could have known that, then realized that it was just the most logical reason for him having a key and walking into the house like he still lived there. A previous foster kid might still be considered part of the family even after having aged out. No reason for her to be concerned about that. Maybe Heather had even mentioned Gabriel's name in passing. Some minor comment about Gabriel, a foster child who had lived there a year ago. So it made sense to Katt.

"Yeah, I used to be," he confirmed. It was a dangerous thing to say. If she didn't want help getting back to her mom, she could turn on Gabriel. She could tell Heather or the social worker or the police that he had been there and had been trying to get her away.

But it kept her calm. Kept everything safe and making sense.

"Heather's out right now," she said. "But she'll probably just be an hour, if you want to wait."

"Actually… I came here to see you."

"To see me?" Katt's brow furrowed with confusion. "Why would you want to see me?"

"I'm part of an organization… that tries to reunite foster kids with their parents."

"Reunite them? Isn't that part of Social Services' job?"

"You'd think," Gabriel said wryly. He didn't say anything else, letting her think about it. Katt set her sketch pad down.

"You don't think they're going to send me back to my mom?"

Gabriel folded his arms. "What do you think?"

"If they let her out of jail, don't you think they'll let me go home?"

"They didn't tell you that she's been released?"

"What?" Katt shook her head. "Who told you that?"

"I saw her. She's out."

"You saw her…?"

Gabriel nodded. "She's back home. I stopped by and saw her."

"And she's trying to get me back, right? She'll get them to take me back."

"If Social Services considers it, that will take a year and a half to two years, at least. But they're not considering it right now. They're planning just to let you age out in foster care."

"That doesn't make sense."

"It does to them. They don't have to decide whether you're being abused or not. They keep collecting government funding while you're in foster care, and everybody's happy." Gabriel's mouth twisted into a sarcastic sneer.

"Come over here." Katt indicated the foot of her bed and turned her head stiffly. "This position is hurting my neck."

Gabriel felt awkward sitting on a girl's bed, but he obliged, sitting down at her level, so she didn't have to tilt her head up to look at him. He examined Katt, finally close enough to get a really good look at her.

Katt's skin was pale and fragile looking, almost transparent. There was a scar along the bottom of her chin, but her face was mostly unmarked. Her hands and arms were marked with scars, and there were a couple of deep black bruises. There were raw-looking IV scars on both arms. Katt looked down at her arms self-consciously.

"I haven't seen my mom for weeks," Katt said. "So there shouldn't be any bruises or injuries. Not if she was abusing me."

"You can't convince Social Services," Gabriel said. "You can lead a horse to water, but you can't make it drink."

"You're just a kid," Katt said. "You're hardly any older than I am. How do you know so much about it? And how do you know anything about me and my mom?"

Gabriel shifted for a more comfortable position. "We call it the underground railway. Freeing kids from their foster homes and helping them get back to their parents. We have an organization. People who help, pass on messages, provide information or transportation. Medical kidnap is a lot more widespread than you would think. People are becoming more aware of it, and they want to do something about it."

"They can't just take me away, and then refuse to give me back without a reason, when they know my injuries were caused by EDS."

"That's what I thought too. They couldn't just take me away for no reason. They couldn't keep me away when they didn't have any proof. But you know what… they make their own rules. They don't have to prove anything. And they can take years deciding there wasn't actually any abuse."

Katt looked around the room. Her eyes finally went back to Gabriel.

"What did my mom say?"

"She didn't believe that Social Services would keep you away either. She still thinks that they will return her. I let her know how to get ahold of me if she changes her mind in the next couple of weeks."

"Yeah. What about me? Are you going to let me know how to get you?"

Gabriel rubbed the back of his neck. "It's a little riskier if I give you any information. Heather or your social worker could come across it. There's already a huge risk with me coming here and letting you know who I am. You can't tell anyone."

"So what if I want your help? How would I get you?"

"Help with what? I can't take you back to your mom if she doesn't cooperate. You can't go home."

"Why not?"

"Because when Heather reports that you've run away, that's where they're going to look for you. You need to get a new identity and move far away. And you can't do that without your mom."

"I could," Katt insisted.

"You want to leave here and not go to your mom?" Gabriel challenged.

"Well… no…"

He nodded understandingly. "It's not so easy if you don't have somewhere to go."

"Did you go back to your mom?"

"No. I ran away, but I couldn't go back to her. The network wasn't set up yet and Social Services was monitoring her. I've had to focus on helping other kids get away… Getting close to my mom would put her in too much danger."

She cocked her head. "What kind of danger?"

Gabriel shifted uncomfortably. "I'll have to explain that another time," he said. "It's a long story."

Katt gazed at him. "Okay." She nodded. "So… you want something to eat?"

Gabriel was taken aback. "What?"

"I'm hungry. Let's get something to eat. Teenage boys are always hungry, aren't they?"

Gabriel shrugged. "I could eat."

She got up off of the bed. When she stood up, one knee sagged suddenly, and she caught herself on the bedside table. Gabriel didn't step in and offer to help, even though he felt like he should. He just stood back, waiting. Katt steadied herself, eased her knee back up into position, and in a moment was walking ahead of him out the door and down the hall to the kitchen.

Katt rifled the fridge, looking through leftovers and pulling out some fruit and drinks.

"I dunno. What do you like? Do you want some warmed-up spaghetti, or just an apple?"

"Are there granola bars?"

Katt looked uncertain. Gabriel went over to one of the cupboards to check. He pulled out a box. "These ones."

"Oh. Help yourself."

Katt looked at the box, but decided against one for herself and had an apple and some cheese instead. They both sat down at the table. Gabriel opened the granola bar and took a bite. He grimaced, chewing carefully.

"I think this must be the same box she had when I was here!"

"Do you want something else?"

"No, it's okay." He worked on it. "I just have to be careful not to break my teeth!"

Katt laughed. Gabriel watched her cut up the apple and cut off some thin slices of cheese.

"So…" Katt trailed off, thinking things through. "I just stay here and see if my mom changes her mind? And if she does, she'll get in contact with you?"

Gabriel nodded. "She'll probably come around in a few days. Right now she thinks that Social Services is just going to send you back, and everything will be the same again. After them stalling a while and not returning her calls, she might start to get the idea."

"Does it really take that long for them to send kids back? Even though they know they're not being abused?"

"You still could be being abused."

Katt bit into a piece of apple with cheese laid over it. "I suppose."

"Are you?"

"Am I what? Abused?" Katt laughed. "No! Why would you ask that?"

"Because I don't want to be complicit in returning any kids to abusers. I want you to go home to a loving family, not to someone who is going to hurt you."

Her expression softened a little at that. "No, my mom doesn't hurt me. She's great. She takes care of me. She's my best friend and I really, really love her."

"Yeah. Well…" Gabriel took one more bite of the stale granola bar and chewed. "I'd better be getting on my way. I don't want to get caught. You won't tell anybody, right? I mean, Heather is sympathetic to your case, but she can't knowingly let you run away. You've got to keep this quiet. And I'll be back or get you a message when I hear from your mother. Do you have a cell phone?" He already knew that she did.

"Yeah." Katt gave Gabriel the number. He wrote it in his notepad and slid it back away into his pocket.

"Thanks," Katt said. "I guess… I'll be hearing from you."

CHAPTER THIRTEEN

Gabriel walked to the bus stop, deep in thought. He checked up and down the street but didn't pay close attention to what was going on as he went to the familiar bench to wait. He heard Renata's voice in his head, telling him that he was being too predictable, choosing the same way to get into and out of the neighborhood twice in a row. Using his key at the Foegels' house twice. Telling Katt his name and admitting that he had once been a foster child there. He was getting sloppy, and he was going to get caught.

Gabriel pushed the thoughts away irritably. He had too much else to worry about. He was going to have to work out all the details around Katt's extraction. It wasn't easy with her being home all the time. It was easier when a child was coming and going to school and other activities. Or when the foster parents both worked outside of the home and weren't around as much as Heather. And he still felt like he needed to do a little bit more background checking to ensure that Katt wasn't abused. The bruises and scars were real. He couldn't ignore them. He realized that she had a disability and that was the reason for the severity of the injuries, but he had to be sure her mother wouldn't hurt her.

Gabriel was walking up to the bus stop. He was brought up short, freezing where he was and staring at the other figure already waiting for the bus. A teenager or young adult, a little taller than Gabriel, in a gray hoodie that was pulled up over his head. It might not be so startling if it was a cold or drizzly day, but it was warm, and the sun was beating down on Gabriel's head. Too hot to be dressed like that.

He remembered the boy he had seen walking down the street and stopping to look at the Foegels' house when Gabriel had been watching it earlier.

It was nothing. It was somebody who lived in the neighborhood. Why wouldn't he walk past the Foegels' house? Why wouldn't he take the bus from one place to another? Gabriel was doing the same, wasn't he?

But Gabriel didn't go on to the bus stop. He stood there for a moment looking at the hooded boy. Then he decided he was too conspicuous standing there, and he turned the corner and went the other way. He would have to use another route to get out of the area. He shouldn't have planned to use the same way twice in the first place. It was sloppy, just like the voice in his head had said.

He needed to be more careful. A lot more careful.

———

It was over a week before Gabriel got a postcard in his mailbox. He had been checking it every day, varying his arrival time, his route, and the way that he dressed when he went to check it. All he had gotten were flyers and advertising circulars. Then finally, a postcard of the Statue of Liberty. Gabriel slid it out from between a couple of glossy flyers, which he tossed in the garbage beneath the post office boxes, already filled with identical flyers from other mailboxes.

He flipped it over to read the message on the back.

I wish I could see the ocean again.

"Yes!"

He had known it would come, but he was pleased all the same. A new extraction and transfer always sent his heart racing. All the planning and coordination to bring it off. Knowing that he had made a difference to one more family. The little thrill of danger.

Gabriel hit the street. He waited until he was a few blocks away to tear up the postcard and sprinkle it into several garbage cans. He would need to wait a day or two. He couldn't show up at Karina's house at a predictable time. And maybe he wouldn't meet her there at all. He could watch her and follow her to some appropriate meeting place away from her house. Then no one would remember his being there more than once when the police questioned the neighbors.

Katt and Karina. There was a soft place in his heart for a single mother with one child. There was a special relationship when it was just one parent and child. Especially a child who was medically fragile like Katt and spent a lot of time sick at home or in the hospital. Like Katt had said, she and her mother were best friends. They depended on each other. Moving a larger family was complicated, and there was a different kind of satisfaction that came from pulling it off, but Gabriel got just a bit more of a kick out of reuniting a single mother and child.

———

Karina tended to drive most places, which made it difficult for Gabriel to follow her to any destination on foot. It was only by luck that Gabriel was at the convenience store close to Karina's house to get a snack and boost his blood sugar when Karina pulled in to fill up. Gabriel watched her pump the gas and then walk up to the cashier. Karina picked up a candy bar and paid for it at the same time. While she did, Gabriel went outside and was standing by her car waiting for her when she finished.

Karina just about dropped the candy bar when she saw him standing there. She actually did drop it, but managed to fumble a catch before it hit the ground. Then she just stood there and looked at him with her mouth open.

"We don't really want to attract attention," Gabriel said, his voice low and casual. "Maybe smile and say 'hi' like we know each other."

She pasted a fake smile on her face.

"Uh, hi! I didn't expect to see you here."

"No, that's pretty obvious. There's a mall near here, over past main. Can you meet me in the food court there in half an hour?"

"Why don't I just drive us there now?"

"Because I don't want anyone to remember seeing you pick up some black dude at the gas station when you disappear."

"Oh… okay, I guess that makes sense. What if someone sees me lunching at the mall with some black dude?"

It was funny the way she said it. Gabriel grinned.

"We'll work it out. There's a long counter with bar stools. We'll sit there and act like we're each eating alone."

"Okay. I guess… I'll see you in thirty minutes, then."

Gabriel nodded. "See you."

He walked away and didn't look back.

———

He had misjudged, and it was more like forty-five minutes when he finally got to the food court and looked around for Karina. He had not ended up buying anything at the convenience store, and his sugar was too low to have walked that far. Karina was sitting at the counter and there were seats to her right and left. But the food court was filling up fast enough that it wouldn't look odd if he sat beside her. Not like they were the only two people sitting there, pretending not to be together.

Karina's expression was anxious. When she saw him approaching, her face smoothed. She smiled a little and nodded. Gabriel ordered an orange juice and small fries and put them on the counter before sliding onto one of the stools beside Karina. Karina was not supposed to be looking like she knew him, but she darted a look of concern at him.

"Are you okay?"

Gabriel picked up the orange juice, his hand shaking obviously. "Blood sugar's too low," he explained and took a long sip. "It will be okay in a few minutes."

"Are you diabetic?"

"No. I have something called mitochondrial disorder. My cells don't produce energy the way they should and it causes a lot of complications."

"Can I help you? Should I get you something? French fries probably aren't the best fuel."

"You sound like my mom."

"Then I'm probably right."

"Yeah. I'll have something else later. This is just for an energy boost." He looked at the cup in front of her. "Coffee's probably not the best choice for you, either, already being so jittery."

"Coffee helps to calm me down. I'm not jittery; I'm just… anxious."

For a few minutes, they were quiet. Gabriel ate a few fries and had some more juice.

"So you believe me?" he asked. "About the fact that they don't plan to return Katt to you?"

She nodded, eyes distant. "I thought it was logical… prove that she has this disease, and they would understand where her injuries came from, and they would send her back to me. But every time I talk to them… they tell me they're working on it. Please be patient while we work it through the system… I asked them why they needed to do anything other than just bring her back to me… and they kept saying that they needed to finish their investigation and go through the proper channels. What investigation? The charges have been dropped. I was cleared!"

Gabriel sipped slowly on his juice.

"But you're not cleared in Social Services' minds."

"I see that. And I don't want to wait two or three years to have her in my life again. She needs me. And I… I love her so much, I can't be separated from her for so long."

"Yeah. I know."

"So… what do I do?"

Gabriel let his breath out. He gathered his thoughts and began to tell her what things she would need to do to prepare. Getting identification. What resources he could offer. What to take.

"You can't tell anyone what you're planning," he warned. "No one. Even in the organization, everyone doesn't know everyone else's part. We'll have people to take Katt along the railway, but no one will know her identity or anything more than their own part in the transfer."

CHAPTER FOURTEEN

Gabriel waited at the coffee shop, watching the sidewalk outside for anyone suspicious. No one had taken any notice of him. No one gave him a second look. He shifted in his chair. He hadn't slept well the night before. He was always too hyped up the night before they started a new transfer. All of the things that could go wrong. All the detailed plans that had been made. No matter how well you planned a trip, something unexpected always happened. Someone didn't show up. You attracted the attention of some sharp-eyed cop. A bus ran late and missed a transfer. There was so much that could go wrong.

He watched a slim blonde teenager with an older redheaded woman come into the coffee shop. They went directly to the cashier to place an order. But the blonde couldn't help looking around the cafe and spotted Gabriel. Her expression was anxious, her movements jerky. If her flaxen hair and milky white complexion didn't attract attention, her furtive manner did. Gabriel grimaced.

The redhead finished paying for their drinks, and they joined Gabriel at his table. Gabriel waited until they were both sitting down and had had a chance to taste their coffees.

"You need to take a deep breath," he told Katt. "Everybody can tell something is wrong. You're attracting attention."

"I can't help it!" Katt protested. She breathed in short gasps. "I'm scared.

I don't know what I'm doing here. This is all… it's so bizarre. I've never done anything like this before."

"I know." Gabriel remembered how nervous he had been when he had run with Renata. She had gotten after him too, counseling him just to relax and quit attracting attention to himself. Learning to be unobtrusive and invisible was a skill learned over time. Most people couldn't just shut off their nervous gestures on command. "It will get easier. But you need to try. We don't want people to remember you. You don't want them looking at you wondering what is going on."

Katt took a sip of her coffee. "I know. I'm doing my best."

Gabriel nodded. He glanced down at the backpack she had set on the floor beside her foot. "You got everything you were told?"

"One change of clothes, my meds, food, a little cash." Katt nodded jerkily. She looked at the backpack and licked her lips.

The cash had been the hardest part for Gabriel when he had run. Renata had insisted on it. Gabriel didn't have any money and the only way for him to get any was to steal it. In the end, he had, but he'd felt so guilty about it. He still felt guilty thinking about it. He had thought about leaving money for Collin when he had returned to talk to Katt. Paying Collin back for the money Gabriel had stolen from him. But if he'd done that, he would have left tracks. Given himself away. Collin wasn't likely to tell Heather about it. He wasn't about to tell her about the drug money that Gabriel had taken in the first place, and why would he tell her about money that had miraculously appeared to repay it? But it was too risky. Maybe someday when a foster child's life was not on the line. Someday when he didn't have any other reason to be in Heather's house.

"I know," Gabriel told her. "It's hard. But it's the only way." Gabriel turned to Joan, the redhead, to take some of the pressure off of Katt. "How did it go?"

"Nobody followed us. It went smoothly… once I convinced her to come with me." She gave a little laugh.

"Why weren't *you* there?" Katt demanded. "I was expecting you, not a stranger. Someone just shows up at my house and expects me to go away with them?"

Gabriel looked at Katt. "Sorry, I couldn't be there. But I didn't want to be seen in that neighborhood again. Going into the house three times… someone would remember. Too risky."

"Three times?" Katt repeated.

Gabriel realized that she didn't know about the first time. About him going in and looking through her stuff and Heather's papers. He didn't fill her in. She didn't need to know he had searched her room.

"We have to be careful not to attract attention," he repeated. "There are a lot of people in our network. You have to be willing to trust whoever we send. Joan got you here safely."

"Yeah," Katt agreed. "But how am I supposed to know who I can trust? What if she had been… somebody bad, instead of someone who was helping you?"

"She knew your name and that you were supposed to leave today. Someone outside of the network wouldn't know that you were scheduled to leave today."

"Unless there was a leak. A mole in your network."

"True," Gabriel agreed. He took a drink of his apple juice, which was room temperature from sitting there so long.

"Then how can I know who to trust? Shouldn't you have… passwords or safe words? Some kind of security?"

"There will be certain crossing points where we have check phrases to make sure it is safe before proceeding. But you need to rely on your instincts for this trip. If you get a bad feeling about someone, don't go with them. If we have to backtrack and pick you up another way, we will. If you feel safe, go ahead. Sometimes we end up relying on helpful strangers. If we had a mole, they'd know the passwords, wouldn't they?"

Katt frowned, thinking about it. "Well… yes, I guess so."

"Then you can't tell a mole from a friend, or a spy from a stranger, except by your gut. Learn to trust it."

"I can't do that!" Katt protested. "I get really anxious. Paranoid about stuff that is actually safe. I talk myself into freaking out about things that aren't really there. I can't trust my gut."

Gabriel smiled.

"Renata, the girl who thought up the underground railway, she is paranoid. I mean really, clinically, paranoid. If we have to scrap a transfer because you don't think we've taken enough precautions, or something doesn't feel right, then we scrap it. I don't care if it's paranoia. I'd rather you were safe."

"So if I didn't show up here with Joan, you wouldn't have been mad?"

"No. We would have set up a fallback plan. We'd just try again."

Katt pondered on this, taking another drink of her coffee. "So we're doing this? I'm running away, to another state, to live under an assumed identity?"

Joan nodded. "Not getting cold feet, are you?"

Katt folded her arms across her chest. "Hell, yeah!"

They all laughed. Gabriel opened his notepad. "Tell me if you want out. You can go back and live with Heather until you're eighteen if that's what you want. Then you keep your own name and you haven't broken any laws. You'll be safe, and you can decide to reunite with your mom once you're an adult."

"No. No way. I can't wait that long. Besides, without her to look out for me, Social Services is likely to kill me. They just… don't get it."

"Kids are five times more likely to die in foster care," Gabriel acknowledged. "It's not quite the safe haven it's supposed to be. At least they didn't have you in a research program. Yet. The mito protocol they put me on made me so sick. I'm sure it would have killed me, sooner or later."

"I have to see my mom," Katt reiterated, choosing to ignore the dire statistics. "I miss her so bad."

Gabriel looked over the cryptic notes that he had scratched out.

"This might be a stupid question," he said. "But… are you safe to travel? I mean… You've got a broken foot. Broken ribs. Bleeding ulcer. I don't know what else. Are you okay to travel now? Or should we be waiting until you heal?"

"I can't run. But then, I can't when I don't have a cast on, either." Gabriel nodded. "I don't know… I guess so. No one has told me not to travel. I'm not going to be on a plane, am I?" The anxiety which had previously faded was back full-force. "I don't know if I could fly on a plane."

"Security is too tight for air travel," Gabriel said. "Too risky that they'd spot your fake ID. Maybe if we had someone with a small private plane, we could risk it, but I don't think you need to worry about that."

"I might get blood clots or burst an artery or something. I don't think the change in air pressure would be good for me."

"Shouldn't be a problem," Gabriel assured her. "We're not going to ask you to fly."

"Okay."

"So you're okay for normal activities, then? Walking, driving, sleeping rough?"

"Is that like camping?"

Gabriel exchanged a look with Joan. "Without the campfire and the s'mores," he told Katt.

"Okay... I'll do my best."

———

They had separated from Joan, and it was just Gabriel and Katt for the next leg of the journey. Katt couldn't help glancing sidelong at Gabriel whenever he wasn't looking in her direction. He was only a couple of years older than she was, but he seemed so mature. He had been on his own for at least a year, and he was running some complicated rescue network all on his own. Katt couldn't even imagine herself doing something like that.

If she'd been asked, she would have thought she would feel awkward being alone with him. A young woman and a young man, depending on each other, all alone... if it were a comic book, the two of them would have been a romantic couple by the third panel. Obviously. But she didn't feel that way around Gabriel. She didn't feel like he had the slightest interest in her that way. He was interested in her well-being, but not romantically. While she felt like she should be awkward left alone with him, it was the opposite. She was relieved when they had separated from Joan. She trusted Gabriel.

In spite of her anxiety levels, maybe she could trust her gut. She knew that he was just trying to help her, and she knew that he had the skills and resources to help. She didn't doubt it.

They started off walking, and between the sidelong glances Katt threw at Gabriel, she knew that he was watching her. Their progress was slow, Katt hobbling along with the cast.

"Would it be better if you had crutches?" Gabriel suggested.

"No. I'm too scared they're going to dislocate my shoulders. And they pull on my ribs."

"What about the kind that goes around you wrist instead of under your armpits?"

"Well... I haven't tried those. But I don't know if my wrists would be strong enough..."

Gabriel shrugged. "Okay. Just thought I'd check. Better if you don't, then. But you have to let me know if we're doing too much walking. Or if you need a rest. I can't go for long anyway, with my mito, but if your foot starts to ache, you need to let me know, okay?"

Katt nodded. "Sure."

"I mean it. Don't be brave and push through it. It's better for us to go slow than fast. Fast attracts attention."

"Okay. I promise I'll tell you."

What was more likely to be a problem than her foot, protected by the cast, was the backpack over Katt's shoulders. It was way too heavy and felt like it was trying to pull her apart. Her shoulders, her back, her ribs and sternum, everything felt like it was being gradually pried apart.

Katt readjusted the weight of the backpack and settled it on her shoulders again. She was glad that she hadn't stuffed anything else in it. As well as the list Gabriel had texted her, she had to include her sketch pad and pencils and a few graphic novels. And a few more clothes than he had suggested. She'd probably included too many snacks, worried that she would go hungry or that the ulcer would get worse if she didn't eat when she was supposed to. The bag was heavy.

Katt didn't have to lug around a heavy backpack when she went to and from school. Karina had purchased a second copy of each of her textbooks to keep at home, so she never had to bring them back and forth. And unlike the other students, Katt had special permission to go to her locker between each class so that she only had to carry one subject with her at a time. That had kept her loads lighter than those of the rest of the kids. But maybe she should have gotten used to the heavier weight, built up the muscles in her shoulders so that she could carry a backpack on the underground railway without feeling like it was going to break her in pieces.

They stopped and rested at a bus stop, and each had a small snack. Katt thought that Gabriel was looking exhausted. He closed his eyes for a few minutes, not talking. Katt let him rest, studying him while he couldn't see her.

A bus was pulling up to the stop.

"Are we catching a bus or just resting?" Katt asked.

Gabriel opened his eyes and looked at the approaching vehicle. "Yeah, let's catch it. I wasn't planning to, but I could use a rest."

"Where are we going?" Katt stood up and reached to pick up her backpack, but her shoulder clicked, and Katt knew she wasn't going to be able to lift it up. Not with one arm. Not in that position.

"Right now, we're just losing ourselves in the city," Gabriel said. He handed Katt two bus tickets and picked up her backpack, his own still on his back. Katt went up into the bus ahead of him, just about tripping on the top step as she got in. The stairs were very steep. Gabriel followed her, making no comment on her stumbling. Katt selected a seat and Gabriel sat next to her, setting her bag down gently on her knees, and sliding his own off of his shoulders to do the same. "Social Services has two options to consider. Either you're headed for home, or you got on the underground railway. Your mom has instructions to stay home and not pack any bags or give any indication that she's going to be leaving town in the next few days. So it will look like you are running for home. If they figure out you're on the underground railway, they'll be watching departure points, looking for us to leave the city. So we're going to stay away from them for a while. Just keep a really low profile. We'll try to coordinate leaving the city before your mom leaves."

"So where are we going now? Why do we have to go anywhere?"

"You need to get used to sleeping rough and blending in with a crowd. We need to keep moving so that anyone who tries to track or follow us will lose the trail."

"We're not going anywhere, then? This is all just random?"

Gabriel yawned and nodded, putting his head back. He closed his eyes. "If we don't know where we're going, neither does anyone else."

"You want me to wake you up?"

"Mmm. Yeah, maybe. I'll just take a short nap. Half an hour. I didn't sleep very well last night."

"I'm way too hyped up to sleep."

He didn't respond. Maybe he didn't even hear. Katt watched their progress out the windows. She watched the people getting on and off the bus. She and Karina played a game sometimes, people watching. They would sit at the food court or one of the benches at the mall, and pick out various interesting people. They would make up stories about them. Names, professions, backgrounds, what they were at the mall for. Sometimes their stories would weave together, with their characters involved with each other somehow. It gave Katt a feeling that everyone was interconnected. It was just a matter of figuring out how.

A group of high school students got on the bus. Gabriel's eyes fluttered open for a moment, glancing over them, then they closed again. Katt picked out a skinny boy with bad acne to make up a story about. The underdog. He hung around the edges of the group, pretending that he was part of it, but he wasn't really. The other kids were friends with each other, more tightly-knit, but he was the outsider. Katt looked at the other members of the group, giving them names and making up things about them. The high-school quarterback. The girl who would be pregnant before the year was out. The latchkey kid who hid an alcohol addiction.

Her eyes landed on a boy in a hoodie and their eyes connected.

It was just for an instant. She thought she recognized him. Then he turned to talk to someone else, and she shook the feeling off. She was just being paranoid, seeing things where there was nothing to see. Like Gabriel said, she needed to be casual and relaxed and not attract attention to herself.

Katt looked over at Gabriel, but his eyes were still closed. He didn't have a gut instinct that there was anything wrong. He was the one with experience and Katt needed to follow his lead.

She closed her own eyes, not sleeping, but working through the story about the boy with acne. She would give him a superpower. Something nobody else knew about. They didn't look at him, ignored him. Discounted him. She'd give him invisibility. He wasn't just an outsider to the group; he was invisible to them. And that gave him power over them. That's how he would defeat them in the end.

———

Gabriel forced his eyes to open, knowing that he'd been asleep for longer than he had intended. He rubbed them, sending shots of pain into the back of his skull. He looked out the window for a moment, trying to gauge where they were. Then he looked around at the occupants of the bus and at Katt.

"Hey. You should have woke me. I didn't mean to sleep for that long."

She shrugged. "You needed it. And you said we weren't actually going anywhere."

Gabriel stretched. It was true, but if he'd been awake, he would have disembarked sooner. There were too few people on the bus. They were no longer part of a crowd. And Gabriel sleeping for so long might have attracted attention. There were no school kids on the bus, so Katt and Gabriel stood out. He pulled the cord to request the next stop. There was a ding and the stop requested light turned on.

"Time to go?"

"Yeah."

Gabriel cast his eyes around the bus again as they got up and headed for the back door. Looking to see if anyone were watching them. Looking to see if the bus driver had noticed them. No one seemed to be paying any attention. Gabriel let out his breath in relief.

When he got off the bus, he held the door open for Katt and waited while she maneuvered awkwardly at the bottom of the stair. There was a big step down from the bus to the curb and she didn't seem to know whether to step down on her cast or to stand on the cast and put the other foot down first. Gabriel waited, not wanting to make her even more awkward by giving her advice or hurrying her along.

Katt landed in what was almost a two-footed landing, and then stood there with her eyes wide, making sure she wasn't injured and trying to get her bearings.

"You okay?" Gabriel asked.

"Uh… yeah. Sorry. Which way?"

Gabriel looked up and down the street. "Why don't you decide?"

"What? I don't know where to go. You're supposed to be my guide, aren't you?"

He smiled. "You need to develop your street sense. After you're with your mom, you're going to need to be aware and keep your eyes open for anything suspicious or threatening. You might as well start now."

Katt looked around her, wide-eyed, as the bus pulled away from the curb. She watched it go.

"I would have stayed on the bus. I feel… exposed out here."

Gabriel nodded. "Yeah. Right now you are. Standing out in the open, looking like you don't have anywhere to go. You look… tentative and lost."

Katt readjusted the straps on her backpack. "I guess that's 'cause I am. I have no idea where I am. Where am I supposed to go? Shouldn't we have lunch soon?"

Gabriel looked at his watch. "Sure, lunch would be good. I'll start you off with an easy choice. Do you want to eat something you brought in your backpack or do you want to buy something?"

Katt looked pained, shifting the weight of her backpack again, first pulling on the shoulder straps, and then reaching behind her to boost it upward from the bottom.

"I think… maybe I'd better lighten my load. Something from my backpack."

"Okay." Gabriel looked around. It was a light industrial area, but he could see a residential neighborhood that started a couple of blocks away. "Let's head that way. We'll find a playground or something and have a picnic."

Katt nodded. Gabriel could see her grinding her teeth, her jaw tight. They were silent as they covered the empty blocks, exposed, no cover, no other teenagers around. No one else out for a pleasant walk. Gabriel figured Katt was getting pretty anxious, though trying her best to hide it. When they entered the tree-lined residential street, Gabriel gave a little sigh of relief. It was a young neighborhood; the houses were tall and only a few years old, there were tricycles and other kids' toys on the lawns and sidewalks.

Gabriel looked for an area where teenagers might hang out. Some little nook that was sheltered from the view of adults. Near a convenience store where they might go to spend their hard-earned money. Maybe a playground or dry pond where they showed off daring skateboard or bike tricks. A library where a girl might tutor guys who were having trouble in English language arts.

There was a bit of graffiti on the end of a shed that they approached, and Gabriel looked around, eyes sharp. There was a footpath that led past it and between two houses, intersecting with an alley.

"This way." They followed the path through the alley and out into a cul-de-sac. At the center of the crescent was not only a park, but a water feature, a little pond with a few ducks floating on it, fat from bread crumbs thrown by residents. There were a couple of benches built to overlook the pond. "There. Let's sit down."

Katt stood beside the bench, not moving. Gabriel swung his backpack off and put it down beside the bench with a sigh. It felt good to get it off. He looked at Katt.

"So, what have you got to eat?"

Katt looked at Gabriel. He couldn't quite identify her expression. Her face looked pinched. Maybe she was still feeling anxious and exposed. He had led the way to the park, but he hadn't asked her if it was okay with her. Maybe she had a feeling about it.

"Katt?"

It took a long time for Katt to focus her gaze on Gabriel. She seemed to be coming from somewhere far away.

"I need help," she said.

"Sure. What's wrong?"

She brought one hand up and crossed it over her body to touch the opposite strap on her backpack.

"There's a problem… with my backpack."

Gabriel reached over to help her take it off. She angled her body away from him.

"I don't… it's…" She plucked at the strap. "If you could… slide this one off. No… lift it up… and then…" She yelped, her body jerking. Gabriel pulled the backpack up, taking all of the weight off of her and trying to see what was wrong. Katt was as pale as a ghost and he saw her eyes roll up. He pulled the backpack the rest of the way off and dropped it. Gabriel grabbed Katt and guided her onto the seat of the bench. He kept his hands there, just an inch away from her, waiting for her to either faint away completely or straighten back up again.

"Katt! Katt, are you okay?"

She moaned a little. She gave a little shoulder-roll, and Gabriel watched one of her shoulders lift and rotate and snap into place. He felt a little sick at the sight. Katt rubbed the shoulder with her other hand, then brought her hand up to her face, wiping sweat from her forehead.

"It's okay."

"You're okay now? Are you sure? What happened?"

She wiggled, using the same hand to rub her back, following the length of the spine. Gabriel had no idea how she could twist her arm into that position.

"My back too," Katt grunted. "Do you think you could kind of… just… rub your hand alone my spine, and see if it pops back?"

"I'm not a chiropractor! I don't want to hurt you. Spines are delicate; I could do real damage…"

"I'm not saying to try to manipulate it. Just… rub along it firmly… it will probably just roll into place itself…" She arched her back and wriggled, her face a grimace of pain.

Gabriel was tentative, not wanting to touch her. But he tried to do what she said, feeling firmly along the length of her spine. Katt gave a squirm, and Gabriel felt a series of cracks, then she relaxed. Katt sighed.

"Oh, wow."

"Are you all right?"

"Yeah." She rubbed her face. "Yeah, that's better."

"What happened?"

"The backpack is pulling everything out of joint."

"Ouch. That doesn't sound good."

"No."

Gabriel delved into his backpack for one of his snacks and then bent over hers. "What do you want me to get you?"

"Uh… juice box. And some crackers."

Gabriel found what she wanted and handed it to her.

"Liquids are heavy to carry," he said. "Bring a refillable bottle and just fill up with water wherever you stop. It's free. If you want, you can add some flavor to it; they make little packets or bottles that are really light."

"Oh. Okay."

She opened the package of crackers and poked the straw into her juice box.

"Why didn't you tell me the backpack was bothering you?"

Katt glanced at him. "I have to be able to carry my own stuff. You can't carry both. It will tire you out too fast."

She had figured out his mito too quickly. It was true; he couldn't carry both bags more than a few steps. But she couldn't carry it either. He should have remembered the story of how she had broken her foot. Taking a jug of milk out of the fridge had dislocated her shoulder. So how could he expect her to carry a heavy backpack like that?

"We'll figure something out," he told her. "And you have to tell me when there's a problem. Before you get hurt. What do you think is going to happen if you break a bone out here? Or I have to call an ambulance for you? I already have one friend locked up in hospital. I don't want you there too."

As soon as he said it, he regretted it. He didn't want to have to explain about Renata. But Katt was already looking at him, her eyes full of questions.

"Locked up in hospital?" she repeated.

"Yes. Just like you would be if they caught you after you ran away. They wouldn't just leave you free to run again."

"What happened to your friend? She ran away?"

"Yes. That's not why she's locked up, exactly. I mean, there's that, because Social Services doesn't want her to run away again. But she's locked up now because…" Gabriel shrugged, his face getting warm. "She's in psych. She's… not stable right now."

"Oh. I'm sorry. That must be hard."

"It is. I haven't been able to see her for a long time."

"She can't have any visitors?"

"It's limited. She can have some… but I can't go there or they'd arrest me."

"For what?"

Gabriel just looked at her.

"For what you're doing now?" Katt demanded. "How is helping me illegal?"

"I'm either kidnapping or I'm abetting a runaway. And I ran away myself. I've done plenty of other illegal activities while saving kids like you."

Katt munched on crackers, thinking about that. "You must really believe in what you're doing," she said finally.

Gabriel breathed out slowly and nodded. "I do."

———

They went on. Gabriel went through Katt's backpack and they abandoned whatever of her food was too heavy. He redistributed the contents of her backpack, making her tie an extra sweater around her waist and carry her sketchpad and pencils. He looked through the graphic novels.

"These are pretty heavy."

Katt sighed. "I can't get rid of them; they're all I have."

Gabriel knew how it felt to have nothing. To hold onto little, inconsequential things because he had to have something to call his own.

"Can you carry them comfortably in your hand? With your sketchpad?"

They experimented. Katt could carry three of them with her sketchpad. Gabriel put the others in his own pack. He weighed her backpack thoughtfully.

"I'll carry it for a while," he said. "We'll switch off. But you have to tell me the minute it starts to bother you. No waiting until you're hurting. We'll try to replace it soon with a bag that has wheels, so you can pull it on the sidewalk without carrying its weight."

Katt's eyes brightened. "That's a good idea! I didn't think of that!"

They started walking again. Not back the way they had come, but cutting across the community looking for a new major street or bus route. Gabriel pulled on a hat. Something to change his appearance and help to cover his face. Katt had the sweater around her waist, and after a while, he had her put it on. He didn't know whether it would help if the police were trying to track them, but Renata had insisted, and it seemed like a good practice. It certainly couldn't hurt.

Gabriel watched out the window when they got on another bus. They would need to find somewhere to sleep before it got dark. He knew the city pretty well, and as they traveled, drew a map in his mind to the nearest safe sleeping spots. They couldn't use a shelter, not yet. If Social Services put out missing persons posters, the shelters would be on the lookout for Katt. But no one regulated where they could sleep rough.

He remembered the first few nights he had slept outdoors with Renata. It had been pretty tough. Katt was not going to be comfortable.

CHAPTER FIFTEEN

Katt was secretly glad that Gabriel's disease stopped him from being able to walk for too long at a time. Her foot was aching a little. And her ribs heated up whenever she walked for long, especially if it were her turn to carry the pack. She didn't put it on her back again, but carried it at her side, like a suitcase. That seemed to be easier on her shoulders and back. For short periods of time.

Gabriel was looking drawn and tired by the time that he told her it was time to eat a supper and get set for sleep. This time, Katt was hungry and wanted hot food. More crackers weren't going to cut it. They stopped at a fast food restaurant and shopped the value menu. Greasy, horribly processed food, but Katt needed something warm in her stomach. Gabriel ate little, his eyes traveling over the other patrons of the restaurant and outside to the sidewalk, making sure that they weren't being watched or followed.

She felt safe with him there, watching over her. That's why she had been so upset over Joan being the one who had picked her up at the house. She hadn't felt safe with Joan like she did with Gabriel. Katt didn't know anything about Joan, but she didn't think that Joan was another runaway foster child. She was someone who was sympathetic to the cause, but Katt didn't get the feeling that she had ever been on the run herself.

"Where are we going to sleep?"

Gabriel took a bite of his hamburger, his eyes returning to Katt. "We're going to be sleeping rough for a few days. I know it isn't going to be comfortable for you, but we can't go somewhere we might be identified. We need to stay under the radar. Away from shelters and hostels."

"What about a hotel?"

"If I check into a hotel with you, the manager is going to be calling the police."

"Why? They'll see that I'm there by choice. You don't have a gun on me."

"An older black dude with a young, vulnerable, frail-looking white girl like you? No one is going to be asking questions. They're going to assume that I'm a pedophile and you're in danger. Even sleeping rough, we're going to have to be careful. Make it obvious that you're protected, without making people think that I'm… going to take advantage of you."

Katt tried to process this. "How are we going to do that?"

"I'm not sure, exactly. Body language, mostly. You're going to need to look like you're comfortable with me. Like a brother. That you're not afraid of anybody else and that you're not vulnerable to me. And as long as we're around other people, and not off on our own, they'll be able to see that I'm not taking advantage of you."

Katt hadn't really thought about how their relationship would look to other people. She tried to imagine what they looked like walking down the street and sitting on the bus together. Were people looking at them, thinking that Gabriel had salacious thoughts about her? Or that Katt had been taken in by him and needed to be straightened out? Did people automatically think that they were a couple, rather than just casual acquaintances? She didn't think so. She wasn't holding Gabriel's hand or spending all her time staring into his dark brown eyes. He didn't put his arm around her when they walked, or kiss her. They didn't sit close together like a romantic couple.

Katt's cheeks burned thinking about it. She took a drink of her pop, trying to cool herself off. Gabriel looked away from her, a slight smile quirking the corner of his mouth.

"Sorry," he said. "Is it going to be all awkward now?"

"Obviously, no one has told you how awkward I am all the time," Katt said, trying to make light of it. "No one is going to think that we're a couple. I'm too much of a geek to be in any kind of a relationship."

"Oh, really?" Gabriel said. He looked like he was going to say something more, then closed his lips together in a thin line, looking intently outside.

Katt finished the rest of her meal in silence. She looked out the window. Night was beginning to fall.

"So, do you have somewhere in mind close to here?" she asked. "I'm getting pretty tired."

She wasn't that tired, but she knew that he was. Katt was mentally tired. Wrung out from spending all day on the run. But her body wasn't exhausted like Gabriel's obviously was.

"Yeah. There's a park near here. Renata and I stayed there one night. It will be good."

"Lead the way," Katt invited. She stood up and picked up her pack. Gabriel shifted his own backpack onto his shoulders and headed out. The park he had spoken of was only a few blocks away. Far enough that Katt's arms and ribs were hurting again, but she didn't say anything to Gabriel or ask him to take her pack.

It was a treed area. There were homeless people setting up tents or laying out bedrolls. Some people had big carts full of supplies and possessions. Others seemed to have nothing, just lying down on the bare ground in the clothing they had on.

Gabriel delved into his pack for a ground sheet and spread it out. He had a couple of thin blankets, but not a lot could be packed into a backpack. Not when he had to carry clothes and food as well.

"The ground gets cold at night," he told Katt. "The groundsheet helps keep some of the moisture and coldness out, but we'll need to cuddle up to conserve body heat as much as we can. I promise I won't do anything to take advantage of you. Just lying together to keep each other warm. Put on all of the clothes that you can to keep yourself warm. Even if you're too warm right now, you won't be in an hour or two. If anyone comes around offering blankets, take two."

Katt nodded her understanding. There wasn't much for her to do as he prepared their sleeping area. She pulled on her sweater and coat. She hadn't packed any blanket or bedding. It hadn't been on the list that he'd texted her. When Gabriel finished, he motioned to the groundsheet. "This is it. Come lie down."

He lay down himself, putting his backpack under his head like a pillow. Katt followed suit. It was still light out. Too early to be going to bed.

Gabriel pulled the blankets over the two of them, and snuggled up to her, putting his arm around her. But as he had promised, he didn't do anything more. No squirming or roving hands. He held perfectly still and just let her lie there against him, like a pillow or a big brother. Katt closed her eyes and thought of her mother.

"We went camping in the Grand Canyon once," she told Gabriel. "Me and my mom. It was so amazing there. The stars… you've never seen stars like that before. The whole sky was just… swimming with them. That was the most amazing vacation I've ever been on."

"Sounds cool," Gabriel said. "I'd like to do that someday. Maybe with my mom… when it's safe…"

"You could do it anytime, couldn't you? Just tell her to meet you there. Who would know the difference? Who would stop you?"

"Hmm. Depends. I don't know whether they're still monitoring her phones or not. They could be listening in, and then they'd know where to look for me. Put her in jail for helping a fugitive."

Katt shifted and turned her head to look at him.

"You mean you can't even call your mom? You can't even talk to her on the phone?"

"No. I could use a burner phone so that they couldn't trace my call, but they could still take it out on her. Say that she knew something about where I was or had helped me. I can't do anything to get her in trouble. I don't want her going to jail."

"Yeah." Katt completely understood his position. She felt horribly guilty for Karina having been jailed. Katt knew that it was her fault that her mother had been put there. Even though she had done everything she could to convince the police and Social Services that Karina hadn't done anything and that they should let her go, it was still because of Katt and her stupid body with its bruises and scars that Karina had been put in jail in the first place. And she felt horrible about it. Like Gabriel, she would do whatever she had to to keep it from happening again. Even if it meant not talking to Karina.

But she didn't have to worry about that. Gabriel and his underground railway were in place, and they were going to take Katt to her mother and reunite them. She didn't have to live like Gabriel, forever on the run and not able to see his mother.

Katt turned onto her back, uncomfortable lying on her side for long. She breathed slowly, one hand over her ribs.

"Are you okay?" Gabriel asked.

"Yeah… just a bit sore. The ground is… really hard."

"Yep," he agreed. "Just imagine that you're on that vacation with your mom, in the Grand Canyon. Sleeping under the stars."

"I can see a few stars. Not very many, though."

"Too much light pollution. Can't see very many in the city."

"Yeah."

There were a lot of people around them. Making noises. Grumbling and muttering, arguing, yelling. As the darkness fell, Katt waited for them to all settle in and quiet down. But the noise level stayed pretty high.

Gabriel's breathing was long and even. She couldn't believe that he had fallen asleep already. It couldn't have even been ten o'clock yet. Katt listened to his breath rasp, trying to match her breathing to his and lull herself to sleep. She had to move again, her spine hurting. But she couldn't switch to a position that didn't hurt her broken ribs. The ground was hard and unforgiving.

Gabriel's breath caught, and she knew that he was awake again, listening to her moving around.

"Sorry," she apologized. "I didn't mean to wake you up. Just looking for a comfortable position."

"It's okay. Come lean against me. I'm soft."

She tried lying on her uninjured side, resting against him. He was warm and soft, but she still couldn't stay in that position for long before moving around restlessly again. Gabriel didn't criticize her. She heard his breathing settle back into a sleeping pattern once more.

As it got later and later, her body more and more exhausted, Katt expected sleep just to catch up to her and overcome the discomfort. But it never did. She jumped at noises that were too sudden or too loud. Her back hurt. Her ribs hurt. Every joint in her body hurt. She had a headache from lack of sleep, and a black mood settled over her. She was never going to get to sleep again. How was she supposed to survive the ride on the underground railway if she had to stay awake the whole time? They were going to have to find a bed of some kind. She couldn't live like that. She'd be dead before she got back to her mother.

As it grew later and later, Katt's anger turned into despair. She cried silently, careful not to wake Gabriel. A couple of times during the night he reached out to her, holding her and trying to calm her. But she didn't know whether he were actually awake and aware that it was her, or if it were just an automatic reaction. Was he thinking of her? Or was he thinking of Renata? Or another kid he'd rescued. There must be quite a list now. Was he so careful and attentive to each one of them? Or was he attracted to Katt even though he said he wasn't?

When people started to move around again, packing up their bedrolls and tents, Katt was still awake. She couldn't figure out why they were all moving and congregating when it wasn't even light out yet. Gabriel awoke beside her. He glanced around and looked at his watch. He grunted.

"Time to pack up."

"It's not morning yet."

"Police will start rousting us before the morning commuters. The law says we have the right to sleep, but we're not allowed to become an eyesore for the people who really count."

Katt rubbed her eyes. "That's stupid."

"Tell that to the cops." Gabriel stretched and rubbed his joints, then got to his feet and pulled the blankets off of Katt. "Actually, don't."

Katt sighed. She knew that she should help, but all she could manage was to get to her feet so that Gabriel could pick up the ground sheet they had been lying on. He didn't complain about her not helping.

"We'll go get some coffee," he told her. "Warm up the stiff joints. You'll feel better once you've been up for a while."

She wondered just how much he could tell by looking at her when it was so dark out. Had she given away how rough she was feeling, or did he just know from experience? Katt didn't imagine that too many people felt chipper after a night sleeping on the ground and waking up at five o'clock in the morning.

Gabriel led the way, shouldering his backpack and picking up Katt's as well. She followed him without a word. They walked past a couple of fast food restaurants and coffee shops where homeless people were already lining up for coffee, eventually stopping at one that was farther away, where there was no one else who was obviously down on their luck. Gabriel gave a bit of a groan as he put down Katt's backpack. It had obviously gotten heavy during their walk, even though he was freshly rested.

Katt gave him a few dollars to help pay for their coffees. She had brought money with her as instructed and couldn't let him pay for everything.

"You want any solid food?" Gabriel asked. "Or just coffee?"

"Just coffee."

He nodded. In a few minutes, they were both sitting down in a booth, backpacks hidden at their feet, sipping their grande javas.

"You have circles under your eyes," Gabriel observed. "Didn't sleep very well, hey?"

"No." Katt hesitated before revealing more. "I didn't sleep at all."

Gabriel's brows went up. "Not at all? Were you that uncomfortable?"

Katt nodded, staring down at her cup. Gabriel thought about this, a frown line creasing his forehead.

"That's no good. Hopefully, you can catch a nap or two while we're traveling today, but you need to be able to be alert. You can't spot danger if you're half asleep. You said you'd gone camping, so I didn't think sleeping on the ground would be as much of a problem for you."

"My ribs were bothering. I couldn't get comfortable."

"Did you take painkillers before bed? What have you got?"

"Tylenol. Some other pills from the hospital, but they didn't give me very many."

"Take them tonight to make sure you can get a good sleep. If you run out, we'll find something."

Katt didn't like to think of how they would 'find something.' What did that mean? Steal something? Buy street drugs? Maybe they had a doctor on their payroll?

"Okay."

Gabriel was staring out the window into the early-morning darkness.

"You went to the Grand Canyon with your mom. What else do the two of you like to do together?"

Katt's thoughts were drawn away from their immediate worries. "Oh… well, we couldn't really afford to do a lot. The Grand Canyon was a big thing, and we only did it once. We do some urban hiking… bird watching… we can't do anything too difficult, in case I fall."

"You know lots of different kinds of birds?"

"Yeah, I guess. It's amazing what you can see, right in the middle of the city. We keep a log book, and some sightings you can list online so that other birdwatchers or people who track migration patterns can see them. It's fun to share them with others."

"Cool. That sounds like fun. And it's good that you stay active, and don't just hide at home so that you don't get hurt."

"Yeah. I could never do gymnastics or a contact sport. I'd be dead. Walking down the sidewalk… I can usually manage that. Though I do fall down sometimes. My knee will give out, or I'll trip over a crack. Or get distracted by a sighting and blunder right over one of those low fences and end up flat on my face."

He laughed, then covered his mouth. "Sorry. I could just see it."

Katt smiled. It was nice sitting with him there, like they were friends, discussing her shortcomings without being judgmental about them. The kids at school and the teachers and doctors were always criticizing her for being so clumsy and doing things to hurt herself. With Gabriel, it was different. She didn't think that it was just because she had a diagnosis now and he knew about it. There was more to it than that. He was accepting of her, the whole package, flaws and all. She supposed it was because of his own illness. He didn't pretend to be macho or have unlimited energy. He was just Gabriel, a guy who was trying to make it from one day to the next in spite of his challenges. And to accomplish something important.

"You like comic books too," Gabriel commented.

"Yeah. Graphic novels. Reading and drawing. I can do that without hurting myself. As long as I don't have my arm in a sling."

"You'll have to show me some of your stuff."

The coffee was helping Katt perk up a bit. And maybe the conversation and being on her feet instead of lying down completely frustrated was part of it too. She was starting to feel clear-headed and more like herself.

"What are we doing today? Still not leaving town or going to a shelter?"

"I know it's annoying to have to wait around when you really want to get out of here and meet up with your mom. But if we can stay under the radar for these first few days, when they are looking hard and watching exit routes, it will be easier when we do try to head out of the city. They'll figure that we're already gone and will have to expand the search outward. They don't have the resources to keep up an intense search or to keep people watching the buses."

"Will they even do anything?" Katt asked. "I mean… a foster kid runs away… that must happen a lot. Do the police really care about teenagers who left on their own?"

Gabriel nodded. "It varies. If you were a repeat runner, they wouldn't put much manpower on it. But you haven't run before and aren't high-risk. If they figure I'm involved, they will put extra manpower on it, so hopefully Heather can keep that part quiet. Chances are, there won't be a huge search or alerts on the TV."

"How would Heather know that you were involved? And if she did, why would she keep it quiet instead of putting the police onto you?"

Gabriel considered his answer. He tapped his cup against the table, and she could see that he was uncomfortable. Gabriel gave a little grimace.

"Heather was the one who gave us a heads-up about your case."

Katt was floored. "What?"

"Yeah. She couldn't reach out to me, but she contacted Renata, and then Renata passed the information onto me." He took a sip of his drink. "No matter what happens, you can't let anyone know that she was involved. There would be huge repercussions. It was pretty brave of her to put us onto you in the first place. She can't afford to have a lot of kids disappear from her care."

"Have there been others?"

"Just you and me. If she starting losing kids left and right, she'd lose her license. Maybe get sent to jail."

Katt shook her head in disbelief. "I won't tell anyone," she promised. "Heather! I would never have guessed."

"She knew they wouldn't get you back to your mom. That they never intended to."

"I owe her a big thank you… can you tell her, if you see her?"

"I won't see her. I can't have any contact with her. It would be too risky for both of us."

———

Sitting on the bench in the afternoon sun had done Katt in. Gabriel let her sleep, thinking through the next few days and how they would get Katt to her mother with the least amount of risk. He had watched Katt's eyelids flutter in the bright sun, closing for longer each time until her head lolled down and she was completely out. She leaned against him, and he put his arm around her to keep her from falling over or waking up. Her head rested on his shoulder, warm and comfortable. He stroked her fine, blond hair.

She was pretty, in spite of her geekiness. Maybe the contrast of the soft blond hair and fair skin with her clumsy, comic-book-loving persona magnified her natural beauty. Despite the fact that she was on the run, that she hadn't slept all night, and that she was in more pain than she wanted to admit, she still exuded an ethereal beauty that begged a second look. It wasn't easy to stay invisible with her at his side. People would remember seeing her. And that made the operation that much more dangerous.

Katt shifted and snuggled against him. Gabriel knew that they should get on their way before too long. Mothers walking through the park with their children in strollers would start to get anxious about a couple of shiftless teens hanging around and might call the police or Social Services. He rubbed Katt's shoulder to see if she would wake up. After a few minutes, her head started to bob up, until she was awake enough to sit up by herself and rub her bruised-looking eyes.

"How long was I asleep?"

"Not that long… but we've been here as long as we should be. We need to get on our way."

"Okay." Katt yawned. She stretched her legs out in front of her and rubbed her knees.

Gabriel watched her slowly get to her feet and get stabilized. She winced as she shifted her position.

"What hurts?" he asked.

Katt looked at him, opening her mouth to argue. Then she shrugged. "Aside from my ribs and my knees… my toes are really bothering. I think I have blisters, but I'm afraid to look."

"Sit back down."

"We should go on. You said."

"Not without taking care of feet first. Isn't that the first rule of hiking? Take care of your feet. First rule of being homeless, too. You're not going to be any good if you end up with an infection. And blisters are no fun. I've got first aid supplies. We'll take care of them."

Katt sat back down on the bench and Gabriel removed the big sock stretched over her cast, and the shoe and sock on the other foot. Katt avoided looking at her feet.

"How bad are they?"

"You should have told me about this earlier. I thought we already covered this when we talked about carrying your backpack when it was hurting your shoulders."

Gabriel's tone was sharper than he intended. But her feet were a mess. Not just blistered, but her toenails had cut into her other toes, shredding the thin, fragile skin. By the blackened dried blood, they had not just been bleeding from that day's walk, but from the previous day's activities as well. Gabriel opened up his pack to dig out medical supplies.

"Sorry," Katt said in a small voice.

He nodded, focusing on the job at hand. Cleaning them up with alcohol wipes, which he knew stung like the dickens. Clipping the nails as short as he dared so that they wouldn't cut the adjacent toes. Wrapping each toe with gauze for protection, thin and flat so that it wouldn't cause more blisters. They were going to have to be careful and not walk too much. Her skin wasn't going to callous and harden up.

"I wasn't expecting a pedicure," Katt said, as he clipped the nails on her broken foot.

"I've worn all kinds of hats with this job."

"Are they really bad?"

Gabriel sighed. "Yes."

"Crap. I'm sorry…"

"You want to end up back in hospital? I can't do anything for you if you have to go in for treatment. You're going to get caught."

"I don't need to go to hospital…?"

"I hope not. But if you had just gone on and not gotten these cleaned up… you'd end up infected."

"Yeah. I just thought…"

"You need to tell me. Just like I told you yesterday. Get a pair of clean socks from your bag."

Katt obeyed. Gabriel finished with her feet and put her shoe back on. He folded his arms and looked down at her. Katt raised her eyes tentatively.

"What?"

"What else? I mean it, you tell me any and all issues."

"There isn't anything else. My ribs. My knees and ankles are sore from walking, but they're okay. And I'm still tired."

"Yeah. I have to figure out what to do about sleeping tonight."

CHAPTER SIXTEEN

Who is the guy in the gray hoodie?"

Gabriel's head snapped around, and he stared at Katt. "What?"

Katt walked slowly, carefully laying each foot down heel to toe in a straight line.

"The boy in the gray hoodie. He talked to me at the hospital and I've seen him around Heather's neighborhood. He's one of your guys, right?"

"I never sent anyone to talk to you at the hospital." Gabriel's eyes were quick, and worry lines creased his forehead. "I didn't know about you until after you went to Heather's."

"But he knew about medical kidnap. He came to talk to me about it and said that there would be people to help me."

"I don't know who you're talking about… that doesn't make any sense. What did he look like?"

Katt frowned and thought back. It seemed like a long time ago now and he had seemed almost like an apparition.

"He's… he's taller than you. White. Dark hair. Kind of sad and serious-looking."

"And explain to me what happened… was he a patient at the hospital?"

"No. He just came in one day. I was pretty sick. I had an infection. I would have thought that I had imagined it, only I've seen the same guy again. Just hanging out. He's never talked to me again."

"And he talked to you about medical kidnap?"

"Yeah. And the underground railway."

"Did he call it that?" Gabriel asked urgently. "He called it the underground railway?"

Katt tried to remember. It seemed like a long time ago, and she had been fighting a fever at the time.

"I… I'm pretty sure he did," she said.

"That… doesn't make sense. No one talked to me about you until later, when Heather went to Renata. Nobody in the network said that they had contacted you. How could he know about the underground railway?"

"Other people must know about what you are doing."

"Yeah, but… we're the only ones who call it that, internally. No one else would know that."

"Then he was someone from the railway… or a spy who heard it called that."

Gabriel swore. He cracked his knuckles, making Katt wince.

"You've seen him since then? In the neighborhood?" Gabriel repeated, sounding like he had just heard this information for the first time.

"Yes. A couple of times."

"A gray hoodie," Gabriel said slowly. "A boy a little older than me in a gray hoodie… I thought maybe he was a friend of Collin's."

"You saw him?"

"I saw him. Hanging around the house. Two times."

"I think I might have seen him on the bus, too, when we left."

"And he wasn't one of Collin's friends? You're sure?" Gabriel pressed urgently.

"No, they weren't ever together. And it was the same guy as I saw at the hospital. I'm sure of it." Talking about it was making her more sure. She couldn't have sworn to it ten minutes before, but she knew it now. It had been the same boy. The boy who had approached her at the hospital.

Gabriel bit his thumbnail, frowning furiously. His jaw was clenched, and he ground his teeth, the back of his jaw working back and forth.

"Renata would know," he muttered. "It's gotta be one of her contacts. She knows everyone," he said rapidly, "she knows a ton of people that I don't know. It must be one of hers."

"Can you ask her about it?"

Gabriel breathed heavily and seemed to be having difficulty catching his breath. Katt's blood pressure was rising just being around him. Her heart thumped hard in her chest and started her ribs pulsing as well. It wouldn't help anything if they both decided to have a panic attack, so she tried to keep her calm.

"Why don't you just call Renata?"

"I can't call her very often… and she had no phone privileges last time I called. Out here," he looked around, "I'm going to have to use a burner. No other phones available."

"You could use mine."

"No, can't let them ping you. It's not turned on, is it?"

Katt shook her head. She thought it was ridiculous to have to turn it off so that no one could trace her. No one was going to be spending any time trying to trace her calls. One runaway teen didn't rank that much bother.

Gabriel seemed to have made up his mind. He put down his backpack and poked around in it until he found a prepaid phone still encased in its plastic bubble. Katt watched Gabriel wrestle it open and slide the SIM card into place. He powered the phone on, and when the splash screen finished loading, he took a few deep breaths.

"It's okay," Katt assured him. She reached over and patted his arm. Gabriel grasped her hand and squeezed it lightly for a moment. Then he blew out his breath once more and dialed Renata's number from memory.

They both waited. Gabriel connected and asked for Renata. He looked surprised at not having to argue with anyone. He raised an eyebrow at Katt. "They said they'd get her." He waited, a frown on his face.

"Hey," his voice went down a few notches in a relieved sigh. "How are you doing?"

Katt couldn't hear Renata's answer, so she watched Gabriel's face intently, trying to gather everything she could from his expression.

"You're okay now?" he asked. He nodded at her answer. "So I'm working on that transfer. Yeah. Okay so far, but… there's been someone else involved… I don't know; that's why I'm calling. A guy. I didn't get a good look at him. Taller than me, bit broader… he's been hanging around the Foegels'; might have been there when she left. But he talked to her at the hospital too."

"Talked to her?" Renata's answering squawk was loud enough that Katt could hear it. Gabriel winced and nodded.

"He was in her hospital room and he talked to her about the underground railway."

Katt couldn't make out the words, but Renata's voice was loud, the words all running together in a rapid stream. Gabriel made soothing noises, trying to break in on her rant.

"Ren—Renata… yeah… Ren… Don't freak out on me; they're going to think you have to be sedated… Just calm down… Who do you think it is? It's somebody we know, or he wouldn't know about the underground railway. Even if it's someone from the police or Social Services, it's got to be someone we know. Somebody with a connection."

He listened to her response.

"I never got a look at his face; he wears a hoodie pulled down. It's gotta be someone you've talked to… No one else told you about our transfer? Only Heather?"

Gabriel listened for a bit, then nodded.

"Yeah. We'll be careful. Thanks… take care…"

After she had hung up, Gabriel stood there for a few minutes in silence, staring at the darkened screen. He sat down on the sidewalk, putting his hat down for change and dropping his head into his hands.

"I can't go on right now… I have to think…"

Katt stared at him. "What are you talking about? We can't just… stop here."

Katt realized that he was shaking, and she pressed her lips shut. If Gabriel said he couldn't go on, he couldn't go on. The adrenaline rush had probably burned through all of his energy reserves. He needed to rest and refuel.

"What do you need?" Katt asked. She bent over his backpack and opened it, feeling for his food supplies. "We gotta get some sugar into you. Am I right?" She nudged him when he didn't answer. "Gabriel!"

Gabriel moaned, but he nodded slightly.

"Okay. There's some granola bars in here, is that what you want? Is there enough sugar in them for you?"

He didn't answer. Katt ripped one of them open and pressed it on him, pulling one hand away from his face and placing the sticky granola bar into it. She kept digging and found an applesauce cup as well.

"Here. This too."

As Gabriel ate, she sat down next to him, folding her sweater to sit on. Gabriel rubbed at his temples. His hands seemed steadier.

"Are you okay?"

"Give me a few more minutes."

It was hard just to sit there and wait, but Katt didn't know what else to do. Gabriel had been the strong and experienced one, the person that she could depend on up until then. As much as she just wanted to let go and panic, she refused to let her emotions take over. She had to hold things together until Gabriel figured out what to do.

"When's the last time you saw him?" Gabriel asked.

"On the bus. After I met up with you."

"You haven't seen him again since then?"

"Not for sure… a couple of times… I'm just not certain."

"What did he seem like? When you were in hospital, and he talked to you? Did you trust him? Believe him?"

"I don't know. He seemed trustworthy… but I didn't understand what he was saying. I didn't really believe him."

"Did he give you any names? Did he say my name or Renata's?"

"No, I don't think so. He just said… there were people who could help me. He said someone would be in contact. That's it."

"How were you supposed to get ahold of him?"

"I asked, but he said there wasn't any way I could. He just said someone would be in touch."

"And no one ever got ahold of you after that? You didn't hear anything else?"

"Well, you did. I just thought…" Katt trailed off. "I assumed that you and he were part of the same organization. That he sent you, or you knew him…"

Gabriel looked around as if the other boy might be watching them or walking by at that moment. Katt's skin goosebumped. Were they being watched? Was he watching them while they talked about him?

"I don't know who he is," Gabriel said. "But we'd better keep an eye out for him."

———

It had been a long time since Gabriel had booked a motel room and actually slept in a bed. But he was worried about Katt. She needed to sleep, and with her broken ribs, sleeping on the ground again seemed like a bad idea. And there were also her toes. While the temperature wasn't likely to get below freezing, even just cool temperatures could slow the circulation to her digits, and who knew what damage that could cause to fragile Katt. He didn't want to contemplate her getting gangrene or losing her toes because he hadn't taken care of her properly.

Gabriel left Katt at a nearby fast food restaurant while he negotiated a price for the room and put his money down. He didn't want them to see Katt or to realize that Gabriel was not alone. He didn't need them calling the police because they thought Katt needed to be protected from him.

Motels were expensive. He didn't normally blow that much money at once. And he and Katt had been paying for restaurant food as well. Usually, Gabriel relied on his purchased snacks and on meals rescued from dumpsters or garbage cans. So far he hadn't had the courage to suggest that course of action to Katt. Rescuing boys was easier. They were less likely to be grossed out.

Returning to the restaurant, Gabriel gave Katt the room key and had her return to the motel on her own. He followed at a distance, watching for the mysterious boy in the gray hoodie. He waited outside in the parking lot, out of sight, watching for anyone suspicious. Particularly for anyone in a dark gray hoodie, looking for his quarry.

Night started to fall, and Gabriel was glad that Katt was settled in the motel room. She needed a good sleep and to know that she was safe for a night. It had been the right choice, even if it was a drain on their resources. The streetlights started to go on as it got darker. Gabriel stuck to the shadows, still watching the parking lot of the motel, watching people come and go. Everyone seemed to belong. Gabriel was the only one hanging around looking suspicious. He was about to give up his surveillance and join Katt in the motel room when a movement across the parking lot attracted his attention.

He hadn't seen the boy approach. Gabriel wondered if he had been there for as long as Gabriel had, watching the motel surreptitiously the whole time. He didn't seem aware of Gabriel's position opposite him.

The boy started to slink around the edge of the parking lot, sliding along in front of the windows with a quick glance past the curtain in each lit window. The hoodie was pulled up over his head, his face lost in shadows. Gabriel frowned, watching him. There was something familiar about the figure. Not just because Gabriel had seen him outside the Foegels' house. Something that went further back than that. Something that was more familiar, but just out of his grasp.

The figure was making its way toward Katt's room. In another minute, he would be there, and there would be some crack or gap in the curtains that would allow him to see into the room and identify her. Gabriel moved to intercept the boy. He didn't know what he was going to do. He wasn't armed. He wasn't a fighter. In a struggle, he wouldn't last thirty seconds. But hopefully, just confronting the stranger would be enough to scare him off. Then Gabriel would grab Katt and they would run. They would double back on their trail and find another place to sleep. It might mean sleeping outdoors again, but they obviously couldn't stay at the motel once they were discovered.

Gabriel darted into a hallway that divided the front of the motel from the back and waited for the hooded figure to make his way past the opening. His whole body was tensed for action. The instant he saw the hooded figure step past on the sidewalk, he reached out and yanked the hood back.

CHAPTER SEVENTEEN

Katt heard a scuffle and raised voices near the door of the motel. She stood close to the window, trying to peek out and see what was going on. Was it Gabriel, or some unrelated confrontation, maybe a drunk or a domestic dispute? She couldn't see anything. Katt's heart was racing. She tried to control her breathing, even though she knew it was silly to think that it would be detectable from outside. There was a thud, someone being pushed against the motel door, and Katt let out a little yelp before she could stop herself. There was a hard knock on the door.

"Katt, open up," Gabriel's voice commanded.

She tried to see out the peephole, but they were too close to it to be able to make anything out. Katt didn't know whether she should obey Gabriel and open it or not. What if someone were holding a gun to his head?

"Katt! Open the door!" Gabriel repeated.

She turned the bolt and opened the door. Gabriel practically fell in, and with him was the boy in the gray hoodie, though it had fallen from his head now and Katt could see his face clearly for once. Gabriel was holding the boy by the arm. He pushed him in, shoving him down on the bed and standing over him.

"What the hell is going on?" Gabriel demanded. His gaze flickered to Katt. "Shut the door," he told her in a hiss and then glared at the hooded boy again. "Explain!"

"Nice to see you too, Gabriel."

"You've been stalking us! What, are you working for the clinic now? Informing for the police? Huh? Who knows we're here?"

"Just me. No one else."

The stranger didn't seem worried or upset by Gabriel's reaction. He was perfectly calm. He didn't try to get up from the bed and didn't argue with Gabriel.

"Tell me what's going on!"

"Why don't you introduce me to Katt?"

Gabriel looked at Katt again.

"Katt… this is Ray Prosper."

The name meant nothing to Katt. It just confirmed what she had already figured out, that Gabriel and hoodie boy knew each other.

"Ray was one of us. But we thought he was dead."

They were all silent, looking at each other. Katt's head whirled in confusion. Ray was supposed to be dead? What did 'one of us' mean? A kid who had been medically kidnapped? A helper on the underground railway? Why had they thought he was dead?

"Can I get up?" Ray asked.

Gabriel didn't say anything. Ray sat up slowly. It wasn't like Gabriel was holding a gun on him. It wasn't like Gabriel could do anything to stop him if he tried. Though Gabriel was worked up, he was obviously smaller than Ray and not as well-built. Ray looked street-worn, but not sick.

Gabriel swore, looking at Ray.

"We thought you were *dead*," he repeated. "How come you never called? How could you never contact us again? You had to know what we were thinking."

"It's a long story."

"We've got all night."

Ray rubbed the back of his neck, considering. Katt looked around and sat down on a chair. Her legs were feeling weak and wobbly. She looked over at Gabriel. If she were tired and shaken, he should be even more so. He was the one who had been standing outside forever, the one who had wrestled Ray into the room. His chest was rising and falling quickly with his breathing. Katt didn't know a lot about mitochondrial disease, but she had comprehended enough about what Gabriel had explained to her to know that each of those breaths represented a depletion in his cellular energy. His excitement was causing him to use up his stored energy faster than his body would be able to replace it.

"Gabriel…"

Both boys turned to look at her.

"If it's safe, you should sit down. Before…"

Ray looked at Gabriel, nodding.

"Take a load off, bro. Slow down. Recharge."

Gabriel's response to Ray was almost a snarl, but he took their advice, sitting down on the other chair, taking a couple of long, calming breaths.

He looked at Ray, and didn't shout at him this time, but his expression said it all. He wanted the story.

"When I talked to you, I thought I was going home," Ray said slowly. He rubbed his face like he was just waking up, blinking owlishly. "I thought… Nick was right. We weren't getting anywhere. I wanted to sleep in a bed. To stop running around. Even if I couldn't go home to my family, at least I could stop having to hide and be paranoid all the time. It was wearing, all of the stress. Not having anywhere to go. Renata acting like there was a bogeyman around every corner…"

So Ray had known Gabriel and Renata both. Katt fit together what pieces she could. He had been on the run with them before Renata went to hospital.

"Renata was more right than any of us knew," Gabriel said.

Ray gave a nod.

"She had a meltdown when you said you were going home," Gabriel informed Ray. "She ended up back in hospital. That was your fault."

"That was just Renata's brain," Ray disagreed. "She was already headed back. She was off her meds, and she was losing more and more control every day. We could all see it. It was only a matter of time before she blew."

"But it was because of you that she did."

Ray shrugged. "I hung up with you—with Renata. I turned back to talk to Nick, and someone shoved past me. I couldn't see Nick. He'd been there talking to me just a minute before."

Ray's voice was thick with emotion. Gabriel stared at him, hanging on every word. It seemed as if all of the air had left the room. None of them breathed.

"I… I looked around. Tried to find him. There was this little hallway, back to a janitor's closet or something. Little square tiles on the floor. Nick was curled up there, on his side. I thought he was sick. Having some kind of episode."

Ray buried his face in his hands. His raggedly-cut hair spilled down over his forehead as he choked for breath. Katt wanted to do something to help him. The scowl was gone from Gabriel's face, his pain matching Ray's.

"I knelt down beside him, calling his name, trying to comfort him. I was worried about whether I should call an ambulance. What if they locked him up? Used chemical restraints? He was already in rough shape after being on the run. We all were. But… it was too late. He couldn't hear me. There was nothing I could do for him. He was gone. Still warm, but… the life just gone from his body." Ray could barely speak. His body shook with sobs.

"You had just been talking to him," Gabriel said. "What happened? What could have happened that fast?"

Ray wiped his eyes and swiped at his nose with the sleeve of his hoodie. Katt thought she should get up and get him tissues from the bathroom, but she was spellbound. She couldn't move.

"You'd know better than me," Ray said. "I didn't exactly have the inside track. All I knew was that they'd gotten to him. I had to disappear. Before they could get to me."

Gabriel swallowed. He was holding it together better than Ray, but it was obvious that he was shaken.

"They insisted it was natural causes. Just the course of his disease. When they went back for a second look, after Renata was attacked at the hospital, they did an autopsy. But they couldn't come up with anything. They found one needle mark. But no toxins. Nothing that could explain him just… dying. It could have been something natural that he was allergic to, like Renata, but they said there was no allergic response. It didn't look like anaphylaxis. Just like… he'd stopped breathing."

"If it was someone from the mito clinic, it could have been some experimental drug. Something that would kill one of us, but not one of them. Something they found in the course of their research."

Gabriel nodded his agreement. "Did you see anyone? Did you see who did it? You should have gone to the police."

"Yeah, because they were doing such a bang-up job protecting you and Renny," Ray sneered. "I knew my only chance was to disappear. Drop completely out of sight until the whole thing blew over and nobody was talking about it anymore. I knew I wasn't safe while I was visible. Going home wouldn't help. I couldn't just go back and follow the protocol and pretend that nothing had happened."

Ray looked over at Katt. He obviously sensed her confusion. She was trying to follow the narrative but was missing key portions of the story.

"We all have mitochondrial disease," he told her. "We were all on an experimental protocol at a research clinic. When we went public about medical kidnap, trying to blow the whole thing open so that people would see what was happening, they… tried to kill us. With Nick, they succeeded."

"They just about got Renata when she was in hospital, under police guard," Gabriel contributed. "A doctor from the clinic showed up and tried to put something in her feeding tube that she was allergic to. It would have killed her in seconds."

"Why would they do that?" Katt demanded, her voice a high squeak. What they were talking about was bizarre, unbelievable.

"They were making millions of dollars off of the research. It didn't matter if they ever found a cure or not. All they had to do was keep the program filled. And with us trying to put an end to medical kidnap, to take all of those experimental subjects away from them… they reacted. They had to shut us up."

"What exactly did you do that threatened their program?"

Ray and Gabriel looked at each other. It was Gabriel who answered.

"Uh… we… went on national TV to tell our story. Exposed them all. By name, if we could."

"And you didn't think anything would happen to you?"

Both boys shook their heads and shrugged. "We thought…" Ray struggled to answer. "We thought we could shut them down. It never occurred to any of us that they would resort to violence. We were out of state. Out of their reach, we thought. The only thing we were worried about was if we would get apprehended by Social Services. Not killed. No one thought they would kill."

"How could you let us think you were dead?" Gabriel demanded of Ray. "All of these months… you could at least have told us you were alive!"

"I didn't want to get back in the line of fire. They've already got Renata under wraps. With your work… you're going to get caught sooner or later. You're not as invisible as you think. The only reason they haven't caught you is because they're not really trying at this point. You've left the mito clinic alone and are just working on the railway… just saving one kid at a time and staying out of the limelight. Social Services isn't even trying to track you down. It's better for them if you stay quiet."

Gabriel's face flashed anger. "I'm making a difference! I'm still working on our vision!"

"Yeah, but as long as you're not cutting into their bottom line, they don't care. What do they care about one kid here and there? They've got a whole industry. It's like spending all of your money chasing down the old ladies tasting grapes at the grocery store. You just raise the price of grapes to cover your shrinkage."

"Then why are *you* still hiding?" Gabriel challenged.

"Well…" Ray had the grace to look sheepish. "Just because they're not putting that much effort into it doesn't mean they won't stumble across one of us if we're careless. I've got no desire to stay in residential care until I age out."

"How old *are* you?" Katt asked. "You look older than eighteen."

"I've got a few more months." Ray looked at Gabriel. "That means if they arrested me, they'd lay charges as an adult. With you, they could still go with charging you as a juvenile. But for me… they're not going to lay juvenile charges against someone a few months from turning eighteen."

"What are they going to charge you with? What have you been doing other than following us around?"

"Look, if you want me to get lost, I will." Ray's tone was tired and subdued. It wasn't a challenge or a threat. If they didn't want him around, he would just walk away.

Gabriel frowned and rubbed his forehead. "How did you even follow us? How did you know where I was? About Katt?"

"I've been hanging around the hospital. Thought I might be able to help out with the underground railway. Help funnel people in. I figured Katt needed help. That's all."

"So what were you going to do? You didn't contact anyone."

"I was still watching and investigating. You rush into things too fast. How much time did you take making sure that you weren't going to be sending her back to an abusive parent?"

"How much investigating did *you* do?"

"I was working on it. Then there you were, extracting her without knowing anything."

"I knew she had EDS. You wouldn't have known anything about that."

"I had my suspicions when I saw her in hospital."

"You know what Ehlers-Danlos is?" Katt broke in. "I haven't met anyone who knew anything about it firsthand."

"Sure," Ray nodded briefly. "I had a girlfriend with it."

"Really? What was she like?"

Gabriel gave a snort of disgust and turned away to open his backpack. Katt joined Ray on the bed, eager to hear about someone else who had actually been through the same thing as she had.

She was only vaguely aware of Gabriel as he had a snack and left Ray and Katt to speak. It wasn't until she got up to go to the bathroom that she realized he was curled up on the motel room floor, fast asleep.

"Oh! What time is it? I totally lost track..." Katt rubbed her eyes and looked around for a clock.

"Eleven," Ray said. "We'd better hit the sack too, and I gotta take my meds. You want to check to make sure he's okay?"

Katt bent over Gabriel, unsure of what to do. She didn't want to wake him up, but if he'd crashed after the altercation with Ray, he might need attention. She touched the side of his neck, looking for his pulse. Gabriel's skin was cool to the touch. Katt didn't manage to find his pulse, but he shifted and turned, pulling away from her, so she knew he was still okay.

"I have to go," she gestured to the bathroom. "Could you put a blanket over him? He's cold."

When she returned, Ray had taken Gabriel's own blankets from his backpack and put them over him. Ray motioned to the bed. "Are you okay to share? I'll stay on my own side, and I'll try not to hog the blankets."

"Uh..." Katt shrugged, not wanting to make a big deal of it. If a boy had asked her a few days ago if he could crawl into bed with her, she would have made a big fuss. But what was she going to do, make him sleep on the floor too, while she took the whole bed like a princess? "Yeah, sure."

"You don't know how good it's gonna be to sleep on a mattress for once," Ray exulted, stripping off the hoodie, and then a t-shirt. Katt watched him kick off his shoes and strip off his socks. He looked at her, becoming aware of her gaze. Katt tore her eyes away from him, trying to act casual. She didn't have any pajamas, and she wasn't about to take off her shirt. But she did take off her shoe and socks and retreated to the bathroom to remove her bra. Ray had turned off all the lights but the lamp beside the bed and was under the covers, facing away from her. Katt crept into the other side of the bed and tried to lie very still.

———

Katt woke up several times in the night. There were footsteps and doors opening and closing as neighbors came and went. Gabriel and Ray were each up to the bathroom at least once. But she was so tired after not sleeping the previous night, that Katt just kept her eyes closed and went back to sleep. Even in the morning, as the room got warmer and the sun filled the room, she just pulled a blanket over her head and went back to sleep. She wasn't the one in charge. She was going to get as much sleep as she possibly could.

"Rise and shine, you guys. Time to get on your feet. We gotta check out or pay for another night."

Katt yawned, reluctant to open her eyes.

"And if they figure out we slept three in here, they'll charge us extra. So let's go," Gabriel ordered.

"Have some compassion," Ray said. "She's worn out."

It wasn't until then that Katt realized the warm lump she was sleeping against was not her blankets, but Ray. She cracked open her eyes and looked at him, his face two inches from hers. Katt startled and pulled back from him. Ray laughed.

"Morning, sunshine."

Katt cleared her throat. "Good morning!" She laughed at herself. "Did I squash you all night?"

"It was very nice. It's been a long time since I had any company."

Katt knew her face was getting red. She got up quickly and retreated to the bathroom, which she hogged for the next half hour. She finally got up the courage to face the boys again and walked out as if it were perfectly natural for her to wake up in a motel room with two boys who were almost strangers. Ray looked at his watch.

"I know we've only got about ten minutes, but do you mind if I take a quick shower? I haven't had a hot shower in months."

Gabriel nodded. "Yeah. Just be quick."

Ray was in and out of the shower in less than the allotted ten minutes. He and Gabriel started talking as soon as Ray stepped out of the bathroom, as if they had been making plans all night and were just formalizing them now.

"If anyone other than Heather suspects that I was helping Katt out, they'll be looking for the two of us together," Gabriel said. "No one will be expecting you, because, among other things, no one knows you're even alive. So you need to be the one to take her out of town."

"She needs to dye her hair," Ray inserted, nodding. "Maybe cut it short or tuck it up under a hat. If they're looking for long blond hair with a black boy, and they see a bobbed brunette who happens to be on the same bus as a random white boy, they're not going to have a clue."

"As long as they don't recognize her face from missing persons posters."

"We have to take that chance. You got a hat?" Ray asked Katt. "Or a hoodie? Guess you could borrow my hoodie."

"It would swim on her," Gabriel disagreed. "Just attract more attention to her."

"Wouldn't matter if they couldn't recognize her face."

"She'd end up getting it caught on something. Tripping over it."

Ray laughed, but Katt nodded her head. "He's probably right. I'm really klutzy. I'd get it caught in the bus door, and it would drag me down the street. I could pick up a hat, though. And hair dye. I have enough money. Does that mean we could get out of town today? And not have to wait another day?"

Gabriel and Ray looked at each other, considering.

"Yeah," Gabriel said. "I think it could work. I'm a bit worried about the cast, though. They know they're looking for someone in a cast."

Ray shrugged. "Stay in a crowd. She moves pretty good, doesn't lag behind. It's the best we can do. As long as Social Services doesn't know you're involved, they're going to be watching for Katt to go back to her mom, not to be heading out of town. Runaways always head for home."

Katt looked back and forth between Ray and Gabriel. "So? Everyone is agreed, then? We can leave today?"

Both boys nodded.

"We have to disguise you first," Gabriel said. "But I think we can do it."

Gabriel and Ray had switched positions. The previous day, Gabriel and Katt had traveled together, and Ray had trailed them, though they weren't aware of it at the time. Now it was Ray and Katt together, and Gabriel followed at a distance, keeping an eye out for anyone who might be paying too much attention to the couple. Cops, social workers, anyone who might have a reason to report them for some imagined infraction. Ray wasn't as likely to be reported as Gabriel was. Gabriel let them get out of sight for a minute or two at a time, not following them in a straight line, weaving in and out for a quick check and then falling back again.

Ray seemed to find it a lot easier to talk to girls than Gabriel did. It came more naturally for him, whereas Gabriel was always trying to figure out what to talk about next. Ray walked closer to Katt than Gabriel would have, and occasionally put his hand around behind her back and rested it on her shoulder as they walked. Gabriel was always trying to project that he was not romantically involved with Katt, not wanting to draw the attention of people who objected to mixed-race relationships, but Ray seemed to melt into a pseudo-boyfriend role, acting like he and Katt had known each other forever and were completely comfortable with each other. Gabriel walked up to them as they stopped to rest on a bench. He sat on the bench that was back-to-back with theirs, not saying anything to acknowledge them, but listening to their conversation.

Ray was talking again with Katt about EDS. To begin with, Gabriel had thought that Ray's claim to have had a girlfriend with EDS was just crap. Just Ray pretending that he knew something before Gabriel did, acting like he knew more than anyone else. But his conversations about his 'ex' and her Ehlers-Danlos seemed to be just as natural as the rest of his conversation with Katt.

"There's pros and cons of being in a relationship where you both have a disability," Ray commented. "On one hand, it's great, because they understand that you have to compensate, that you have limitations sometimes. And if you both have to stop to take breaks, you can just hold hands and have a nice time, without worrying about the other person getting impatient."

Katt nodded, listening raptly. Gabriel didn't get the impression that she'd ever had a boyfriend. Maybe not even a best friend. She and her mom were so close; Gabriel figured it was probably the only real relationship she had.

"But it can suck too. When you're too tired to do something, and the other person can't do anything for you. When you get sick at different times and can't see each other for a month. When you're both on crutches and neither one can carry the other's books." He laughed.

Gabriel could see where he was coming from. Katt patted Ray's leg. He had his arm around her shoulders again.

"I bet you carried her books anyway," she said.

"Well, I did my best."

"Would you want to get involved with another girl with—a disability—again? Or would you avoid it? Stick with someone… normal?"

Ray took his time in answering. If it had been Gabriel, he would have rushed in to answer, filling the silence with whatever prattle came to his mind. But Ray held back, and Katt waited, not prompting him again.

"I don't know," Ray said. "What's normal? Everyone has their own strengths and weaknesses. I don't think I'd rush into another relationship with someone with physical issues… but I wouldn't avoid it either. Just take my time and see what happened."

Katt nodded, looking satisfied with the answer. Neither of them looked at Gabriel, still pretending that he wasn't there. Which was what they were supposed to be doing; but Gabriel still felt rejected, somehow.

They were silent for a while. Ray moved, rolling his shoulders. He pulled out his water bottle, and Gabriel saw him palm a couple of pills before taking a drink to chase them down. Katt didn't appear to have noticed.

"Well, kid, time to be getting on our way again," Ray said, ruffling Katt's new dark auburn hair. "Can't spend too much time sitting around. How are you feeling?"

"I'm good."

"Ribs?"

"Sore, but not too bad."

"Shoulders?"

"Fine." Ray had helped Katt to find a backpack with wheels on it, which she could pull behind her when the sidewalk was smooth and level.

"Feet?"

Katt gave a grimace. "They're still pretty sore today."

"Do I need to look at them? Any new blisters?"

"No. They're okay. Just hurting from yesterday."

Ray nodded. "Anything else?" he prompted. Gabriel admired his persistence. If he'd been that patient and persistent with Katt, maybe she would have told him about the problems with her shoulders and her feet before she hurt herself.

Katt shook her head. "When are we going to get lunch?"

Ray glanced over his shoulder at Gabriel, but quickly forced his eyes back away and answered without consulting with him. "Not for a couple more hours. If you need something, you'd better get a snack from your bag."

Katt turned to unzip her bag and find something. "What about you? Don't you need something to keep your energy up?"

"I did not long ago. I'm okay. Did you take your meds this morning?"

"Yes, mom."

Ray smiled at her. "Good. We've got to make sure you take care of yourself. It's easy to let yourself get run down when you're on the lam."

"Is that supposed to make you sound tough?" she teased. "Because I'm not buying it."

"That's what I get for showing you my sensitive side."

CHAPTER EIGHTEEN

Everything had gone smoothly. Which either meant that they were on a roll and everything would go fine, or that they were due for everything to fall apart. Gabriel wasn't sure which. Thinking like Renata about anything that could go wrong, he was pretty sure that everything was going to fall apart.

He hung back at the bus depot, watching Katt and Ray buy tickets separately and board the bus to sit alone as if they didn't know each other. Everything smooth as silk. But Gabriel couldn't get the feeling of dread out of his stomach. The bus depot was one of the pinch points in the transfer. In order for them to get out of town, they needed to have an egress point. Sometimes they could find someone who would drive them from one town to the next, or preferably over state lines, before putting them on another bus. But mostly their volunteers operated in their own city and didn't expose themselves. Driving a transfer over a state line could escalate charges from abetting a runaway to kidnapping, and people didn't want to risk that.

Gabriel bought a ticket for another bus and went to sit down. None of them were going to be leaving immediately, so he figured he might as well close his eyes.

The bus trip went off without a hitch. Katt boarded first and found a seat, so she was already sitting down when Ray got onto the same bus and sat down without looking at her. Even though she knew that he wasn't supposed to acknowledge her presence, she was surprised that his eyes didn't even flick to her once. He was good at what he did. Gabriel was too, of course. Katt wouldn't see him again until they reached their destination. He was on a later bus, so she wouldn't see him again until after disembarking.

Even though Katt had slept pretty well at the motel, she was still exhausted, so she made the most of her time on the bus and closed her eyes to go to sleep. She wouldn't be getting off for a few hours.

She dozed for most of the trip, sleeping for a while, then waking and watching out the window, then falling asleep again. She watched the desert flow by outside the windows and remembered that vacation to the Grand Canyon. It was a mile marker in her life. One of those things that she looked back on in life. Other events were often measured by it. That was before the Grand Canyon vacation, or that was after. The bus ride would be another. That was before she ran away. That was after. Even her name would change. She wasn't Katt Lindholm any longer. Katt Lindholm had ceased to exist.

When the bus pulled into the final depot and everybody who remained got up to disembark, Katt felt a sense of let-down. After such a momentous change in her life, there should be something more to mark the change. Not just stepping off a bus into a new world.

"Katt Lindholm?"

Katt turned her head as she stepped off the bus, even though she knew that wasn't her name anymore. A security guard stood there, along with a woman in a suit. Neither was smiling. Katt swallowed and turned her head back away like she hadn't heard them and was just going on like the rest of the passengers. But the guard grabbed her by the arm and pulled her out of the line of the exiting passengers. Katt resisted, but he was strong and determined.

"No, you don't, you're coming with us."

"Are you sure it's her?" asked the woman, following as the guard pulled Katt farther away from the other passengers. Away from Ray. He didn't reveal himself. There was nothing he could do. He couldn't grab her and run away with her. Jump on a motorbike like the spy in some espionage movie.

Katt tried to resist the guard's pull, but there was no point. He was too strong and determined, and she didn't want another dislocation.

"Are you sure? It doesn't really look like her," the woman persisted, looking down at her phone.

"It's her," the guard growled. "Isn't it, Katt?"

"I…" Katt's mouth was full of cotton. "I don't know what you're talking about. You've made a mistake."

He made a growling noise in his throat and continued to pull her along. Into a hallway that led away from the public area that the rest of the passengers were going down, into a series of dimly-lit hallways and rooms where only authorized personnel were allowed. Staff rooms. Administrative offices. It was an interesting peek behind the scenes. Katt was aware that she was trying to distract herself from the reality of the situation.

She had been caught. They were going to call the police or to put her on a return bus to meet the police back on the other end. Gabriel was not going to be happy. After all their careful planning, how had it happened? Had she done something to give herself away? Was it the cast? The bus driver must have recognized her for her to be met on the other end.

Katt tried to think of a swear word that was bad enough to use in the circumstances. It was so bad she didn't know whether there was one.

She had been caught.

She was going back.

But likely not to the Foegels. Instead, she'd be sent to a residential facility that she couldn't run away from. An institutional setting where she would have a dorm room and no privacy. Everything would be regimented. A prison.

"In here." The guard pushed on Katt's arm and opened a door, revealing a bare room, just a table and two chairs. Green walls, hard tiled floor.

"You're making a mistake," Katt protested, as he pushed her in ahead of himself.

The woman followed and watched as the guard checked Katt's pockets and sat her in one of the chairs. Katt looked at the bracket attached to the top of the table and wondered idly what it was for. In answer to her unspoken question, the guard put a handcuff over one of Katt's wrists, ran the chain through the bracket on the table, and put the other handcuff around Katt's other wrist. She pulled against the bracket.

"No. No, there's been some kind of mistake. I haven't done anything wrong."

The guard was an older man, graying around the temples, not much taller than Katt. He gave a short bark of laughter and shook his head. "Runaways. You always think you are going to get away with it. You think we don't read the bulletins? Changing your hair color is going to confuse us?"

"Just leave her in here," the woman in the suit said. "I don't know how long they'll take to pick her up. Might be a while."

The guard grunted. He double-checked the handcuffs. Then they left her alone, pulling the door shut behind them.

Katt sat there, devastated. She had let herself believe that Gabriel and Ray could whisk her away and get her back to her mother. They had done it for other kids, why wouldn't they be able to do it for her? It didn't matter that she had to take on a new identity and move away from her childhood home. All that mattered was that she would be able to be with Karina again, living her normal life instead of being trapped in a foster home with people who didn't understand her and who had no history with her.

Hot tears ran down Katt's face. She sniffled and tried to wipe them away with her shoulder. How could she have gotten caught? She'd done everything right. She listened to everything the boys told her. She was stuck, chained up like a criminal. At least Gabriel and Ray hadn't been caught. Katt knew things would be worse for them than for her. Running around wouldn't likely get her put in jail. Locked up in a residential treatment program, maybe, but not in jail.

Katt pulled on the handcuffs, wanting to wipe her face. She wiggled her fingers. One of the talents she had was the ability to fit her hands through very narrow openings. The guard hadn't counted on her hypermobile joints when he had handcuffed her. Katt squeezed her fingers together and inched them through the bracelet of the handcuffs. She wiped away the tears on her cheeks and rubbed her eyes. She squeezed her other hand through the other handcuff.

She massaged the joints on each hand in turn. Then she looked at the closed door. Had the guard locked it? Why would he bother, with Katt securely chained to the table? Katt slowly rose from her chair and crept to the door, ears alert for any sounds from the hallway. She peeked out the narrow window with wires running through it. There didn't appear to be anyone in the hall. The handle turned easily in her hand. Katt pushed the door open and stepped out into the hallway. She closed the door again and headed the way she had come from. She couldn't remember all of the turns, but she could hear arrival and departure announcements over the public address system, and walked toward the sound. She passed a couple of bus depot workers on the way out, but apparently no one thought anything of an unescorted teen walking through the staff corridors. No one challenged her.

She finally got back to the main hall and let out a sigh of relief. She looked around, wary of running back into the guard or anyone else who might recognize her. Gabriel and Ray were still there, standing on the other side of the room talking to each other, their expressions worried. Ray had both his backpack and Katt's bag. Katt walked over to them and picked up her bag. Gabriel and Ray looked at her with their mouths hanging open.

"What the—?" Ray was the first to get any sounds out.

Katt raised her eyebrows, looking at him innocently.

"They let you go?" Gabriel demanded. "How did you get out?"

She smiled. "Apparently hyperflexible joints make it hard to keep you in handcuffs."

Ray shook his head, admiration shining in his eyes. It was Gabriel who nudged them to move. "We'd better not hang around here. They're going to figure out that you're missing before too long. And they won't leave you alone the next time."

"Let's scram," Ray agreed.

They each collected their bags and made a beeline for the door. They were tense for a few minutes as they hiked away from the bus depot, then Gabriel let out a long sigh.

"That was too close," he said. "I thought you were a lost cause. I haven't ever had anyone taken off a bus before!"

"Well, there's a first time for everything," Katt said. She was feeling excited and light after the escape. She too had been sure she was a goner.

"You just pulled out of the cuffs?" Ray asked, dumbfounded.

"Well, I had to sort of squish my hand up," Katt demonstrated.

Ray's eyes got big. "That's sick!"

Katt laughed. "We did it! We got away! Everything worked out."

"Everything didn't work out," Gabriel corrected. "We failed. You got caught. We just lucked out when you were able to escape from the handcuffs."

"And now we can meet up with my mom, right? She's here?"

"She won't be here yet. We didn't want her to leave town until you were safely out of the way so that they would still be watching your house instead of focused on escape routes. Now that you're out, she can leave in a day or two. We'll send her a message letting her know. But you're still going to have to stay under cover for a few days and make sure you don't get picked up again."

Katt shook her head. Two more nights sleeping on the ground or in motels? Two more days of keeping on the move, changing her appearance frequently, and not looking suspicious? She didn't feel nearly as adventurous as she had when she'd started out. She had thought that it would be fun and exciting. But it was uncomfortable and nerve-wracking. She just wanted it to end and to be with her mother again.

"And when we meet up, we'll be able to settle down and live like normal people again, right? No more running?"

"As long as her new identifications hold out. We have to make sure everything is high quality and will pass so that she can get a job and health care coverage and all."

"It will be so nice to get a place of our own and sleep in my own bed every night." Katt shook her head. "I never realized what a luxury it was just to sleep in your own bed. I mean, I always missed it when I was at the hospital, and it felt so good to go home and be back where I belonged. But even sleeping at Heather's... it's not the same. It wasn't mine. Wasn't comfortable like my own place."

Gabriel's face was pinched. He didn't look at her, staring on ahead like he was scouting out their next step.

"Oh... I'm sorry," Katt apologized. "I wasn't even thinking. You and your mom... you guys don't have a home to go to. That was a really thoughtless thing to say."

Gabriel nodded in acknowledgment.

"Let's split up," he said. "They're going to be searching the area looking for the two of you. You should come with me. Change your shirt. Ray—"

"They didn't identify me," Ray cut in. "Just her. So either one of us can go with her."

Gabriel stopped short and looked at him. "Yeah... you're right. Katt, who do you want to go with?"

"Why do we have to split up? If they're just looking for me alone, then the more people I'm with, the safer I am. Right? They don't know I'm with anyone."

Ray and Gabriel looked at each other. Katt got the feeling that Ray would have liked her to himself, but she felt bad about Gabriel. It had been his plan, and Ray had sort of hijacked it showing up like he had. She didn't want Gabriel to have to be alone.

"I suppose," Ray agreed.

Gabriel nodded.

"We should go somewhere kids hang out," Katt suggested. "So we blend in."

"School?" Gabriel suggested.

Katt wrinkled her nose. "Who wants to go to a school? I don't want to go there even if I'm not going to classes. What about the mall? A movie?" She smiled. "Do you know how long it's been since I went to a movie?"

"Probably not as long as us," Ray countered.

"I don't know…" Gabriel hedged.

"Why not? Who's going to be looking for me in a dark movie theater? Or shopping at the mall?"

"It's not likely, but still…"

"Let's do it, then! We can find a theater, right?"

———

Katt's plan took their minds off of the search that the bus depot guard would inevitably initiate when they discovered that she had walked off, focused instead on finding a theater and getting there. Gabriel was used to looking for places where he could sleep or panhandle without standing out from the city's homeless. People didn't look at the homeless; they were invisible. That's what Gabriel had done with Renata, and it seemed like the most sensible approach when they didn't have anywhere else to go. Finding areas where homeless congregated was second nature to him now. Finding a movie theater without a map was a different set of skills.

They eventually did find one. After wandering around the mall for a bit, window shopping and blending in with the other teens, they went to the theater and looked at the billboard and movie posters.

"What do you like?" Ray asked.

"Superheroes," Katt said immediately, pointing to the latest Marvel release. "That work for you guys? You don't want to watch a chick flick, do you?"

"Superheroes works for me! Gabe?"

"Sure," Gabriel agreed. "Looks good."

"Refreshments?" Ray asked after they purchased their tickets.

Gabriel didn't like the rate they were running through their money. First a motel room and then movie tickets.

"Refreshments are so expensive," he said. "We gotta watch the money…"

"I'll cover them," Ray said.

"Where did you get that kind of money?"

"Odd jobs. You sure don't get it begging."

"No," Gabriel agreed.

"So? What do you guys want?" Ray prompted, looking at the various combos on the price board.

Gabriel let Katt and Ray work it out without his input. Eventually, they were sitting in the dimly-lit theater waiting for the movie to start. Gabriel helped himself to some popcorn.

"So what's with you and superheroes?" Ray asked, obviously having noticed Katt's comic books at some point. "Most girls don't go for them."

"I don't know why not," Katt said. "Buff guys in tights. Who wouldn't go for that?"

Ray snorted. Gabriel smiled. At least she was honest. In Gabriel's experience girls said that they were looking for sensitive guys, but wouldn't look twice at a skinny, sensitive guy like Gabriel. Their heads were turned by the jocks.

The lights went down, and the music started. Gabriel tried to put everything else aside and just immerse himself in the movie.

About an hour into the movie, he could no longer ignore the growing pain in his stomach. He put his hand over it, trying to calm the rumbling and writhing. But it wasn't working. He got up and slid past Katt and Ray, murmuring an apology.

"You okay?" Ray asked.

Gabriel didn't respond, too intent on getting past him and to the restroom before it was too late. He made a dash once he got out of the theater and barely made it to the toilet in time.

He should have known better than to eat greasy, junky food. He tried to eat healthily to keep his energy up and his body functioning the best that it could. Even though he lived a nomadic life, he didn't eat a lot of fast food. He'd choose sub sandwiches over burgers, and he tried to get fresh fruits and vegetables whenever he could.

He shouldn't have had the junk food; it was too hard on his system.

"Gabe? Hey, man, are you okay?"

Gabriel rested his head against the side of the stall. "You shouldn't have left Katt alone."

"She's watching a movie. Nothing is going to happen. What's up? You didn't come back, and we got worried."

"Sick," Gabriel said. "Stupid. Shouldn't have had the junk food."

"You allergic to something?"

"Yeah, but I don't know what would have been in it. Just the oil, I think. Too rich for me."

Gabriel held his breath and suppressed his gag reflex, trying to resist throwing up again. Not while Ray was there.

"Can I get you something? Do anything for you?"

"No, just go watch the movie. Tell me what happens."

"I'll stay with you."

"No. Leave me alone. I'll be okay; I didn't eat that much."

Ray still lingered. "Watch your sugars and electrolytes," he warned. "You don't want to end up in hospital."

"Yeah… can't really do anything about that when I'm puking."

"I can check back in a few minutes, make sure you're okay."

"Just go, Ray. I'll come back, or I'll see you when it's over."

"Okay…" Ray finally departed, leaving Gabriel alone with his rebellious body.

———

Gabriel didn't come back in for the end of the movie. Katt waited in the lobby, people pushing and shoving their way past, while Ray went back into the restroom to see how Gabriel was doing. Katt's stomach wasn't feeling great either, but with the amount of junk she had crammed into it, that was no great surprise. She'd be okay once she had a chance to digest it.

She stood with her arms folded across it, waiting.

The lobby had emptied out, and the next movie showing started before

Ray and Gabriel came out. Gabriel was walking under his own power, which was a relief. Katt had been worried that they'd have to call an ambulance for him. His complexion was too dark for him to be pale, but he did not look well. Katt stepped forward to meet them.

"Hey. You okay? I'm so sorry; I never wanted you to get sick. Just thought we'd have a little fun. Pretend we were normal teenagers for once."

"Not your fault," Gabriel said, and attempted a smile. "Don't worry about it. Sometimes our bodies don't work right. At least you didn't fall on the stairs and break something else, right? A bit of an upset stomach, that's nothing."

"It's not nothing," Ray clucked over Gabriel like a mother hen. "Not when you could go hypo on me or lapse into a coma if your sodium is too low. Or faint from dehydration. We need to get something into you."

"Not when I just got everything out. I can't eat anything yet. I'll just throw it up again."

"Can you drink? Just a few sips? Some juice or a sports drink?"

"Just leave it alone for a while," Gabriel protested.

Katt thought it was cute, Ray fussing over Gabriel like that.

"It's getting late," she pointed out. "We should be finding somewhere to sleep for the night."

Gabriel took a long breath. Ray reached toward him to steady him, then withdrew his hand and tried to look nonchalant.

"No hotels tonight," Gabriel said. "They already know you're in town. There will be alerts out. Maybe TV spots. We can't afford to be seen checking into a motel."

Katt sighed and nodded. She had already known he would say that.

"Okay. So where do we go?"

CHAPTER NINETEEN

Katt was awake, but her head was muzzy, and she didn't know at first why she was awake or where she was. She knew that it was a big day, but she couldn't remember why. She lay still for a while, blinking and rubbing her eyes. Then she remembered. Karina. She was supposed to be meeting up with her mother. That was why it was such a special day. Katt rolled over to look at the boys.

"Are you awake?" she whispered.

Gabriel moved. He propped himself up on his elbow to look at her.

"You're awake early."

"I can't help it. I get to see my mom today!"

"If everything works out," he cautioned. "Sometimes it takes a day or two to connect properly. Something goes wrong… we have to be cautious."

"I know. But it could be today!"

"What could be today?" Ray grumbled, sounding barely awake. "What's going on?"

"Katt's just excited," Gabriel said. "You can sleep a bit longer."

Ray cleared his throat and rolled over, shutting them out. He pulled his sleeping bag up over his head. Katt envied his fancy sleeping bag. High tech fabric that was really warm but rolled into a tiny bundle. He said he worked odd jobs, and she wondered what exactly he did. She supposed he didn't have to pay for a house or a car, so he had the money he needed for a sleeping bag.

"Warm me up?" she whispered to Gabriel.

He shuffled closer to her and put his arm around her to hold her close. Katt wedged her cold feet under his legs. They lay still for a long time, not asleep, but not talking or getting up either. Just letting the time pass until they had to get up.

Finally, Gabriel sighed. "Time to get moving," he suggested. He sat up and reached over Katt to shake Ray by the shoulder. "Up and at 'em, Ray. Early bird gets the worm."

"No worms for me," Ray grunted.

"Come on. We're getting up. We'll go catch some breakfast before the morning commuters."

"Told you I don't want any worms."

But by the time Gabriel and Katt had finished folding up their groundsheet and blankets, Ray was out of his sleeping bag and yawning loudly as he got his things packed up.

"I need coffee," he said. "A great big, dark roast coffee with tons of sugar."

"Not good for you," Gabriel said. "You should take better care of yourself. Caffeine and refined sugar aren't good for your mito."

"Maybe not. But that's what I'm having."

Gabriel shrugged. "We'll find a coffee shop. We'll have to wait a few hours before we can start pulling things together."

———

Gabriel looked down at the phone to read the text.

"Everything seems to be clear," he said cautiously.

"Let's go, then," Katt said, trying to keep her voice from going up several notches, and failing.

Ray gave her a grin. "Not that you're excited or anything."

"Of course I'm excited! I haven't seen her since I went into the hospital for a broken foot. All they had to do was put a cast on it and send me home, and instead I've had this whole thing to deal with! Medical kidnap? I'd never even heard of it before. I thought that all kids who were in foster care were abused or orphans, not that you could get put there just for being sick."

Gabriel's eyes were on the park downhill from them. Moving from the cars to the mothers with strollers and the joggers. There were children playing in the playground. It was an idyllic scene. Since it was a Saturday, no one would be surprised to see three teens at the park when they should be in school. Katt looked at him, waiting for his signal. He shook his head, seeming reluctant to move.

"Just a few more minutes," he said.

"Come on," Ray complained. "You've done a dozen of these and it's always worked out. You can see everything is clear. No police cars. Nobody hanging around that shouldn't be. It's just Katt meeting up with her mom. It will be fine."

Gabriel sighed. "Okay. Fine. Let's move. Ray, you stay up here, keep a lookout."

Ray shrugged. Gabriel motioned to Katt.

"Okay, let's go."

She followed him eagerly. Katt couldn't see her mother yet, but knew she was down there. Karina had changed cars, so Katt wasn't sure what she had pulled up in. A helper had texted Gabriel to let him know that she was there. No direct contact between them.

Gabriel's eyes swiveled back and forth as he made his way down the hill. He was making Katt nervous with his paranoia. Everything seemed to be going smoothly.

Katt looked for her mother. Where was Karina? She tripped and stumbled, and Gabriel put a hand on her arm to steady her.

"Don't fall down the hill," he advised.

"Thanks."

"I don't see her, do you?"

"No. Not yet. But we know she's here."

Gabriel looked down at his phone again. Then looked around. "Let's head over there, toward the parking lot. Easy exit if we have to get out of there."

"In what car?"

He grimaced and didn't answer.

"Is that her?" Gabriel pointed at a woman in a sun hat, facing away from them. Katt couldn't see her face, but she had Karina's height and build. And squinting, Katt could see an elbow brace on her arm.

"Yeah, I think that's her."

They headed for her. Katt picked up her pace, leaving Gabriel slightly behind her. She wanted so much just to be with her mom. To hold her in her arms again.

"Mom!"

The figure did not turn around. She appeared to be intent on watching a little girl on a tricycle the other direction.

"Mommy! Karina!"

"Katt," Gabriel called to her warningly.

Katt didn't turn around. She was about three steps from the woman in the sun hat when she realized that it wasn't Karina. The woman turned around. She was a stranger. But instead of looking at Katt questioningly, wondering why the girl was coming up to her, her eyes were sharp and knowing.

Katt whirled around to warn Gabriel. But it was too late. There was a man standing with Gabriel, one hand on his arm, stopping him from going anywhere.

"Katt Lindholm," the woman said. "Nice of you to come."

"Who are you? What's going on here?"

"My name is Valerie Beal. And what's going on here is that you're going back home. You've had a nice little adventure, but it's over."

"I don't want to go back to foster care," Katt said in frustration. "I want to be with my mom!"

Beal grabbed Katt's arm with a firm grasp. Katt didn't jerk away. She didn't need to dislocate her arm fighting back.

"You're coming with me. Just behave yourself if you don't want to get hurt."

Katt let the woman pull her toward the parking lot, looking back over her shoulder at Gabriel. His face was impassive. The man holding onto him was speaking. As Katt watched, he put handcuffs over Gabriel's wrists and pulled his arms behind his back. Arresting him? What for?

They were both escorted to cars in the parking lot. Katt was put in the front seat of what she assumed was a social worker's car. Gabriel was put into the back seat of a dark sedan with bars on the inside of the back windows.

"What's going on?" Katt asked. "What are you doing with Gabriel?"

"Gabriel is under arrest for kidnapping. Now you stay put," Beal told Katt in a sharp tone. "If you try to jump out of this car while it's moving, how many bones do you think you're going to break?"

Katt hadn't even considered jumping out of the car. But the social worker was right. Katt would break every bone in her body if she tried something like that.

Beal tore off her sun hat and threw it into the back seat before sitting down behind the steering wheel.

"What's going to happen to me?" Katt asked as they pulled out of the parking lot.

"You're going back to Social Services in your own state. What they do with you is up to them, not me."

"Why can't I go back to my mom? She didn't do anything to hurt me!"

"Honey, you're talking to the wrong person. I don't have anything to do with it. It's my job to take you into custody and turn you over to your own Social Services. That's the extent of my involvement. I don't know anything about your and your mother."

Katt slumped back in her seat and closed her eyes, unable to believe what was happening. After all the planning, all the running, all the discomfort, she was right back where she had started. And probably worse off. They wouldn't be likely to put her back into a foster home where she could just run again. She would be put into residential care, something secure.

Even thinking about her own circumstances, she couldn't help worrying about Gabriel as well. Kidnapping? Could they really convict him of kidnapping? She had gone with him willingly. He had been helping her out. Katt couldn't bear the thought of Gabriel going to prison for helping her.

Katt covered her face, trying to keep her composure.

———

Gabriel wished that he could slip out of handcuffs like Katt had. After sitting in the car for an hour with his hands cuffed behind his back, he was stiff and sore. As the hours drew on, it became excruciating.

"Can you take the handcuffs off?" he asked Boden, not for the first time. "My arms are killing me."

"Policy," Boden said indifferently. "Anyone we transport has to be handcuffed."

"Then could you handcuff them in front? Please?"

"Nope."

Gabriel shifted around, trying to find a position that would ease the pressure, but he couldn't find any way to sit that would be more comfortable. If they were traveling all the way back home, Gabriel knew he was going to be stuck there for several more hours.

"Please, can't you do something? This is killing me!"

"You'll survive."

Gabriel felt sympathy for Katt. He could only imagine she had felt the same way when the backpack had been pulling her arms and back out of joint. She had dealt with it, and he would have to do the same.

He wasn't belted in, so Gabriel tried lying down across the seat.

"Get up," Boden snapped.

Gabriel ignored him, trying to get comfortable across the molded seat. Boden touched the brakes a couple of times in an attempt to persuade Gabriel to sit back up, but when Gabriel refused, he didn't stop the car. He made a noise of exasperation and kept driving. It was going to be a long ride, and Gabriel guessed that he didn't want to stop every five minutes to force his passenger to sit up.

Katt had expected that the social worker was going to drive her all the way home, or if not, would put her onto a bus to be met at the other end, but neither assumption was right. Katt's stomach roiled when the car pulled up in front of a youth detention facility.

"What's going on?"

Beal didn't answer. She got out of the car, and when Katt didn't get out on her own, went around to the passenger side and opened it. She grabbed Katt by the arm and pulled. Katt got out as gracefully as she could, eager to avoid having her arm pulled from its socket by the social worker.

"What are we doing here?" Katt asked. "I don't understand."

"You're a runaway. This is where you're being held until you can be dealt with."

"I didn't do anything wrong. I just wanted to see my mom!"

"I already told you, I've got nothing to do with it. I'm just doing what

I've been ordered on this end. What happens after that is out of my hands. Give your excuses to someone in your own jurisdiction. My only job is to send you back."

"Then what am I doing here?" Katt gestured to the building as they walked up the sidewalk.

Beal just scowled and didn't answer again. As they drew up to the entrance, Beal grabbed Katt's arm again, holding onto her firmly.

"I'm coming. You don't have to grab me," Katt protested.

"I'll grab you if I like, Miss Lindholm."

Katt felt her face flush as she bit back an angry retort. She steeled herself not to pull away and injure herself. They walked in the door, and there was nobody at the reception desk. Beal and Katt waited for a few minutes before a woman with a uniform and a plastic ID tag returned to the desk. Katt could just make out LANE in block letters. Lane raised her eyebrows, looking them over.

"I wasn't expecting any new admittances."

"This is Katt Lindholm. Out of state runaway. She's being kept here while we wait for transfer."

"They're picking her up?"

"Yup."

That meant that Katt was going to be staying there for a number of hours. Maybe even overnight, if her transportation didn't want to drive both directions in one day.

Lane studied Katt.

"Why isn't she in handcuffs?"

"This one's double-jointed. She slips them off."

The receptionist looked pleased with this. "An escape artist! Well, then, I guess she's not going to the dorms. I've got a transfer cell right here," she nodded to a closed door. "That will be perfect for her."

Beal nodded. "Good. She needs to be kept secure." She indicated Katt's bag, which she had brought in with her from the car. "I assume she's got a change of clothes in there. And I understand she's on medications." Beal turned her eyes to Katt. "You got all your meds in there?"

Katt nodded. "Yes."

"Okay," Lane nodded. "I'll get her out of the way and then you and I can get all of the admittance papers filled out."

Beal let go of Katt's arm when Lane came around the desk. Katt rubbed her arm and pushed her sleeve back to look at the red fingermarks Beal had left behind. Lane's eyes fixed on the bruises, and instead of grabbing Katt, she motioned for her to walk ahead of her to the heavy door. Katt watched her punch the four-digit passcode into the keypad, and then Lane opened the door and motioned her through.

There were three small cells side-by-side on the other side of the door. Barely big enough for a cot and a metal, lidless toilet. The cells were separated from each other and from the front by metal bars, just like a jail on TV. They looked old and worn like they'd been in use for a hundred years. Katt wondered how old the facility was and what the dorms Lane had referred to looked like. Not like these cells, she expected.

Lane opened the door on the far left cell and Katt stepped in. Lane left Katt's backpack against the far wall, out of reach.

"You're lucky. You're alone in here today," Lane commented. "You can catch up on your sleep. Dinner isn't for a few hours, and asking about it won't bring it any faster. You want to yell and make a bunch of noise; you go right ahead. No one in the general population is going to hear you, and I'm not going to be inclined to do you any favors."

"Can I make a phone call?" Katt couldn't think of anyone to call. It was really just a test question, to see what her rights were and how likely Lane would be to respond to requests.

"Phone call? No, you can't make a phone call. You're not under arrest; you're in protective custody." Lane locked the cell door with a manual key. "Who would you call, your fairy godmother? Wishing isn't going to get you out of here. You want to make a phone call; you're going to have to wait until you're settled on the other end."

Katt sat down on the cot. It was worn and lumpy, but at least looked like it was supplied with clean sheets.

"Any more questions?" Lane demanded.

Katt shook her head. "No."

"Good. I'll be back to check on you in a while."

She went back through the heavy security door after punching her code into the keypad. The door closed with a whoosh, like an airlock. For a moment, Katt held her breath, like there might not be enough oxygen left to breathe. But that was silly, of course. The room had a supply of fresh air. She didn't need to worry about suffocating in the tiny, close cell. She was perfectly safe there.

<hr>

CHAPTER TWENTY

<hr>

Gabriel wasn't sure how he had fallen asleep during the most uncomfortable car ride of his life. But when he woke up, it was dark and the car had stopped. He waited for it to start again if it had merely stopped at a stop light. Or for Boden's clipped query whether he needed a pit stop, which had been repeated several times along the way. But the engine stopped, and Boden didn't ask him whether he needed to get out. The back door opened, and Boden grasped Gabriel's arm to pull him upright.

"Wakey, wakey. Time to get up, sunshine."

Gabriel struggled to get his feet back on the floorboards and right himself. He blinked, looking around.

"Where are we?"

"Time to put you up for the night. Court tomorrow."

Gabriel's arms were asleep. His body ached. Boden had offered a couple of times to buy Gabriel a burger or pop, but Gabriel had refused, not wanting to end up sick. His stomach hurt with hunger, and if he didn't have something soon, his blood sugar was going to be a problem. He was surprised that it hadn't been yet, but he had been asleep, so maybe his body was in hibernation mode, conserving glucose.

Boden levered Gabriel out of the back seat and gave him a moment to get his land legs before leading him into the holding facility. There were lights all the way around the building, and as they walked out of the parking lot toward the building, it was almost as bright as noonday. Gabriel blinked, waiting for his eyes to adjust.

There were several checkpoints along the way where Boden was required to show his identification and whatever papers he had on Gabriel and to explain yet again what he was there for.

Eventually, they found their way to a holding cell for Gabriel. He looked it over and didn't care about the size or the claustrophobic closeness of the walls. All he cared about was that there was a bed to sleep on, no one else to harass him, and that they would release his arms from the handcuffs. The guard who took charge of him from Boden watched as the cuffs were removed and Gabriel stiffly moved his arms around and rubbed his burning shoulders with numb fingers.

"Has he been searched?"

"No. Did a pat-down, that's all."

"Put your hands on the wall," the guard told Gabriel.

He obeyed, but couldn't hold his weight on his arms when the guard tried to move his feet back.

"Ow—I can't—I'm going to fall."

"You're fine, just hold still."

Gabriel's arms collapsed, and he went down, banging his head on the wall on the way to the floor. The guard put his foot in the middle of Gabriel's back, pinning him down as if he thought it was some kind of ploy to get away. Gabriel painfully brought his hands behind his head.

"I've been in handcuffs all day," he explained, trying to keep the whine out of his voice. "My arms are useless."

"Hold still."

Gabriel complied. The guard frisked him thoroughly and turned his pockets inside-out while he lay on the floor.

"You can't leave a prisoner in handcuffs all day," he told Boden.

"My rules say he's got to be in handcuffs while being transported. It hasn't been *all* day."

The guard grabbed Gabriel's jacket and shirt in the middle of his back and hoisted him back to his feet that way. Gabriel rubbed his forehead where it had bashed the wall and the guard pushed his hand away to take a look at it.

"No stitches," he grunted. "I'll get you an ice pack. Sit down in there."

Gabriel entered the narrow cell and sat down as he was told.

"I need something to eat," he said, holding his head in his hands, elbows resting on his knees.

"Dinner's done. You'll have to wait until breakfast now."

"I have a medical condition," Gabriel said. "I can't fast for that long. I'll go into hypoglycemic shock."

"You didn't feed him either?" the guard challenged Boden.

"I offered more than once. He said no."

"No junk food," Gabriel corrected. "I have to be really careful what I eat. Or I'll be sick and end up in hospital."

"What are you, vegetarian?" The way he sneered, Gabriel had very little doubt what the guard thought of the vegetarian lifestyle.

"No. Just… no dairy, and not a bunch of oil or processed junk. I have a mitochondrial disorder."

He didn't expect the guard to know what that meant, just that it would sound official and intimidating enough that he would take Gabriel seriously. The guard's eyes snapped to Gabriel's face.

"I have a niece with mitochondrial disease!"

Gabriel was pleasantly surprised. "So you know I'm not just making it up. You wouldn't want someone to ignore your niece's mitochondrial disease and not give her what she needed, would you?"

"No, I wouldn't," the guard agreed. "Anyone who mistreats her had better be ready to answer to Uncle Arch." His eyes went over Gabriel, and Gabriel wondered what tell-tale signs he was looking for. You couldn't usually tell a mito kid just by looking at them. But most were thin like Gabriel, cells starving for energy. "What do you need?"

"There's food in my bag. I always carry safe snacks."

The guard moved toward Gabriel's backpack. "You don't need something hot?"

"No. Just something to keep my blood sugar up."

Boden shifted boredly, letting out a loud sigh. Arch flashed him a look. "This is your prisoner. I would think you'd want to see he was being treated properly. You don't want to be hit with human rights violations, do you?"

"Looks fine to me. If you'll sign my papers, I'll leave him to you. Then you can chat or have a nice little tea party. I don't care."

Arch gestured for Boden's clipboard, and went through it, signing everything off. "Transfer complete. Go back the way you came, and they'll see you out."

Boden left. Arch rolled his eyes at Gabriel and bent over his backpack again. "Gotta be careful of these dangerous criminals."

———

For the first little while, Katt just sat, waiting. She tried lying down to nap, but her body was too hyped up and wired to sleep. She had been so close to getting back together with her mom. Would she ever get another chance? Or was she doomed to be locked up until she turned eighteen, just to prevent her from having any possible contact with her mother?

Katt got up and paced the cell. There wasn't really enough room to pace. There was barely enough room to take two steps, turn around, and take two more. Katt walked up to the bars and stared out between them. Freedom was just two doors away. Through the security door, past the reception desk, and out the front doors. If Lane were away from the reception desk, Katt could just walk out. Except for the small matter of the bars.

Lane had mockingly called her an escape artist. It had been surprisingly easy to slip out of the handcuffs at the bus depot. But the iron bars were another matter. She couldn't exactly squeeze her body through those.

Katt had watched contortionists on TV with Karina. She remembered debate about whether Harry Houdini were double-jointed, and that was how he had been able to get out of some of the impossible spaces that he'd been able to escape from. Katt had watched a video on the computer about a contortionist who could pass his entire body through a tennis racket. With no strings, of course. It had been sickening to see him popping his shoulders out of joint and bending his ribcage to an impossible size to thread himself through it.

A consumer report on infant cribs said that the bars had to be close enough that you could not pass a pop can between the bars to pass safety standards. Otherwise, a baby's body could conceivably fit through, but not his head, and he would strangle. Katt touched her head to the bars. They were just far enough apart that she could pass her head through. It would be tight over her ears, but they were flexible. Was it possible that the bars had been built to some older safety standard, too wide to be considered secure for juveniles? Were they wide enough to let a slim body through?

Katt experimentally put her leg through up to the pelvis. Her arm up to the shoulder. Both seemed to allow enough wiggle room to push through. But what if she got stuck halfway through? What if there weren't enough room for her ribcage? She'd certainly look like a fool if Lane came back in to check on her and found her hung up on the bars. They'd have to call the fire department to saw the bars apart and get her out.

Katt went back to the cot and lay down, closing her eyes and thinking about it. She had been so close to reaching her mother. The security door opened and Lane looked in on her.

"You need anything?" she asked.

Katt didn't answer, pretending to be asleep. The woman withdrew, letting the door swing shut behind her. Katt cracked her eyes open and watched until Lane disappeared from the window slit in the door. Then she got up again. She didn't have a watch on, but it seemed to her that Lane was checking on her about every half hour.

If Katt had a superpower, it was flexibility. That and her size might work in her favor. She approached the bars again and tried to determine the best way to get herself through the bars. Shoulder first, leading with the side her hurt ribs were on to ensure they wouldn't get stuck when she was halfway through. Anything that didn't fit through she could just dislocate. She'd have to push through the pain until she was through and could pop any joints back in again.

She could do it. Just like the guy with the tennis racket.

Katt took a few deep breaths and smoothed her ears back in preparation. Then she started working her way through. Arm and leg, shoulder. Her ribs protested as she squeezed them through. Katt blew out all her breath and held her abs tight, pushing steadily. The first half of her rib cage slid through. Katt worked her head through without bruising her ears too badly, and her sternum made a popping noise. Concentrating next on her pelvis, Katt wiggled and worked her lower body through. The other half of her rib cage did catch, and Katt was glad she'd put her injured side through first, as it took a good deal of breathing, scrunching, and squeezing to get the second half through.

Then she was free and standing on the other side of the bars. Katt popped her sternum back in and straightened various other joints to make sure that they were properly connected. The worst part was done. The second part of her escape was just a walk from one door to the other, and straight out of the building.

She looked through the window and found that she had a good view of the reception desk. Lane worked on various jobs, moving back and forth from the computer to surveillance monitors to stacks of paperwork. She had been away from the desk when Katt had arrived with the social worker, and Katt was counting on the fact that she would leave it again. It would be no good if she just continued to work at the desk until it was time to check on Katt, and found her standing outside the cell. Katt had no way to fight Lane or run from her. If she didn't leave the desk, Katt was sunk.

Time passed slowly, and Katt's internal clock was ticking loudly, reminding her that Lane was due to check on her again soon, and then all chance at escape would be gone.

Then Lane stepped around her desk and disappeared from sight. Katt pushed down the handle of the door and shoved the door, but it didn't open. Katt swore softly to herself. She had forgotten about the security code. She'd watched Lane enter it several times, but hadn't been paying close enough attention. Katt closed her eyes and tried to picture Lane's fingers moving over the keys. The beeps had all been the same tone. There had been lights beside the keys so that she could see which ones had been pushed. Katt tried one four-digit combination, but the final light flashed red and gave a 'negative' tone to let her know she'd messed it up.

"Come on. I saw it…"

Katt was watching for Lane to come back, her heart pounding. She tried another quartet. Negative. Another. The last light turned green and the door clicked. Katt shoved it open. She didn't even look in the direction Lane had gone. She didn't have time. If she were going to get caught, she was going to get caught. It wasn't going to be because she had looked back. Katt grabbed her backpack at the last instant and hurried through the security door to the exit door of the building. In five seconds, she was in the cool air, free once more.

———

Gabriel ate his snacks, rubbed his shoulders and arms a bit more, and went to sleep on the cot. No amount of pacing or worrying was going to get him out of there, so he figured he might as well get what sleep he could.

It was a good thing that he had slept both on the car ride and when he got there, because wake-up call for the bus to the courthouse came at about four in the morning. Gabriel dragged himself out of bed and followed the instructions he was given, which included showering for his court appearance and working his way through a breakfast that was both cold and greasy and didn't include the use of a fork. Gabriel wiped his fingers on his pants in disgust and requested food from his backpack. But Arch was no longer on duty, and the guard who was supervising Gabriel had no sympathy for inmates who claimed to be sick or on special diets.

He was handcuffed again to be taken to the courthouse, but instead of having his hands chained behind his back, he and the other prisoners were given a 'four piece suit,' with ankle chains and wrist chains both anchored to a waist chain. It was awkward, and the noise of the chains made Gabriel grit his teeth, but his shoulders were sore, and he hadn't been looking forward to having his hands chained behind his back again.

Even though they had to get up early for transportation to court, it appeared that their court appearances were sprinkled throughout the day. Gabriel sat on a hard bench, waiting, as the first couple of prisoners were taken from the holding room. He hoped that his hearing wasn't scheduled for the end of the day.

Then his name was called. Gabriel raised his hand to identify himself, and the guard unlocked him from the anchor and escorted him to a small courtroom. The courthouse was vaguely familiar, and Gabriel frowned, looking around. He didn't remember well, but it was the same building he had been taken to by Heather Foegel to attend a hearing of his own case and maybe to get a chance to speak to the judge, which hadn't happened. His mom had been there. But she wouldn't be there this time. She wouldn't even know he was there.

Gabriel was taken to the defense table. A young lawyer joined him after a few minutes, introducing himself hurriedly as David Jessup. He looked over a file he'd obviously just been given on Gabriel. One computer-printed page was in the file folder. Not much for him to work on. He would have no idea what the case was about unless he and Gabriel could talk somewhere.

The prosecutor arrived, hopefully just as uninformed as the defense, and then Social Services. There were social workers and police officers, all talking with each other, their voices blending together.

"All rise for Judge Deidre Whittaker," the bailiff announced.

Gabriel was already on his feet. He stared at her as she walked into the room. An older woman, gray-haired, her face wrinkled but not severe-looking. She was short, with a slight build. A strange mixture of soft, grandmotherly packaging combined with steel.

"Thank you. Be seated," she said, without looking at the audience.

Gabriel lowered himself to his seat. The bailiff read off the style of cause, and the judge looked up, as shocked to hear Gabriel Tate's name as he was to hear hers. They had talked before but never met face-to-face. She had introduced herself to him as Judge Dee-Dee. Renata was familiar with Judge Dee-Dee and gave good reports on her. Judge Dee-Dee had been the one to put Renata's mother in prison, though she had expressed her regrets to Gabriel at having been forced by the evidence to do so.

"Gabriel Tate," Judge Dee-Dee repeated. She looked at Gabriel. Their eyes met for a long moment. Her eyes dropped back to the paperwork. "What are the charges?"

The prosecutor reeled off a list of charges, with kidnapping heading the list. Judge Dee-Dee paged through the reports that had been given to her, making brief notes.

"Kidnapping requires that the perpetrator was acting against the will of the victim," she said crisply. "What evidence is there that Mr. Tate was acting against the will of Miss… Lindholm?"

"He took a minor across state lines," the prosecutor said. "Moving the victim across state lines without the consent of the guardian constitutes—"

"Not in my courtroom it doesn't," Judge Dee-Dee replied evenly. "In my courtroom, we refer to the Penal Code, which requires the movement of the victim to be against the victim's will."

"But in the case of a minor, the guardian's consent has to be considered, and that—"

"How old was the victim?"

The prosecutor stopped and looked down at his paperwork, not familiar enough with the details of the case to answer immediately.

"Uh… Miss Lindholm is fifteen."

"Which puts her under the statute for kidnapping, not child kidnapping."

The prosecutor looked over his shoulder at the social workers and cops for help, but none of them were able to bail him out.

"Uh… yes, your honor, that would be the case."

"So do you have evidence that Miss Lindholm was restrained or otherwise moved without her consent?"

A few long seconds passed while the lawyer looked at his papers, and looked back at the pool of social workers once more. He shook his head.

"No, your Honor, not at this time."

"When you get that evidence, then you can charge with kidnapping. For now, the charge of kidnapping is dropped."

The man nodded, swallowing.

Gabriel sighed in relief. Kidnapping was a felony charge, and would have meant mandatory prison time. He could have kissed Judge Dee-Dee.

She didn't even look in his direction.

"The next most serious charge is providing shelter to a runaway."

"Yes, your honor," the prosecutor said more confidently, puffing his chest out.

"Would you mind defining 'providing shelter' for me?" Judge Dee-Dee's eyes were still on the papers in front of her, and she didn't look at the lawyer as she asked the question. He fumbled for a response, turning red as he cobbled together a cogent definition for her.

"Uh—I believe the code calls for any person who knowingly harbors a minor without the permission of the minor's guardian…"

"And how does the Code define shelter?"

There was complete silence in the courtroom. Gabriel's lawyer grabbed a well-thumbed copy of the Code out of his briefcase and flipped to the relevant section.

"The person's home or any structure over which the person has any control," he read aloud.

Judge Dee-Dee looked up from her papers at Gabriel's lawyer and studied him.

"Thank you." She turned her head back to the prosecutor. "Mr. Tate harbored Miss Lindholm in his home?"

The lawyer looked uncomfortably at the cadre of social workers, and one of them moved forward to speak to him in a whisper.

"It would appear, your Honor, that Mr. Tate does not have a home of his own…"

"Did he rent an apartment?"

"Mr. Tate is a minor, and therefore can't rent an apartment…"

"Did he harbor her in a backyard shed? A friend's home?"

"He accompanied her from the time that she ran away and helped her to avoid detection by her guardians—"

"But that doesn't meet the definition of providing shelter to a runaway, does it?" Judge Dee-Dee challenged.

The lawyer cleared his throat. "I suppose it would be a stretch."

"That brings us down to contributing to the delinquency of a minor."

"Yes, your Honor." The lawyer brightened at this.

"Do you have examples of the laws that Mr. Tate encouraged Miss Lindholm to break?"

"That's still under investigation at this time. The two of them were only apprehended yesterday."

"I see. Your recommendations for custody arrangements while the situation is investigated?"

"Obviously, we would recommend remanding him to juvenile detention. These charges are very serious and—"

"These charges have been reduced to contributing to delinquency, with no evidence as to what that might involve."

"Yes… but we are talking about a minor child. A girl, in the company of an older male juvenile offender with a record of—"

"What is Mr. Tate's record? His *convictions*."

"He doesn't have any convictions, but he has a history of involvement in kidnappings and providing shelter—"

"But no convictions."

"No."

"Are the police laying any other charges than the ones that have been discussed?"

One of the cops stood up. "We are investigating the other cases and what charges can be laid at this time—"

Judge Dee-Dee's gavel came down, cutting off any further explanation. "Mr. Tate is to be released to the custody of Social Services. He is not," Judge Dee-Dee looked hard at the social worker who had been talking to the prosecuting lawyer. "*Not* to be confined to juvenile detention, but to a suitable foster or group home placement."

Gabriel sagged back in his chair, letting out a sigh of relief. Judge Dee-Dee stood up, pausing before retreating to her chambers. "And I want him examined by a doctor before placement. This is a child with a medical condition who has been homeless for months, and I want him treated as such. I want a report back on his condition and how he got that goose-egg by the end of the day."

There was a buzz of activity from the courtroom as Judge Dee-Dee disappeared. In a few minutes, a guard was unlocking Gabriel's shackles to free his hands and feet. The social worker who had been railing against Gabriel was by his side, looking stunned by the developments.

"Gabriel, if you'll come with me, we need to figure out where we're going to place you…"

He could tell that she was frustrated. The go-to placement for an older juvenile when they didn't know where to put them was juvenile detention for a day or two. Put a scare into them and keep them out of the way until Social Services could figure out a long-term solution. Gabriel got up and let her lead him out of the busy courtroom. Someone handed her Gabriel's backpack, and she shook her head, but shouldered it herself.

"How did you get the goose-egg?"

———

Gabriel sat at the kitchen table at the Young Men's Residential Group Care, which despite its long name was a small, repurposed bungalow with twenty-four-hour supervisors, where he shared a room with two other boys. He wasn't feeling too bad, having fit in a long nap after his visit to the doctor's office, where they declared him to be in good health despite his extended period of homelessness.

He had thought about calling Judge Dee-Dee to thank her for how she had handled his case in her courtroom, but decided that might be considered cheeky or in bad taste. He should just let her continue to act independently, without any implication that she was acting on behalf of the underground railway, which she wasn't.

But he did want to talk to Renata. He was worried about Katt and where Social Services was going to put her. The railway had failed once to get her to her mother. Social Services wouldn't want to give her another chance. But they couldn't keep her locked up for the next two to three years until she aged out, could they?

Ray would call Renata to try to find out what had happened to Gabriel, and Gabriel hoped that he would also give her some details of what had happened to Katt. Or maybe Heather or someone else in the grapevine would have heard.

Gabriel waited until he was alone, though he knew there were still supervisors around to eavesdrop and keep an eye on him. He dialed the hospital and asked for Renata's unit.

"Renata Vega, please."

"She's certainly in demand today," the nurse griped. "What are you doing, planning a birthday party?"

Gabriel's mind flashed back to the previous year. Renata's birthday had passed while they were both in psych together, with no more to mark it than a card from her mother, which she threw away without opening.

"When *is* her birthday?" he asked.

"Renata's?" Gabriel could hear the tapping of computer keys that told him she was looking it up. "Next week, actually. Friday. But I'm afraid there won't be any parties!"

"No," Gabriel agreed. But maybe he could send her a card that she *would* open, or call her on the phone and wish her a happy birthday. If he hadn't gone back underground, maybe he could even try to visit her. "Can I talk to her?"

"I'll have to track her down. She's up and about."

Gabriel waited on hold until the nurse managed to track Renata down and give her the phone.

"Gabe?" Renata answered the phone with his name.

"How did you know it was me?" Gabriel laughed.

"Because I've already talked to everybody else. You were the only one left to call in."

"You talked to everybody?" Gabriel asked. "Does that mean Ray?"

"You might have called me when you found out he was alive."

"Yeah, sorry about that. Things were moving pretty fast. I didn't really have the time."

"So has all the excitement died down now?"

"For now. I'm not sure how long I'm going to stay in place... I feel so exposed."

"Well, the clinic hasn't made any more attempts on my life, and it's all out of the news now, so maybe they don't care anymore. Maybe you're safe."

"Huh. Not sure. And they're still working on charges against me for

Katt and the others. However many they figure I was involved with. So did Ray know… what they did with Katt? Where they moved her to?"

"Chances are they're not going to put a runaway right back in a regular foster home," Renata pointed out.

"No, I know. That's why I'm wondering. Is it someplace… we're going to be able to get her out of? To try again?"

Renata chuckled lowly. Gabriel shifted his grip on the phone. Where had they put Katt? Was she completely out of their reach?

"She escaped custody before they managed to transfer her," Renata said.

"What?" Gabriel couldn't stop the grin from spreading across his face at the news. "Did she slip her handcuffs again?"

"No… she squeezed between the bars of her holding cell and opened a keypad-protected door."

Gabriel laughed aloud. "What I wouldn't do to see that! She squeezed between the bars?"

"She could teach old Renata a few tricks," Renata said. "Here I thought *I* was the master at escaping from secure facilities."

"Well, unless you can learn to bend your bones like her, I don't think she's going to be able to teach you. So she just walked away? Again?"

"I gather from other sources," Renata said, "that there was a surveillance camera on the cells. So she's damn lucky she wasn't spotted sliding out through the bars or waiting for her chance to get out of the room."

"They have video of her squeezing through the bars?"

"They do," Renata concurred. "The only thing they don't have… is her."

"Oh, man." Gabriel wiped at the tears squeezing out the corners of his eyes. "That's priceless. So where is she? Do you know? She didn't exactly have your number to call in and report."

"Ray was there waiting for her. They're together."

Gabriel sighed. "Good. Do we know what happened to her mom? Did she get arrested? I got word that she was in place and everything was clear."

"She didn't make it. When Katt didn't run straight home, the police started intercepting Karina's texts. She never even knew Katt had run."

"So I was texting with the police?"

"Apparently. Hope you didn't say anything incriminating."

Gabriel tried to remember everything he had sent to Katt's mother. He tried to keep all communications pretty cryptic, but he couldn't remember all of what he had said.

"I guess if I had, I'd be in juvie right now instead of being free. I'll have to try to get word to her through other routes. Are Ray and Katt standing by? They're ready if we set up another transfer point?"

"Ray will contact me. We'll work something out."

"Great," Gabriel let out a sigh. "I'm glad we get another try."

___

EPILOGUE

___

Ray took a look around the cafe, but nobody jumped out at him as being suspicious. Katt didn't make any sign that she recognized anyone. He hadn't been expecting to see anyone inside. The hostess came up to them with a wide, white smile.

"Table for two?"

"We're meeting a friend out on the patio," Ray told her.

"Oh, right this way."

Ray tried not to stare at the girl's long, tanned legs as she walked away. He knew that Katt was watching him. And he had a job to do.

The message from Gabriel had been that their next contact would be wearing a hat. Ray wasn't sure what kind of hat he was supposed to be looking for. A baseball cap? A fedora? They didn't want someone who was going to stand out or be memorable if witnesses were questioned by the police.

His heart pounded a couple of extra beats when he saw the woman in a sun hat like the one the social worker had been wearing at the park. But Katt gave a squeal and darted between tables straight for her. It didn't take much to figure out that the woman was not just their next contact on the railway, she was Katt's mother.

"Sick, Gabriel," Ray muttered. "That was a dirty trick!"

He got to the table, where Katt and Karina were hugging, then holding hands, and both talking at once, a mile a minute. People were watching the reunion with a smile, and Ray tried to motion to the two of them to tone it down a little so that they didn't attract so much attention.

He sat down in one chair and Katt sat in another, still holding tightly to one of her mother's hands. Ray noted the elbow brace on Karina's arm. Just like the social worker decoy had been wearing.

"This is Ray," Katt gestured to Ray as he sat down. "He's one of the boys who has been helping me. Him and Gabriel. And others, but mostly it's been Ray and Gabriel."

"Gabriel says hi," Karina said with a warm smile. "To both of you. He filled me in on as many of the details as he could, but you'll need to tell me all about everything!" Karina touched Katt's face, shaking her head in disbelief. "I can't believe that we're finally together and that you're safe. We can start over again."

"You've got everything you need?" Ray asked. He didn't go over the checklist of documents that Karina would have to have arranged to establish their new identities. And he wouldn't be able to ask them where they were going once they left there. He wouldn't likely ever see either one of them again.

"Yes, everything is arranged," Karina agreed. "We're all set."

"You'll need to be extra careful about doctors," Ray warned. "Now that she has a diagnosis, you'll be able to give them a heads-up and explanation of any injuries before they get any ideas in their heads… but there's no guarantee that they're going to believe you. You could end up right back in the same situation again."

Karina nodded seriously. "I know," she agreed. "You don't know how many times I've had to fight with doctors and social workers before. I've always been able to deal with them. But this time… they just did an end run and I never got the chance."

"You'll need to educate them too," Ray said to Katt. "If we're going to stop medical kidnap, we have to spread the word about diseases like this. So that kids get a diagnosis before Social Services swoops in and takes them, instead of after."

"Yeah," she agreed, holding Karina's hand. "I wouldn't wish something like this on anyone."

Ray scraped back his chair to leave the two of them alone.

"You're leaving?" Karina asked. "Stay and have a lemonade, at least."

Ray shook his head. "You guys have a lot of catching up to do. I gotta go wish someone a happy birthday."

Did you enjoy this book? Reviews and recommendations are vital to making a book successful.

Please leave a review at your favorite book store or review site and share it with your friends.

Don't miss the following bonus material:
Sign up for mailing list to get a free ebook
Read a sneak preview chapter
Other books by P.D. Workman
Learn more about the author

Sign up for my mailing list at pdworkman.com and get Gluten-Free Murder for free!

PREVIEW OF PROXY

Leva aimed her phone at Seth as he stood proudly in front of the roller coaster. There were smiles all around, children who were excited at being in the theme park, the dream of every kid in America.

But none were like Seth's. None of the other kids had worked as hard as Seth had to get there. He had fought through his illness, through countless hospital stays, never wavering from his wish to visit Disneyland. His face was pale, his spiky dark-blond hair damp with sweat, and his lanky teenage body too thin, but he had made it there. He'd made it to his goal. And, as he had insisted, not in a wheelchair but under his own power, though she noticed that he was leaning against the signpost for support.

He was her brave boy. Strong in heart, if weak in body.

"I can't believe we're here," Seth said, for about the hundredth time that day. But this time it wasn't just 'here' in Disneyland, it was 'here' in front of the roller coaster he had always wanted to ride. Successfully raising the money to get to the park had been exciting. Entering the grounds had been thrilling. But standing in front of *his* roller coaster was the pinnacle of joy for Seth. "We're finally here!"

"Yes," Leva agreed. "Give me a big smile."

He smiled and gave a thumbs-up. Leva took a couple of shots and then lowered her phone.

"Well, are you ready to actually go on it?" she asked. Roller coasters weren't her thing, and Seth had never been on one. She was still waiting to see if he would go through with it.

Seth looked up and watched the roller coaster go through its loop-the-loop, passengers screaming wildly and waving their arms. He swallowed.

"I have to go on it," he asserted.

"You don't have to. It's up to you. We don't have to go on every ride, you know."

"I know… but I have to go on the roller coaster."

"Only if you want to."

He nodded. His face was sweating and Leva wondered whether it were because he was scared, because of the heat, or because he was sick.

"Are you feeling all right, baby?"

"I'm not a baby," Seth growled.

That, at least, was a normal response for when he was well. When he was sick, he didn't argue about not being her baby. He wanted to be held and nurtured just like any helpless child.

"I'm fourteen," Seth reminded her. "You can't call me a baby." His eyes shot around at passersby to make sure that no one had heard her.

"Sorry," Leva apologized. "You're right. I should be more careful when we're out in public."

He nodded. "Let's get in line."

Leva led him over to the disabled entrance. Seth opened his mouth to argue. He didn't want to look different. He didn't want people looking at him and wondering what was wrong with him that he had access to the disabled line. But when he looked over at the regular line-up and how far back it stretched, his lips pressed together, and he didn't protest. Walking around the park and standing in line was exhausting. If he wanted to be able to continue to live the dream, he had to stick to the short lines.

Leva flashed her pass at the ride attendants to confirm that they were qualified to be in the disabled line. A pretty blond girl who didn't seem like she could be much older than Seth leaned over and opened the gate for them, giving Seth a brilliant smile.

"Come right this way," she offered. "We'll put you on the next car that comes in."

They watched another train rush through the curves of the roller coaster, screams washing over them. They could see the LCD screens displaying everyone's photos as they went through the last curve. Open mouths, flying hair, shrieks of delight.

Seth leaned against the wall; one hand pressed to his stomach. The young woman who had let them in grabbed a wheelchair from a nearby corral.

"Here, sit down. Are you okay?"

Seth tried to wave off the wheelchair, then collapsed into it with a sigh. "Just tired."

"Okay. You sit there until I have a space for you. Give me or Derek a shout if we can get you anything else. Okay?" Her voice was bright and encouraging. No pity here. It was the happiest place on earth. Everyone got the same smiles. Everyone was on equal footing, healthy kids and terminal alike.

Leva moved closer to Seth to rub his shoulders and analyze just how tired he was. She had hoped to be able to put in a little more time; but they had five days to see the park, they didn't have to do everything in one day.

"Don't," Seth protested, slapping her hands away in irritation. His eyes went to the cute blond employee. Not too tired to care what she thought of him.

The next train pulled up and people disembarked in a babble of excited chatter off the opposite side. The girl opened up a cart for Seth and pushed his wheelchair up close to it. When she put the brakes on, Seth was able to get up under his own power and transfer to the seat. Leva climbed in beside him, though she was sure he would rather have had the girl there. Or any girl other than his mother. The employees moved up and down the cars, making sure that everyone was properly buckled and barred in. They were instructed to secure all phones and cameras. Leva pushed hers farther down into her pocket. She'd be devastated if she lost her phone. It would be smashed to bits if it fell from the top of the roller coaster when they went through the loop-the-loop. Everything was stored in the cloud, she supposed, but it would be a lot of work to restore it to another device. She needed to have everything at her fingertips.

"Are you sure you want to do this?" she asked Seth.

He was breathing heavily, almost hyperventilating. His skin was pale and sweaty.

"Are you okay?"

Seth nodded. "Gotta do this," he muttered. He clenched his fingers around the restraining bar, knuckles turning white.

"If you want to do a different ride… you don't have to go on the roller coaster."

"I do," Seth insisted. "I do have to go on it!" He swore. "Just leave me alone, Mom! I can do this. I'm not a baby."

"I know you're not. I'm just worried about you."

"Well, quit it. I'm fine."

"Okay."

She tried not to look at him directly. He was obviously terrified of the roller coaster, but it had been his dream for so long. He had told so many people he was going on it. It would be the first question everyone asked. 'Did you get to go on the roller coaster?' He was locked into it now and didn't see any way out.

Leva put her hand over Seth's and gave it a little reassuring squeeze. Seth moved his hand away in irritation.

There were a number of announcements, a last warning, and then the cars started to move on the track. There was a collective gasp, a held breath in anticipation, and they were on their way. Seth suddenly wasn't so irritated about having his mother next to him and put his hand over Leva's, squeezing tight. She tried to give him a smile and quick words of comfort, but the words were torn from her mouth by a lurch of the cars, and they were racing down the track, in a vortex of sound that made it impossible to talk to each other. Leva did her best just to hold on and suppress her own physical reaction to the movement.

Roller coasters weren't her thing.

It was in the loop-the-loop, the one thing that Seth had been anticipating half his life, that she felt him go limp beside her. Leva tried to turn her head to look at him, to shout out to him, but she couldn't. She was pressed back in her seat by the force of the train going around the loops, and couldn't move to help him.

By the time they got down to the bottom, to the end of the ride, Leva was screaming, yelling for help. Her yells drowned out the thrilled screams of the other passengers and everyone was suddenly looking at her, aware that something was wrong.

It wasn't the pretty blond girl that met them at the exit, but a tall, acne-scarred boy with an overbite who didn't look old enough to ride by himself, let alone be qualified to evaluate a medical emergency.

"Ma'am? Are you okay?"

Leva indicated her motionless son, his head lolling to the side.

"Did he faint? Some people experience syncope when they go through the loop," he told her in a calm voice, reciting the words that had been drilled into him in training. "Does he have any medical conditions?"

"Yes, he has a medical condition!" Leva yelled at him. "That's what I'm trying to tell you! Get an ambulance. He needs to go to the hospital!"

The boy hesitated, his eyes going to Seth and then to the other employees. "I can get some ice and a first aid worker. He'll probably be fine in a couple of minutes."

"It's always the boys that faint," a woman worker said with a laugh.

"Get—an—ambulance!" Leva insisted. "Do it now! Don't stand there laughing at him!"

She fought loose of her restraints so that she could lean closer to Seth. She thrust her fingers into his pulse, her own heart hammering so hard and fast it hurt her chest. She was relieved to feel his pulse still beating. Her body slumped and she let out her breath.

"Is he… he's not dead?" asked the boy with the acne. "He's okay, right?"

"His heart is beating," Leva said, "but it's very weak. Will somebody please call an ambulance?"

"It's on its way," an older employee assured Leva, moving in and taking charge with her calm manner. "Darcy, we're going to need to shut down the ride. See to it. We need to clear a path for the ambulance. First aid workers are here," she observed, waving to the uniformed first-aiders.

"Passed out on the roller coaster?" the male first-aider asked with unconcern. "It happens all the time. Nothing to be worried about, ma'am. He'll just be a little confused…"

He reached for Seth. Leva didn't know if he planned to slap Seth's cheeks or shake him awake, but she pushed him back angrily.

"This is a serious event!" she snapped. "He could die! Does it look to you like he just fainted?"

The man froze, looking at her in alarm. "What…?"

"Seth is a very sick boy! His heart is still beating, which is a good thing since I don't see a portable AED here. Why wouldn't you have an AED at a roller coaster?"

"We do, ma'am. But you said his heart is beating; he doesn't need one...?"

"Where is it? Are you completely incompetent? All of you?"

Someone pushed forward, holding the AED case out in offering like the holy grail. "It's here. Do you need it?"

"Not yet, but we might," Leva snapped. "Help me get him out of the car. Lay him down. Elevate his feet."

"Shouldn't we leave him there?" a girl argued. "I thought you weren't supposed to move anyone."

"This isn't an injury accident. He didn't get *hit* by the roller coaster. Get him out. Lay him down. Get blankets for shock. Don't you have blankets?"

By the time the ambulance got there—nearly fifteen minutes, Leva noted, looking at the time on her phone again—Seth was lying on the concrete, blankets over him even in the sweltering weather, feet elevated, the AED open beside him. The paramedics looked over the scene.

"What happened? What's going on?"

"He has mitochondrial disease," Leva said. "He passed out on the roller coaster. He might have had a heart attack! We've treated for shock."

"The AED hasn't been used?" the paramedic asked.

Everyone shook their heads, looking at each other for approval.

"If you thought he had a heart attack, shouldn't you have hooked up the sensors?"

Leva looked at the open AED box. She had prepared everything in the event that they needed it, monitoring Seth's pulse manually. But the AED would have monitored what kind of rhythm it was. Whether his heart was producing the right electrical impulses, not just beating.

"Doesn't anyone know how to use this thing?" she accused. "Hasn't anyone been trained in what to do?"

The paramedic moved in with his stethoscope, pulling the blankets aside and pressing it to the outside of Seth's t-shirt. He motioned for silence, and the chatter among the employees subsided. Leva held her breath, waiting for his verdict.

"It sounds okay," he said. "We'll hook him up to a monitor when we get him into the ambulance. You're his mother?"

"Yes."

"What can you tell me about his medical condition?"

"Haven't you ever heard of mitochondrial disease?" she challenged.

"I've heard of it. Not in relationship to having a heart attack or fainting riding a roller coaster. Does he have heart problems?"

"Yes, he has a damaged heart from incompetent treatment in the past."

"Should he have been riding a roller coaster with a damaged heart?"

"The doctors cleared him. They said it would be okay."

The paramedic and his partner checked all of Seth's vital signs. "He seems stable. Has he fainted before? Is he prone to seizures?"

"Yes, he's fainted. But if it was just a faint, he'd be awake by now. This is far more serious."

"Has he had seizures?"

"Yes. But this doesn't look like a seizure."

"A seizure doesn't have to look like a tonic-clonic seizure. It can be difficult to detect without proper equipment."

"We need to get him to the hospital," Leva insisted, panic rising.

"Let's do that," the paramedic agreed. He and his partner got the gurney out of the ambulance. They seemed to be moving in slow motion. Leva didn't understand why paramedics and doctors always seemed to move so slowly. On TV, it was always a rush, everybody dove in and did their part, shouting out orders, doing something to make sure that they could save the patient. In Leva's experience, it was never like that. The doctors took hours, sometimes days, to evaluate an adverse event and decide on a course of treatment. Half the time, she was the one who suggested a diagnosis and course of treatment before they could come up with something.

They got Seth onto the gurney and into the ambulance.

"Can I ride with you?" Leva asked, climbing up.

"I'm sorry, ma'am. Policy says that we can't take any passengers. You can meet us at the hospital." He told her which one and asked if she knew her way there.

Leva shook her head. "We're not from here. We came on a vacation. Something special, to celebrate that Seth was doing better. We raised the money to get here with an online fundraiser. We just got here today."

"Okay. Why don't we see if we can get a police officer to escort you over there? Do you want to get your car?"

Leva shook her head. "It's all the way over in the parking lot on the other side of the park. And I'd have to pay for parking at the hospital. It's always such exorbitant prices. Can I leave it here?" Leva asked one of the park employees. "Is it going to get ticketed and towed away if I don't pick it up today?"

"If you'll give me a description and the plate number, I'll take care of it."

Leva had to get out her wallet and check her registration to give him all the details. Her brain wouldn't work. She couldn't even remember the make. The man noted down all the appropriate details.

"Don't you worry about it. It will be there tomorrow. And if you need a ride back here to pick it up, you call this number," he gave her a hospitality card. "A service will pick you up and bring you back here. No charge. I'll tell them to expect your call."

Leva nodded. The paramedic who was going to drive closed the rear doors of the ambulance. "We're going to go on ahead, ma'am. Police will be here in two minutes. We'll meet you in Emergency."

"Okay. Thank you."

In a couple more minutes, the ambulance pulled away, lights flashing but siren off, moving out through the park at a sedate speed.

———

Leva took a picture of Seth in the hospital bed, IV in his arm again, oxygen threaded into his nose. He had machines monitoring both his brain waves and the electrical activity in his heart. He had not woken up. They were running blood tests and had scheduled brain imaging to see if they could figure out what was going on.

She used an editing app to lay the pre-roller coaster picture and the hospital picture side by side, tapped in a status update, and uploaded them to all her social networking sites with one click. Before long, everybody would know as much as she knew. Family and friends would send their encouragement.

Maybe somebody would have additional suggestions of things that the doctors should check for. Theodore Woodward's aphorism always made her shake her head: "When you hear hoofbeats, think of horses, not zebras." Seth had always been her little zebra. Diagnosing him was always just beyond the doctors' reach. A cold or flu virus would land him in the hospital for weeks. His electrolytes went up and down like a yo-yo, completely unpredictable. One day he would seem fine. Strong, acting like a normal teenager, and then the next, at death's door.

Getting a diagnosis of mitochondrial disease had felt like such a victory. Finally, an explanation for everything. But instead of being the end of their journey, it had been another starting point.

So little was understood about how the mitochondria worked, how cellular energy was created and how one little failure of an enzyme or something else in the process could disrupt the entire body. And what course of treatment were they supposed to follow? There were research programs, experimental protocols, the herb and naturopathic route. The optimum diet. Vitamins and how they affected the whole Krebs cycle and might—or might not—fix everything. Diagnosis had brought more questions than answers.

"Mrs. Wilcox?"

Leva looked up at the doctor who hovered over her. She'd been staring down at her phone, willing it to ring. Praying for someone who had a suggestion to call, text, or message her and let her know. She'd completely blocked out everything else. There was a dark cast to his skin. Black hair and dark brown eyes. A young man. Old enough to be a fully-fledged doctor, but not old enough to have his university loans paid off.

"Doctor! I'm sorry, I was somewhere else."

"Understandable. I realize how difficult this has to be for you."

"Oh, I don't think you do," Leva said, shaking her head. "By my count, this is Seth's forty-eighth hospitalization."

His eyes widened at this announcement. "Well, that would explain why my staff says they are having trouble getting me a comprehensive medical history."

He sat on the edge of Seth's bed to talk to her. Leva bit her tongue to keep from telling him how unprofessional that was. At least he had come to talk to her directly, rather than hiding behind a cadre of nurses and interns. He was trying to have a discussion with the one person who could help him, the one person who knew Seth's history like some people knew ancient Roman history or the entire genealogy of the British monarchy. Seth was Leva's obsession. She was the expert on Seth and everything that had happened since he was born.

"He's been diagnosed with mitochondrial disease," Doctor Darvish said. Leva tried to fix his name in her memory so that she would be able to record it and to ask for him again later. Later when he wasn't on duty, and the nurses didn't want to deal with Leva's questions or didn't want to pass on her thoughts and her latest research to him.

"Yes, that's right. Umm… two years ago now. We thought that once he was diagnosed, it would be easy to find the right course of treatment and get him healthy again. But that hasn't been the case."

He nodded sympathetically. "It is new country for us. Being able to diagnose it is a step in the right direction, but finding the appropriate treatment can be elusive."

"So what can you tell me about what happened today?" Leva asked. "He just collapsed. If it had just been a faint, he'd be awake by now. It wasn't heart or a seizure… so what is it?"

"Has this ever happened before?"

"Sometimes if his electrolytes are off. I told the emergency room to test."

"His sodium levels are extremely high. Can you think of any reason that would be?"

"They can be all over the place. He didn't have anything salty at lunch; I don't think. I mean, some junk food, because it was Disneyland, but nothing that should have pushed his electrolytes out of whack. Unless there's a problem with his kidneys…"

"I notice he has a feeding tube."

"He's been through so many crises when he hasn't been able to eat… I prefer the feeding tube over a central line."

"It's unusual to leave it in once the crisis is over."

"Yes. But taking it out and putting it back in multiple times is worse, it increases the chance of infection."

"He's really too old for a feeding tube."

"What does age have to do with it?" Leva demanded. "If he is in a coma like this, how do you propose to give him his nourishment? You know that IV solutions are not sufficient. He has mitochondrial disease; we can't afford to let his cells starve, even for a day."

Darvish's lips pressed together. He didn't agree or disagree. He wrote something down on Seth's chart.

"We're giving him D5W," he said, indicating the IV bag. "But I'm recommending dialysis as well. We don't usually recommend dialysis for high sodium, but cases as acute as this are very dangerous. Outcomes are not good if we don't get control of it."

Leva nodded. She swiped on her phone and entered this new protocol in her health care app.

"But you don't have any idea what might have caused this in the first place?" she asked.

"I'm afraid not. Kids with metabolic disorders can be… challenging to deal with. He hasn't had any fever or diarrhea? No confusion before the ride on the roller coaster?"

"No, he seemed fine. He was anxious about it. Tired. Sweating from the heat. I suppose he might have gotten dehydrated from all the walking around and sweating."

"That could have contributed, but I would have expected something more than that."

"And you don't think it was the roller coaster itself? We checked with all the doctors before we went, and they said it was safe."

"I can't think of anything the roller coaster should have caused other than queasiness or fainting. He didn't throw up? On the roller coaster or earlier in the day?"

"No. Not today. I wish I could point to something that simple."

He nodded and got up from the bed.

"We'll treat him, and try to avoid messing up any other electrolytes in the process. Someone will be coming to take him down to dialysis. The next time you see him, he should be awake."

"Can't I go down to dialysis with him?"

"Sorry, no. Not this time. We've got a flu outbreak, and the unit is under quarantine. No one is allowed in."

"Oh." Leva nodded. "Okay. I guess when he goes down, I'll pop over to the cafeteria and get something to eat."

He nodded and reached out his hand to shake hers.

"Good to meet you, Mrs. Wilcox. Don't you worry; we'll get him fixed up as quickly as we can."

CHAPTER TWO

How is Wilcox doing?" Jahn Darvish asked the nurse over the dialysis unit.

"His levels are normalizing. What the heck happened to throw his numbers off so far?"

"Still investigating that. Is he awake?"

"Not last I saw, but he should be awake before long. You can see if you can rouse him."

Darvish nodded his thanks and went down the row of dialysis beds, smiling at the patients as he went by. He found young Seth Wilcox's bed and shook the boy's arm.

"Seth. Time to wake up now, Seth…"

Seth's head moved slightly, but he didn't open his eyes. Darvish squeezed tighter and shook harder.

"Come on, Seth. Time to wake up. I know you're tired, but I need you to talk to me."

The muscle in Seth's arm tightened, resisting. Dr. Darvish moved to Seth's face, patting him on the cheek, each pat making Seth flinch and squeeze his eyelids closed more tightly.

"Wake up, Seth. Open your eyes now. If you talk to me, I'll let you alone, and you can go back to sleep."

"No," Seth groaned.

"Come on, son. Let's see those baby blues."

Seth's eyes blinked reluctantly open. Darvish gave him a reassuring smile and waited for a few moments for Seth to focus on him and get oriented.

"What happened?" Seth whispered.

"You had a little problem with your electrolytes. What do you remember?"

Seth brought his hand up to his face and rubbed his forehead with a frown. "I don't know. Wasn't I at Disney?"

"Yes, you were. What were you doing there?"

"My mom raised money for me to go. 'Cause that's what I've always wanted. Am I still there? Or am I home?"

"You're still in California. What was the last thing you did at Disneyland?"

Seth cleared his throat, looking around. He rubbed at the oxygen tube feeding into his nose. Not like it was bothering him, or he wanted to pull it out, just feeling with curious fingers to see what was going on.

"We had lunch. Took a break. We were going to go on the roller coaster."

"And did you?"

Seth thought about it, his eyes vague. His brain seemed to be moving very slowly. Whether that was normal or a result of Seth's screwed-up 'lytes, Darvish wasn't sure. He needed to get his hands on as much of Seth's medical history as he could.

"I don't think so," Seth said finally. He turned his head away from Darvish, letting it loll in the opposite direction to get another view of the room. He stared at the dialysis machine. "Why am I on dialysis?"

"There were dangerously high levels of sodium in your blood. I wanted to clean it as quickly as possible to avoid damage to your kidneys. Have you been on dialysis before?"

"Yeah."

Darvish made a note of this on his phone. Not on the official record, but a reminder to himself to follow up on it later.

"What did you have for lunch, Seth?"

Seth continued to stare at the dialysis machine as if mesmerized.

"I don't remember."

"Did your mom buy something? Or did she bring something with her?"

"I don't know. Maybe… I don't know."

"Tell me about your feeding tube."

Seth fingered it under his hospital robe, looking irritated. "I hate it. It gets in the way all the time. People think I'm like a freak. Who wants to be around a guy with a tube coming out of his belly? It's gross."

"I can see how it might put a crimp on relationships," Darvish agreed, giving a nod. "So why do you still have it? You don't need it, do you?"

"No," Seth plucked at it. "I don't need it and I don't want it. You could tell my mom to get rid of it."

"It's your mom's idea?"

"She says I need it when I can't eat."

"That sounds reasonable, doesn't it?"

Seth scowled. He slumped back against his pillow and hit the arm of the bed with his unencumbered hand.

"Did your mom put something in your tube?" Darvish asked. "Maybe she put something down it that she shouldn't have. Something that made you sick."

Seth stared at him without expression.

"Did your mom put something in your feeding tube today?"

Seth shook his head. "I don't remember. She didn't need to. Not when I was feeling okay."

"Has your mom ever put something in your feeding tube that she shouldn't have? Something the doctors didn't know about or approve?"

"She wouldn't do that."

"Maybe an herbal remedy or dietary aid that she read about online. Vitamins or digestive enzymes."

"The doctor has to approve everything."

Darvish nodded. "Okay. Well, you're going to be here for a while longer, so if you want to go back to sleep, you can."

Seth appeared to be more wide awake now, and not inclined to go right back to sleep. He shifted his position.

"Can you sit me up?"

"Sure." Darvish worked the controls to bring Seth up to a sitting position. "How's that?"

"Can I go back today? To Disneyland?"

Darvish couldn't help but laugh at Seth's eagerness. "Sounds like you're already feeling better. I don't think you're going to get back there today.

We'll talk about it tomorrow. Though I'm not sure the roller coaster is a good idea."

"I only have five days. I have to do everything in five days."

"We'll see how you're doing, Seth. We don't want to release you and have you collapse again. It could be even more serious next time."

"I feel fine."

"That's good. I'm glad you're feeling better. But we'll have to watch your levels and make sure that everything is stable. I don't like an episode like this just coming out of nowhere. I'd like to know what caused it."

Seth shook his head. "But I don't know. I just… things like that happen to me. Because of my mito. No one can control it."

———

It was no great surprise to Seth that when he was transferred to a gurney and back to the emergency room bed, that Leva was waiting there, ready to take his picture and post it online to update his status. It was easier than making all those phone calls, he knew, but just once he would have liked her to just leave it alone.

"Smile for me," Leva said, snuggling beside him and holding her phone out in front of them so that she could get them both into the picture. Seth rolled his eyes and didn't smile.

"I don't feel good, Mom. I don't want to smile."

"It just looks better on the posts; then everyone knows that you're doing better. People want to see you happy."

Seth waved her off, not wanting her to take further pictures. "I'm tired. You can take pictures when we go back to Disneyland."

She gave him a big smile. "All ready to go back?"

"The doctor said maybe tomorrow. So I want to sleep and get all better for tomorrow so he says it's okay."

"Okay," Leva agreed. She sat in the chair next to the bed and stroked his hair. "So you're feeling better, baby?"

"Yeah."

"It was pretty scary, you just going limp on the roller coaster like that. I was so afraid that you'd had a heart attack!"

"My heart is okay."

"It could happen," Leva protested. "All the times you've been sick, that puts a lot of stress on your heart. The doctors may say that your heart is fine, but they don't *know*. They can't see it. High sodium could have caused a heart attack too."

"I went on the roller coaster?" Seth asked. "I don't remember."

"You went on the roller coaster. So brave!"

"It's not like I'm five," he grumbled. She always treated him like a baby. Especially when he was sick.

"Shh. Go to sleep. Maybe we can go back tomorrow."

———

Jahn Darvish sat with the hospital social worker, Sia Exler, his boss, Dr. Fraser, and the hospital attorney, Samantha Dreyer, to go over Seth Wilcox's file.

"There is no way these are naturally occurring sodium levels," he said, sliding the first electrolytes report across to Dr. Fraser. "Even in a kid with a mysterious metabolic illness, there's no way his sodium levels spike that fast."

Dr. Fraser nodded, adjusting his half-glasses to review the numbers on the report. "There were no warning signs, Jahn? Diarrhea? Confusion? I wouldn't expect him to be cogent during an episode like that."

"According to the mother, nothing. Acting normally until he collapsed on the roller coaster."

"That seems highly unlikely."

Darvish nodded his agreement. "She says they had lunch shortly before getting onto the roller coaster. I think she injected sodium directly into his feeding tube."

"That would explain the rapid onset."

"Is there any other explanation?" Samantha Dreyer, the lawyer, asked. She was a striking blonde in a conservative navy blazer and skirt.

Fraser and Darvish looked at each other. Neither could come up with a suggestion.

"We're checking out other possibilities. Kidney function. Adrenals. But I think the boy was poisoned. I can't come up with any other explanation."

The social worker was flipping through printed computer pages. "This isn't the first time that he's had high sodium or another electrolyte imbalance," Sia said. "And that suggests that it is part of his disorder."

"Or part of his mother's disorder," Darvish said.

The social worker and lawyer both looked confused. Fraser's mouth twitched. "Be careful, Jahn."

"What do you mean, the mother's disorder?" Sia demanded. "You think this is genetic?"

"No, I think it's the mother. I think this has been going on for some time, and no one has been able to see the forest for the trees."

"What do you mean?"

"The mother. Munchausen by Proxy. She's poisoning him."

"I saw her earlier in the day to see what their needs were while they were away from home," Sia said. "She seemed like a very concerned, attentive mother. I didn't get any vibes."

"Munchausen by Proxy mothers are attentive. They appear very involved in their children's care, very knowledgeable, and very caring. But if they feel they're not getting the attention they deserve, the kid suddenly has a downturn."

"There's no proof," Fraser said.

"This is proof." Darvish tapped the report on Seth's initial electrolytes test. "Right there. Salt poisoning. Not a natural metabolic process."

They sat around the table looking at each other.

"You have to be sure," Samantha warned. "One hundred percent. Munchausen is being used too much these days. Judges are getting leery of it. Stories in the media about using Munchausen by Proxy to get kids away from parents when you can't actually prove abuse. I don't want that stigma attached to any of our files."

"I'll talk to her one more time," Darvish said. "Just to be sure."

———

Proxy, Book #3 of the *Medical Kidnap Files* series by P.D. Workman can be purchased at pdworkman.com

ABOUT THE AUTHOR

Award-winning and USA Today bestselling author P.D. (Pamela) Workman writes riveting mystery/suspense and young adult books dealing with mental illness, addiction, abuse, and other real-life issues. For as long as she can remember, the blank page has held an incredible allure and from a very young age she was trying to write her own books.

Workman wrote her first complete novel at the age of twelve and continued to write as a hobby for many years. She started publishing in 2013. She has won several literary awards from Library Services for Youth in Custody for her young adult fiction. She currently has over 50 published titles and can be found at pdworkman.com.

Born and raised in Alberta, Workman has been married for over 25 years and has one son.

———

Please visit P.D. Workman at pdworkman.com to see what else she is working on, to join her mailing list, and to link to her social networks.

———

If you enjoyed this book, please take the time to recommend it to other purchasers with a review or star rating and share it with your friends!